# THE SCROLLS OF BISHOP EUBULUS

## AND OTHER STORIES

## REBECCA BRADLEY

EDGE SCIENCE FICTION AND FANTASY PUBLISHING
An Imprint of HADES PUBLICATIONS, INC.
CALGARY

# The Scrolls of Bishop Eubulus, and Other Stories



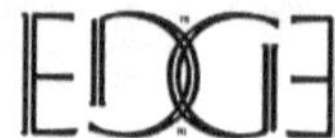

EDGE SCIENCE FICTION AND FANTASY PUBLISHING
An Imprint of HADES PUBLICATIONS, INC.
P.O. Box 1414, Calgary, Alberta, T2P 2L6, Canada

The EDGE Team:
Producer: Brian Hades
Acquisitions Editor: Ella Beaumont
Edited by: Katarina Yerger
Cover Design: Brian Hades
Cover Art: David Wilicome
Book Design: Mark Steele

ISBN: 9781770532489



EDGE Science Fiction and Fantasy Publishing and Hades Publications, Inc. acknowledges the ongoing support of the Alberta Foundation for the Arts and the Canada Council for the Arts for our publishing programme.

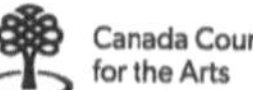


Library and Archives Canada Cataloguing in Publication

Title: The scrolls of Bishop Eubulus, and other stories / Rebecca Bradley.
Names: Bradley, Rebecca, 1952- author
Description: First edition.
Identifiers: Canadiana (print) 20250189755 | Canadiana (ebook) 20250190230 | ISBN 9781770532496 (hardcover) | ISBN 9781770532489 (softcover) | ISBN 9781770532472 (EPUB)
Subjects: LCGFT: Short stories.
Classification: LCC PS8553.R2272 S37 2025 | DDC C813/.54—dc23

FIRST EDITION
(20250513)
Printed in USA
www.edgewebsite.com

# Publisher's Note:

*Picture this: a world where shadows carry secrets, where deserts hum with ancient whispers, and where every corner hides a tale both thrilling and terrifying. In The Scrolls of Bishop Eubulus, and Other Stories, Rebecca Bradley invites you to journey through thirteen extraordinary tales that blend dark fantasy, cosmic horror, and razor-sharp humor into something entirely unforgettable.*

*Step into a haunted room that watches you back, where every breath could be your last. Follow a detective in the aftermath of a zombie apocalypse as he solves murders no one else cares to understand. Venture into the eerie desert sands, where ghosts roam freely, and ancient texts promise salvation—or doom.*

*But this collection isn't just about the unknown; it's about the people who confront it. Cryptozoologists face their worst discoveries, archaeologists awaken horrors buried for centuries, and humanity's First Contact turns hilariously, disastrously wrong.*

*Each story is a portal to a world where the line between the real and the surreal dissolves. These are not just tales—they are living, breathing journeys into the uncanny, the unsettling, and the utterly captivating.*

*Dare to open the pages. Who knows what you'll uncover?*

*Brian Hades, publisher*

# Contents


Miracle, in Sand . . . . . . . . . . . . . . . . . . . . . . . . . . . . . . . . . 1

The New Forty . . . . . . . . . . . . . . . . . . . . . . . . . . . . . . . . . 11

Kids These Days . . . . . . . . . . . . . . . . . . . . . . . . . . . . . . . 21

The Fremont Collection . . . . . . . . . . . . . . . . . . . . . . . . . 31

Condominium . . . . . . . . . . . . . . . . . . . . . . . . . . . . . . . . . 55

Red Carpet . . . . . . . . . . . . . . . . . . . . . . . . . . . . . . . . . . . . 59

An Inspector Calls . . . . . . . . . . . . . . . . . . . . . . . . . . . . . 67

The Scrolls of Bishop Eubulus . . . . . . . . . . . . . . . . . . . 77

Small World . . . . . . . . . . . . . . . . . . . . . . . . . . . . . . . . 127

Operation HAND OF GOD . . . . . . . . . . . . . . . . . . . . 133

The Shrieking Sand . . . . . . . . . . . . . . . . . . . . . . . . . 143

The Hanging Room . . . . . . . . . . . . . . . . . . . . . . . . . 171

Cold Case . . . . . . . . . . . . . . . . . . . . . . . . . . . . . . . . . 187

End Notes

# Dedication

To Robin Eubule, with all my love.

# Acknowledgements

**Many patient people** have helped me refine these stories over the years, and they have my gratitude: my sisters Ellen, Kim, and Allyson; Robin, Kat, Owen, Milo, and Suzanna Thelwall; the late Charles Alverson; Susan Glover; Linda Crosfield; Peter Clarke; Nancy Kilpatrick; and Derek Welsby, the only person I know who has actually driven the Korosko Road. Special thanks to Brian Hades, and to Katarina Yerger, both of whom made the editing process into a happy and productive conversation.

# Miracle, in Sand

**"ULTIMATE THRILLS," says** Leeda, "has a special on executions next month."

"Not my style," I say.

Leeda surveys the prices. "It's good value, Mother. Select from twelve international cuisines for your last meal—unlimited drinks—authentic souvenir blindfold—"

"Souvenir? Is that meant to be funny?"

"No, silly," she says, "they'd laminate it and send it to me. With the firing squad, you get an authentic cigarette."

"Who smokes anymore?"

"It's traditional. What, you're worried about the health risk?" She giggles at her own joke.

I sigh. "Darling, all I want is something a bit scenic. I hate those situational things."

"Well, it's your decision." She sorts through the pile of high-coloured brochures she has picked up from the travel agency: FINAL CURTAIN, WAY TO GO, LAST RESORT. "You know, Mother," she goes on, "if it's scenic you want, these executions have museum-quality scenery and props. NO REPRIEVE has a genuine 18th-century guillotine. Isn't that charming?"

"I'd call it gimmicky."

"Oh, Mother." A wrinkle like a delicate vertical pencil-mark is sketched between Leeda's eyebrows. Time for a trip to the salon. My daughter is only eighty-three, rosy and firm-skinned, but the wrinkle foretells the course of her next three decades: increasingly frequent appointments with her dermadresser, the concentration of her daily dose of vita rising by small increments, her occasional glass of opiette becoming a nightly tipple. As she approaches fifteen-past the century, her spirit will declare a denial of her body, reversing the order of things in the sad old days. In about thirty years, give or take a few, my grandson Cass will drop into some travel agency on her behalf.

"SHARK ATTACK?" she says.

"*No.*"

"Honestly, Mother, there's no pain involved. The package includes a full-body anesthetic."

"I see no thrill in drowning while a fish tears me apart. What else have you got?"

She gives me a look familiar from a hundred thousand dinner tables and gigamarket expeditions across eight decades, a patient look just short of irritation, which says in plain E-Basic I'm being difficult to please. "FAMOUS LAST WORDS?" she suggests. Adolf Hitler glowers from the glossy cover. "*Re-creations of the most memorable deaths of the ages will place you in the flow of history. Be inspired by—*"

"I saw an article about that in *Deathstyle*. Crucifixion without tears, at whatsisname's right hand."

"You mean Christ," she says, consulting the booklet, "but there are others you might like better. QUEEN OF THE NILE—"

"Clasp-an-asp. Repugnant. And I won't go for drinks with Socrates, either."

"THRILLS'N'CHILLS?" she says. "It's a Scott of the Antarctic thing."

"Scott's last camp?"

"Not the real one. A replica about a kilometer away."

"A replica." I sip at my vita, cherry-flavored, but like everything else these days, it tastes of synthesis and dust.

Leeda frowns at the booklet. "Does that matter? Apparently it's nice and easy."

"I'm sure Captain Scott didn't think so."

"Oh, Mother."

She reshuffles her leaflets, while I twirl my glass between fingers as smooth and pink-nailed as her own. The liver-spots and crepe-skin are present only in potential, warded off by vita and dermadressing. A few weeks of neglect, and my decision would be made for me, but that sort of irresponsibility is socially unacceptable.

"All right, this sounds nice. *REST-EE-ZEE. The last word in tranquil terminations for the discriminating thanatone. Fall asleep in a fragrant garden, soothed by birdsong and the tinkling of a tiny fountain. Choice of velour- or silk-finish chaise—*"

"Boring," I cut in. "Next?"

"END ZONE? No, too sporty. SHOP 'TIL YOU DROP? Never mind, I know what you're going to say. Here, you look at them."

She shoves the leaflets across the table. On top, a full-colour holomontage of a broken ship spirals down past a ruptured submarine. A face beams from the porthole of a bathysphere with no visible means of support or salvage. LLOYD'S TRAVEL. On the next, a racing car soars off a cliff. AUTO DA FE. I'm sure the puns are getting worse.

Would it be so very antisocial, I ask myself, to take a modest pill at home among one's loved ones, as they used to do? Yes, I understand the economics of it all. Every year, ten million of us attain the age of thanescence, a 1/115th share of a population stabilized at 1.2 billion. In terms of consumer-base, the death business cannot possibly be a growth industry. Elaboration must be the name of the game—but do they give us what we want, or what they want us to want?

"Mama?"

I look at my daughter across DESIGNER DEATH, thinking it must be fifty years since she called me that. Her face has turned troubled, deepening the shadow-line between her brows.

"Are you sure you're ready, Mama?" she asks.

"Of course I'm ready. I've been fifteen-past for months. Believe me, I'm quite adequately sick of being alive."

Fiddling with the discard pile, she winces at my plainness of speech. I imagine the socially correct term for my stage of life is teetering on her lips.

"Why do you ask?" I peer into her face for any sign of a shameful secret. "You're not imagining you'll grieve for me, are you?"

Now I've shocked her. "Mother, that's a terrible thing to say."

"Then what?"

"It's just," she says, visibly groping, "that I can't help thinking about when Father thanesced. He had everything so well planned, booked his death long before fifteen-past, played in the dance band at his own wake—"

"I know, you told me."

"You should have gone, Mama," she says.

"Darling Leeda, would you embarrass an ex-husband of yours by going to his wake? Anyway, we're talking about my death wish, not his."

"Thanescence, Mama, please." Leeda's fingers are pleating ONE WAY TICKET into lopsided fan-folds. "I'm just worried. All this choice, and nothing resonates."

"Too many awful choices," I say, waving at the leaflets. "Tawdry charades, darling, with costumes and special effects, packaged up expensively like everything else that happens to us. Actually, I do know what I want. I want something *real*."

"Real?"

"Why not? Nothing virtual or holoholic, and especially not one of those stupid play-acting things. I want to do something real. I want a death I can live with."

A pause while Leeda digests this. "You're not making sense," she says finally. She's trying to keep the wariness out of her voice, but I see at once that I've gone too far, that my feeble epigram has frightened her. It has raised the possibility of senility or a related disgrace, the stigma of dermadressers not faithfully visited, vita-glasses not scrupulously drained, sins of omission that might degrade one at last into that worst of modern sociopaths, a burden. She's a dutiful daughter, my Leeda, primed with social conscience. If she convinces herself my mind is going, she will damn the humiliation and turn me in.

"Relax, darling," I say, "you know what nonsense I talk. What else have you got?"

She appears only partly convinced. I try harder, chugging my cherry vita as she spreads out the rest of the leaflets.

"How about a disaster?" she asks, peering sharply across the table.

"Disasters are good," I say.

"ThanatAir is having a sale on airjet crashes. Guaranteed no survivors, and up to two minutes' weightlessness while the jet's in free fall."

"That sounds lovely, darling. But there's always the chance," I say carefully, "that weightlessness might make me nauseous. I wouldn't want to spend my last moments with my nose in a sickbag." Private subtext: there's nothing real about a deliberate catastrophe.

Leeda picks out another glossy booklet from near the bottom of the pile: a tidal wave menacing an active volcano, while a meteor paints a streak across the sky. "How about a natural disaster?" she says.

I say, "*Now* you're talking."

———— «» ————

I take no interest in the details of my wake. It is Leeda who books the floor show and the caterer, her son Cass who selects the dance band and the party pack, his daughter Suzee who frogmarches me to the gigamarket for my wake-wear. I exercise my veto power only once. The cake cannot resemble a volcano. No hot-caramel lava is permitted to flow down its flanks. It is a *real* cake.

At the crowded buffet table, I eat a rollmop and think wistfully of my great-grandfather's wake, back when these rites of passage were conducted with a certain dignity. No floor shows then, no thematic cakes, a more seemly spread of hors-d'oeuvres. How did we come to this?

I drift across the dance floor, shaking hands, kissing air, as the band plays a dance-tempo arrangement of Mozart's Requiem. One of Suzee's lovers fondles me from behind, possibly mistaking me for my great-granddaughter; when he sees who I am, the declared thanatone, he puts his lips close to my ear and whispers, "One for the road?" Alas for his kind intentions, sex is about as interesting to this thanatone as next year's weather forecast. I thank him politely and lose myself among my other guests.

The hearse will come soon. My friends and loved ones will wave me off with their wine-glasses, as custom decrees, and return to the dance floor in my memory. In all but body, I have already left them. I know now that what we call thanescence is nothing so dramatic as a death wish. It is a niggling sense of wrongness at continuing to be alive. That I am drinking is a waste of good wine; that I am breathing, an abuse of good air. Vita may fool the body, blithely overriding the organism's physical obsolescence, but instincts carved out through half a million generations know when it's time to quit. My very DNA is looking pointedly at its watch.

I am comfortable with that imperative. Immortality may sound like a nice idea, but it would not be practical. I spent some eight decades as a human-biomass historian, and this is the essence of what I learned about the vita revolution: that if thanescence had not already been bred into us, we would have been obliged to invent it. One Great Downsizing was horror enough.

———— «» ————

The cathedral windows of the departure lounge look out on the separate ThanatAir terminal, a few hundred meters away across a daisy-chain of landing pads. Five jets are queued up beside it, lovely fragile birds designed for just one flight, their silver sides as brittle as glass. I can make out that four of them are rigged for remote control, but one has a standard cockpit. I suppose thanescent pilots might wonder what it feels like to crash.

In the far corner of the lounge, the POMPEII thanatones are donning their togas, rather too merrily. Alas, it appears they will be housed next to my group on the mountainside. FIT FOR THE GODS, hilarious in grass skirts and leis, and scheduled to be cast into the crater minutes before the eruption, will be camping conveniently closer to the summit.

My group, one of several not in costume, sits primly under a sign saying KABOOM!!! in large fiery letters. One thing I dislike about my impending death is the name of the package. It is not even strictly accurate, since it will be the pyroclastic flow that kills us, not the big kaboom.

By this point, indeed, I'm wondering if I will get my money's worth. KABOOM!!! is not cheap, at least half again the going rate for a Titanic enactment, twice the rate for an execution, six times the average cost of a chaise in a garden. Even so, the departure lounge is more crowded than I had anticipated. Apparently, given the limited supply of natural disasters, we will have to share the south flank with nine other groups of thanatones, as many as will fit comfortably into the destruction zone.

We are paying for the predictive technology, of course, the complex modelling that can pinpoint the time of the eruption to within an astonishingly precise eleven minutes, the track of the pyroclastic flow to within a half-dozen meters. Tsunamis are cheaper, being easier to model; earthquakes cheaper yet, but not very popular, because there is not much to see and no guarantee of a clean death.

And that is not all we are paying for. The fourteen of us under the KABOOM!!! sign will require a support staff of eleven, plus numerous autodispensers to cover the hours after the human servitors depart. Then there are the structures that will house us for three days before the eruption, though they cannot add much to the overhead: preformed styro on plyboard frames, cobbled together in a couple of hours. They are designed to give an illusion of solidity, but their obsolescence is as inbuilt as my own.

————— «» —————

When alarm-lights flash and chimes break into the in-flight entertainment somewhere over the Sahara, it is not unrealistic to become a little excited, even hopeful. The odds against an unscheduled airjet crash are about 3.7 million to one, but such things can happen. I hold my breath—but the contingency systems swing into action, computers override and compensate, and the jet levels off into a semi-powered glide. Damn, I say to myself.

"Damn," mutters the man beside me.

We peer through the porthole together. Below us is a woodgrain pattern of rocky ridges sharpened by the wind, too rough to land on; not far beyond, however, I see classic flat desert, which is, sadly, much more suitable terrain for a forced landing. On the other hand, a great tract of it directly ahead is obscured by the billows of a sandstorm.

"I wonder how dangerous a forced landing would be in a storm like that," I say thoughtfully.

"Possibly very dangerous," says the man beside me.

"I suppose the pilot will try to avoid it, then," I say.

"I suppose he will. If he can." We stare at each other. Suddenly he grins, and after a moment I grin back.

But turning again to the porthole, I see we are already out of any small danger that may have existed a few moments ago, sandstorm or no sandstorm; almost on the ground now, coasting along on the emergency cushion of down-drafted air until the backjets finesse us to a halt. A dense yellow-grey porridge of sand boils outside the glass.

"So much for that," I say.

The man beside me sighs.

The omnivoice chirps, "Gentlepersons, we're experiencing a slight change in our flight plan today, but a replacement jet is already in the air. For your own comfort and safety we'll ask you to remain in your seats, where our friendly flight staff will shortly be bringing you complimentary beverages and snacks."

"Looks like you could get lost pretty quickly out there," says the man beside me.

"People used to," I answer, "with some regularity. I suppose one still could. If one tried."

We watch the aggressive display of wind and sand against the glass. There is something very *real* about it. I notice people getting up from their seats. A red-haired woman who was sitting two rows ahead is already standing at the emergency exit, reading the stencilled instructions. Two flightpersons are hurrying towards her, one with a tray of sushi in his hand.

"It's tempting," the man beside me goes on, "though I rather liked the idea of seeing the eruption."

"This could be better," I tell him.

He frowns at the porthole. "But they'd rescue us, wouldn't they?"

"Not if we walked fast." I stand up and wait for him to let me squeeze by. Instead, he precedes me into the aisle.

Already people are lining up. At the emergency exit, men in togas or tropical shirts are politely restraining several upset flightpersons while the red-haired woman pulls the levers that will pop the lock. There is mild excitement but no panic, except perhaps among the friendly flight staff.

"You can't go out there! We're not licensed for that!"

After a brief discussion, we tie them up using strips torn from the togas and sit them down among the thanatones who really want to see the volcano. Wind devils rampage through the open hatch, filling our eyes with sand and tears. Somebody breaks out the champagne. I drink to the unplanned, the unscripted, the *real*, as I wait my turn to leap out into the storm.

# The New Forty

**The simple truth** is, they lack empathy. Soulless, self-absorbed, prowling the night for good times and quick fixes, nothing in their heads except the urge to pour liquid down their throats and jump on each other like apes in the zoo. Mindless, shameless. And the vampires are just as bad.

Oh, the young!

But I am not as bitter as I may sound. It is only that, after centuries of observation, I understand them a little too well. These days I observe them on talk shows, the youthful of both species, especially the undead. The rising stars of the new-epoch vampire movies, the supermodels of vampire chic, the vamp-rock bands with names like Bloody Waters, The Grateful Undead, Bled Zeppelin. How perfect are their cold, shapely cadavers, and how beautifully they match the new tenor of the world. If there was ever an age when my kind could come from the shadows and blend right in, that time is now.

My kind? *Their* kind, rather. I have no kind. Even among vampires, I am a freak, a sport, an accident. A common slattern the first time around, spawned into a class and age where women did not give birth so much as whelp litters of unplanned annual brats, whose short lives and hacking deaths recapitulated those of their ancestors. Not mine, though. My father died when I was small, my mother when I was perhaps ten—whereas I survived two husbands and all seven of my own poor whelps. Then I plodded on dismal and solitary to the extraordinary age of sixty-four.

Then I became a witch, by definition and through no true fault of mine. In those times, it was enough to be beyond the menses and to live alone, to have wrinkled flesh, grey hair, gaps in one's jaw, and a reputation for wisdom. Perhaps I should have known better than to be wise. They took me for torture and cast me between-times into a cold cell with vermin for company, and my own bodily effluents, from blood to puke, for what is now called interior décor—colour-coordinated wall and floor coverings that reflected the inner me and gave the place atmosphere, in the language of the home-renovation shows to which I am now addicted. One night, they tossed me a cellmate.

We exchanged no words. I never properly saw his face. The mob had beaten him bloodily enough to kill a Christian outright, so his very survival proved him to be a creature of the devil and fodder for the stake. After they clanged the door shut on us, I crawled across the cell to steal his coat and check his pockets, on the chance of a crust of bread. He was sprawled motionless on his belly; but when I turned him over, he struck like a snake, straight for my gullet, biting so deep I heard his teeth click together inside my flesh. I think I bit him back, since the taste of his blood was in my mouth when I woke up, or maybe he bled into me from his many wounds. At any rate, by then he was gone from the cell and I was a twice-born accident, who barely knew my father and never knew my sire.

I knew about the devil, though, and how his minions could come to even virtuous old women in the night to tempt them into vile congress. This, I assumed with shame and fear, was what had happened to me. And it also appeared that the devil took care of his own. Just as the prison door had opened for the Apostle Paul in Philippi, the door to my cell swung obligingly off its hinges, and no living thing stirred in the gaol. I ran off into the dark wood and away from the sleeping town.

So there was I, a babe again, new to the ways of a strange new world—but a babe in a withered body with deep fissures in its face. Yes, I felt a difference as I ran. For the first time in twenty years, my hips and back did not hurt me, my old bones moved easily in their sockets, my breath did not wheeze in my throat. Even the welts and breaks from my torture were miraculously painless. How I ran! First from fear, later from the joy of running freely under an icy moon, setting the farm dogs whining and cringing as I passed. I outran a deer in the king's forest, and—on fresh instinct— caught it with a strength that was novel to me, twisted its beautiful neck, and drank from its throat. So now I was not just a witch but a poacher, eligible for the rope as well as the stake, but I was also a small mewling child overcome with the newness of everything.

Back to the talk shows.

———— «» ————

*"Look, Phil, we have feelings too. We're very sensitive, very nurturing with our young. For us, newborn vampires are like newborn babies. We stay close, we do everything we can to help them through what is often a difficult, highly emotional transition. We teach them…"*

*"…To kill?" says Phil, with the frown that signals he is asking a hard-hitting question. The audience cat-calls and applauds.*

*"Hey," says the strikingly handsome young man. His pale marble skin glows under the studio lights. "I find that remark both vampirist and personally offensive. You're thinking of the bad old days, when we did what we had to, just to survive. That doesn't mean we liked it."*

———— «» ————

Liar. He'd rip the good doctor's throat out if a half- billion people weren't watching, and he'd like it very much. Mortals have not known us long enough to read our body language. And as for *sensitive* and *nurturing*, I saw nothing of those qualities during my own difficult, highly emotional transition. There were many things I had to discover painfully for myself, starting with the fatal nature of sunlight. It was only by luck I did not immolate myself out of sheer ignorance when my first post-mortem sun rose. I hid whimpering under the bracken and dug myself my own little grave in the forest dirt, among the worms and moles; at sundown, I clawed my way out again with still-smarting hands. Beyond a vague theory that I had accidentally sold myself to Satan, I had no idea of what I had become. Not even the sudden attraction to blood—several moles, voles, and a badger had helped me pass that first long day—felt out of the ordinary. Later that night, when the nest tracked me down, I knew only that I should be afraid of them, deathly afraid, yet somehow I was not.

Three handsome youths and two beautiful maids surrounded me among the trees, luminous in the moonlight, richly dressed. Quality folk they looked like, such as I had seen before only as passengers in liveried coaches, holding their noses as they were whisked through the stinking streets of our town. They stared at me with surprise and all-too-evident distaste. Much later, I wondered if one of them was my sire. At the time, I did not know enough to ask the question. Then one of the youths laughed harshly.

"God's truth, who'd have thought *that* was worth turning?"

———— «‹›» ————

*"You have to admit," says Doctor Phil slyly, "that you're all—how shall I put it—a little better-looking than the average human. In fact, I'd say you're all drop-dead gorgeous, no pun intended. So, is becoming a vampire like having a beauty treatment, or what?"*

*"Phil, modesty forbids me to answer that." The vampire laughs, oh so decoratively. Phil and the studio audience laugh along. "But to be perfectly honest, appearance doesn't matter much to us. We can't help what we look like."*

———— «‹›» ————

More lies. Back in the shadow days, only the young and beautiful were candidates for turning. The old, the ugly, the worn, the imperfect, were simply dinner. And now I know how lucky I was, that long-ago moonlit night in the king's forest. Under a different alpha, they might well have torn me to shreds, in the same spirit as humans once exposed nonstandard babies on hillsides. But all I knew of them then was that they were neither gamekeepers nor inquisitors.

"Help me," I said to them, holding out my sun-blistered hands. "Take me with you."

The lad snickered. "Why should we? What use would you be to us?"

"I know things," I faltered. "I'm good with herbs and helping at childbirth. Women come to me for counsel."

Judging by their laughter, they thought that was hilarious. I can see why, in retrospect, but at the time I was stung to anger. I snapped at them, "You could show respect, then, for my grey hairs, and some pity for a poor old woman in distress."

"Grey hairs?" cried one of the girls through her laughter. "Your age is nothing to us, hag. Why, I could be your three-times-great granddam—though I dearly hope I'd never have a grandchild as ugly as you." Then she lifted her head to laugh more freely, giving me a much better view of her teeth.

That is how I learned I had joined the legendary undead; I recognized her for what she was. I ran my tongue around the inside of my own mouth: no teeth had grown back, but the remaining stumps had become long, strong and sharp. The beautiful ones found my howl of discovery very amusing indeed. But when they tired of teasing me—those youths and maids who were old before I was born—they ran off on a further merry chase and left me alone. That was more dreadful to me than their derision. I ran after them.

———— «» ————

*"So you see it as a kind of liberation? An empowerment of the vampire community?"*

*"Absolutely, Phil. An end to centuries of discrimination and ostracism. And—yes—a long-overdue end to the victimization of a misunderstood minority. Believe me, we welcome the opportunity to become full, productive members of society."*

*"And do you see that as a challenge?"*

*"Absolutely, Phil."*

———— «» ————

I am tempted to throw something at the screen. How well they have learned their lessons, these vampires-for-the-21st-century. And how they adore being a demographic. But I could tell them a great deal they do not know about being a minority, a demographic of just one, and that what set me apart from the others was not just my raddled face. I gained the first inkling of this truth on that first night, when I ran wailing after the beautiful ones and caught up with them just after they downed their prey.

He was a lad I knew, one I had helped deliver into this world some sixteen years before. A good enough boy, hardworking and honest, perhaps a little lumpen. He was courting, I knew that too, and in my opinion it was well past time he should be decently married to the blacksmith's middle daughter. All five of them were suckling at him when I crashed through the brush, fastened to his body like piglets to a sow, but he was still alive and conscious. His eyes widened when he saw me. Hope? Appeal? Or did he see me as one of *them*, truly a chattel of the devil, just as the witchfinder had said? The next moment, the alpha made the question moot by biting into the artery at the base of the boy's thick peasant neck.

"Here, Granny," he said, grinning up at me, "I'm of a generous disposition tonight. There's a mouthful or two left in the beast—come see how fine it tastes. And then go away, because the sight of you offends us."

"The beast's name," I said, "was John." I turned and walked into the darkness, and never once looked back.

———— «» ————

*"But you have killed people, right? How do you feel about that now?"*

*"That's an excellent question, Phil. Sure, we've had to kill people in the past, simply to survive. Does that make us evil? I don't think so. It makes us no different from any other nation or ethnic group in the history of the world."*

———— «» ————

For once I agree with my good-looking colleague, whom I last saw in London wearing a fashionable swallowtail coat and chowing down on a thoroughly Dickensian street urchin. The fact is, the youthful of my species are no more evil than the human young they used to be. They are no more than Peter Pan with fangs, butterflies in amber, trapped forever in the borderline psychopathy of youth. They are the ultimate expression of neoteny. Life never gets the chance to knock the stuffing out of them.

But life had already left me with very little stuffing by the time I was turned. I never could bring myself to prey on humans—too much damned empathy to start with, too liberal a schooling in the sharing of mortal pain. After parting from the beautiful ones, I became the terror of small forest creatures as I worked my way slowly across the wilderness of several southern counties. In London I took a new name and became a poor widow from the country—who would notice another ravaged beldame among so many?

In fact, it was not a bad choice of what is now called 'lifestyle.' For many years I supped handsomely on the vermin of Whitechapel and Lambeth and slept in safety in the great underground palace of the London sewers. Plagues and fires came and went, fashions changed and changed again, generations of mortals flowed past me, but the rats and the sewers went on forever. Early in the Regency, I conceived a bright idea: why not dress as a man and work for the borough as a ratcatcher? Why not get paid for what I was already doing? The bounty on the barrowloads of bloodless vermin I delivered became the foundation of my later fortune, now nicely diversified in a number of offshore investment banks.

Naturally, I saw others of my kind in London's rich hunting ground. They rarely saw me, though, since I preferred to observe them discreetly from a distance. Their ethnology became a hobby of mine: their feeding and mating habits, pecking orders, kinship patterns, ritual behaviours. I could write a book on them, and probably will. On the few occasions when they recognized me as undead, they reacted much as my first vampires in the forest had, with a mixture of amusement and distaste.

———— «» ————

*"Now, can I ask you something personal, something that literally millions of women out there are just dying to know?"*

*"Certainly, Phil."*

*The good doctor leans forward. In the audience, and presumably all over the television-viewing world, many women and a not-insignificant number of men lean forward as well. "Do vampires—fall in love?"*

*The vampire closes the gap even further. "Yes, Phil, we totally do fall in love. And we are perfectly capable of forming stable, loving relationships."*

*"Do you, er—go out on dates?"*

*"We most certainly do."*

———— ⟨⟩ ————

Dates? Hunting parties, in the shadow times. Nowadays, courting vampires dance the night away, or go out to dinner in one of those new specialty restaurants. The first cross-species marriages are being watched closely by sociologists and tabloid journalists. Romance is in the air—and not just for the young.

I had long thought I was beyond all that. I was old. Average life expectancy for mortals did not go much beyond fifty until well into the 20th century, and persons of my apparent age were hopelessly over the hill. I began to dress better and more expensively as the 19th century wore on and my pest-control business expanded into a small commercial empire, but I did not dress to attract lovers. Who, apart from the obvious fortune-hunters, would want to court such a withered old crone?

Then a curious thing happened. For whatever suite of reasons, the brief lives of mortals began to stretch. More people began to live beyond their fifties, and then their sixties; more and more began to outlive the biblical threescore and ten. Suddenly, I was surprised to learn from magazines that life began at forty; and then, not much later by vampire standards, that fifty was the new forty. And then it was sixty. Clearly, the boomer generation was starting to catch up with me. As the new millennium approached, I was amazed to find I was a relatively youthful and potentially attractive woman.

———— ⟨⟩ ————

*"Yes, Phil, I think you can safely say the world is seeing a new breed of vampire. And I have high hopes that a brighter future lies ahead for us all."*

———— ⟨⟩ ————

Amen to that. The face-lift did not take, alas, but the dentures make a remarkable difference. Then there is the transforming power of makeup, a clever stylist, and a personal shopper with a taste for good labels. The roses are from a virile gentleman of seventy-six who is happy to give up golfing in the sun for my sake. Tonight, we shall make a little champagne ceremony of his turning. And why not? Immortality, like youth, is wasted on the young.

# Kids These Days

**Moira Baker adjusts** the needle in her son's arm, wipes her daughter's chin where formula has oozed from the corner of her mouth, then shakes the sweat off her own forehead. "Swallow, Amy," she says. "Swallow, Timmy. I know you hate it, guys, but it's good for you, okay?" Patiently she alternates between her son and daughter: inserts nozzle into mouth, squeezes, wipes, instructs to swallow. Not very efficiently, they obey.

Jeff Baker hurries through the kitchen, dressed for work, heavy briefcase under his arm. He pats Amy and Timmy on their heads in passing. "Be good for your mother, kids. You okay, Moira?"

What can they do but be good? What can she be but okay? Moira puts the feeder down long enough to stand up and kiss Jeff goodbye. He looks tired—the plant has lost another technician, the fifth this year, putting even more pressure on the overstressed few who remain. That's how life goes in these days after the world has ended. When he's gone, Moira disconnects the IVs, squeezes a few more mouthfuls into her children, sponges them off, and starts getting them ready for school. Obediently they walk in the direction where she aims them, stand and sit when told to, hold up their arms, insert foot or hand or head into whatever garment is held open for them. Amy can even manage buttons on good days, and this is a good day. Moira hugs her—"Clever girl, Amy!"—and then feels obliged to praise and hug Timmy as well, to be fair. Who knows what they see and hear?

———— «〉» ————

It is a bright September morning, but unseasonably chilly, a broad hint that winter may come early this year.

Moira bundles her children into warm jackets and wraps scarves around their throats. Who needs to be nursing head colds on top of everything else?

She tows them along by their flaccid hands, around the upheavals in the pavement, past the shuttered convenience store, across leaf-littered streets lined with sagging cars. This used to be the sort of greenbelt suburb where the young and prosperous middle classes would cluster for breeding purposes; therefore, with its high concentration of children, it was hit very hard by Bainbridge's Disease. On the Bakers' route to school, a dozen or more expensive swing sets are rusting in overgrown back yards, squeaking monotonously in the light wind. Scattered toys make patches of colour deep in the yellowing grass.

Moira and her children walk past the burnt-out Fraser house, the Aquino house with its boarded windows, and the Zelitsky house, home of Amy's best friend Cortney. Alas, the Zelitskys gave up hope some time ago; the glassless windows stare at Moira across a jungle of old lawn, as blank as the eyes of a latter-day child. The glimpse of faded pink near the sidewalk is Cortney's tricycle, lying right where she left it on the morning of the night she fell ill.

Sukey Chang is waiting on the next corner with Davey, Mickey and Marky, all three of whom are swaying like captive balloons on the ends of their leashes. The twins are in Timmy's class at school, while Davey is a year younger. Today he has a bandage tied around his head like a tennis-player's sweatband, and Sukey looks faintly defiant as she greets Moira. Moira does not ask.

She has long suspected that Sukey loses control now and then. The boys frequently sport bruises or bandages, and Moira has seen Sukey whip Mickey with his own leather leash when he is being more frustrating than usual, but three children must be so much more exhausting than two. Anyway, to whom would Moira report the abuse? As long as Sukey manages to keep going, keep hoping, keep feeding them and cleaning them and leading them to school, her boys are better off than the Swanson twins, or the Clemms, or poor little Cortney Zelitsky with her slashed throat.

Indeed, they are passing the Swanson house now, and out of habit Moira averts her eyes. She is the one who followed her nose into that house to find Sarah Swanson lying in the kitchen with half her head shot off, and the twins caroming aimlessly off the family room walls. Moira was shocked, though not at Sarah's suicide.

No, the shocker was that Sarah left the twins behind, dependent on the dubious care of the Commission for Orphaned and Abandoned Children. In the dry-eyed social morality that has emerged in the wake of Bainbridge's Disease, you are expected to take your children with you when you give up hope. That's what euthypacks are for. Of course Moira often wonders what she herself will do if Jeff ever dies accidentally, as Tom Swanson did, but she knows that, whatever may happen, she will never stop hoping. Never.

———— «» ————

Terrance Street, the most direct route to the school, has been impassable since the gas main exploded a while back—how lucky they all were that the undermanned fire trucks were able to keep the conflagration from crossing Memorial Park. Moira and Sukey tow their children along the detour, past the charred beams and brick piles of the little strip mall and the townhouse complex, and into the schoolyard. This is only the second week of the school term, and attendance is still good.

Moira leads Amy and Timmy to the fenced play area, where twenty or so of their playmates are milling around the monkey bars and the sandbox in a kind of leisurely Brownian motion. She opens the gate and shoves them gently inside. They shuffle straight on for a few steps until Timmy collides softly with Alison Tanner and bounces sideways into Amy. No harm is done. On they go, shuffling and milling, milling and shuffling. Moira shuts the gate and joins the mothers conversing by the door.

School is where the hopes of the parent generation are most clearly expressed. Keeping the bodies going is one matter—working towards a brighter future is quite another. Yes, Bainbridge's prion always heads straight to the frontal lobe; and yes, it multiplies disastrously there, in any brain not mature enough to block it out, severing connections, scrambling neurons, eating souls. Adults, with their fully ripened frontal lobes, are immune to the effects. Back when the pandemic first broke, the oldest victims were in their late teens. The youngest were those conceived after the pandemic's main hammerblow, those whose births were the worst possible news for the human race: a cohort of babies who never ever cried, even as they starved to death because they could not be taught to suckle. After a while, nobody had babies any more.

But that was then, and this is now, and still there is hope! As long as the mothers and fathers of the world can keep their children's bodies functioning, there is hope! Brain damage be damned! Gene therapy is the name of the game now, the magic bullet being cast by the scientists, the test-tube sorcery that someday soon will make the surviving children well again. Moira's faith in the scientists is absolute. She does her part by tending the shells of her children, just as a housekeeper will air, clean, and polish an empty house in the expectation that its owners will soon return. The IVs supply antibiotics to keep them well, vitamins and minerals to nourish them, meds to keep them docile—unsedated, the limbic system tends to kick in a little too primally, and behaviour can turn awkward. The solid food is necessary to keep the gut from closing down, to supply carefully calculated fibre, and to keep the children from eating *other things*.

Meantime, hopeful parents do their best to nurture minds as well as bodies, just in case. Even the scientists cannot say definitively whether some tiny flame of consciousness burns deep in the children's ravaged brains. Talk to them. Read to them. Assume they can hear you. That was the advice handed out in the early days, along with the pamphlets on nutrition, feeding techniques, medication, incontinence control, security. Moira, taking it as her gospel, is tireless in her post-Bainbridgian maternal duties.

———— «» ————

The school door swings wide. Stooped, greying, and unshakeable, Miss Arthur greets the mothers and signals to the volunteers to round up the children and set them walking in her direction. Moira has no duties on this week's roster, though she is down for playground supervision next week and classroom assistance the week after. How lucky they are to have Miss Arthur still willing to serve; so many teachers have simply given up. Moira waves to Amy and Timmy as they pass, thinking what a joyful surprise it will be if someday they wave back. And what she wouldn't give to hear them quarrelling again!

"I don't see Lisa Murray," Sukey says beside her. "Maybe Joshie came down with that bug over the weekend. I know he was feverish on Friday."

"Well, then, it's a good thing if she's kept him home. Coming to Safeway?"

Sukey shakes her head and moves toward the school steps, speaking over her shoulder. "Sorry, Moy, I'm on the roster today. But could you pick me up some candles for Davey's birthday party? I won't have time before tomorrow. See you at twelve."

"Okay." Twelve o'clock is feeding time. Every mother has to come and do her own. Walking towards the school gate, Moira kicks away a picture-memory: Amy, Grade One, two months before Bainbridge's and the end of the world, is waving goodbye to Moira from the same school steps. In her other hand is a lunchbox with a cartoon princess pictured on each side. Inside the lunchbox is a tuna sandwich, an apple, carrot sticks, a box of raisins, and a tiny carton of juice. Timmy, stumping along beside Moira, desperately desires a lunchbox too, but Moira tells him to wait until next year—next year he'll be old enough for kindergarten, and she'll buy him a superhero lunchbox for his morning snack, even though he'll be coming home for lunch…

Moira blinks rapidly, and after a few seconds she has the tears under control. Hope, she tells herself. She looks at her watch. There is more than enough time to get to Safeway, buy birthday candles for Sukey and formula for the kids and a bit of real food for the grownups' dinner—steak, maybe, or anyway what passes for steak these days—and perhaps to go down Sixth and see if there's any sign the library will ever reopen. And it will be a kindness to stop in at Lisa Murray's on the way, to see if Joshie does have the flu, and if Lisa needs anything from the store. Single mothers have a tough time of it in this age of the world. Moira goes out the school gates and down the street, bears left past the ruins of the Well Baby Clinic, and carries on up the hill towards Lisa's upscale condo complex.

Moira would not care to live there herself. The complex is fairly isolated, set off by ruins on one side and the upper edge of Memorial Park on the other, and Lisa and her son Joshie are almost the only tenants left. It is probably safe enough, but it is no longer a pleasant place. Moira follows the cracked sidewalk past the dry swimming pool and deserted playground, along a laneway flanked by graffiti-spattered garden walls. Grass runs riot in all the postage-stamp yards except Lisa's.

The smell hits her as she passes Lisa's open window—a desperately familiar smell. Moira's pace slows for a step or two, then quickens. The outer door is open, but the door to the living room is shut, and she can hear movement behind it. She stops in the hallway, nerving herself. She has a shrewd idea of what she will find.

"No, Joshie, *no*," she says firmly as she steps into the living room. It is clear that his meds have worn off, and that he is, or was, very hungry. Lisa's body, except for the leg Joshie has been able to chew off, is in a tangle between the couch and the coffee table. Keeping a careful eye on Joshie, Moira bends over to inspect the remains. Suicide looks unlikely, she notes; almost certainly natural causes, perhaps a heart attack or a stroke. And judging by the stink and by Joshie's level of limbic distress, it could have happened as early as last Friday.

Joshie approaches, growling deep in his throat, dragging his mother's leg by the ankle behind him. He drops the leg and reaches for Moira, but oh! kids these days are so terribly slow! Evading him easily, Moira backs out of the room. She shuts the door behind her and wedges the handle. Joshie will be safe enough until the Commission's van comes for him, and Lisa is beyond needing protection.

———— «» ————

Between having to stop at the Commission to report an orphaned child and finding a long lineup at the one manned checkout counter at Safeway, Moira barely makes it back to school in time for lunch. The other mothers shake their heads at the news of Lisa's death, but the shakes are perfunctory. What's another death, after all that have gone before? Everyone's affect has long since been hammered flat.

But that evening, Moira is surprised. She mentions Lisa's death to Jeff in passing as he helps bathe and diaper the children for bed. He has been a little gloomy all evening, indeed for the last week or so, and now his mouth goes tight. He drops the IV hookup on Timmy's bed and flops down beside it, closing his hands like shutters over his face.

Moira, taken aback, finishes the IV for him, tucks Timmy into bed and kisses both children goodnight. Then she takes Jeff by the elbow and leads him as she would lead a blind man into the kitchen. His hands are still over his face. She sits him down at the table and puts herself in the chair beside him.

"What's up?" she asks.

Jeff drops his hands and stares at her. "It's too much, Moira. I can't go on."

"Of course you can! Though it is sad, isn't it? But I didn't know you were that fond of Lisa."

"Who? Lisa? This isn't about her. I hardly knew her. It's about the whole damn thing." He leans back in the chair, his eyes screwed shut. "I found out today, Al Burket's putting his affairs in order. I don't know what he's waiting for. They'll be taking the kids with them anyway, so what's the point of tying up loose ends?"

"They're just trying to do things properly. I do think it's a pity, though, when parents give up hope like that."

He opens his eyes and stares dully at the floor. "That's not all. Emily Grissom had a stroke Saturday night—she was dead by the morning. Ben was at work today, but he's pretty cut up. And I bet he'll be reaching for the euthypacks himself before long, since he can't look after that daughter of theirs on his own, and his heart's bad to begin with."

"Don't think about it, Jeff. All we can do is keep on hoping. I know it's sad, but that sort of thing happens all the time."

"That's just the point, damn it! It does happen all the time. Strokes. Heart failure. Kidney failure. Cancer. Sheer bloody exhaustion. We're all dropping in our tracks."

"Poor old Jeff," she says, "you've had such a bad day. You get yourself a drink, and I'll put those steaks on. Just remember, any day now we could get good news from the scientists." She starts to rise, but he leans forward to catch her shoulder and pushes her back into the chair.

"No, Moy. I've been thinking."

"Okay, you sit, I'll get your drink."

"I don't want a drink! I don't want anything! We can't go on, Moira."

"Stop it," she says, starting to worry. "It almost sounds like you're giving up hope on me. As long as there's life, there's hope."

He looks at her wearily. "You call this life?"

"Of course!" she says, making the effort to smile widely, wider, to cheer him up. "We can't give up now. What if we gave up, and the very next day the scientists found the cure? Think of the children."

"The children." He laughs at that, bitterly and mirthlessly, and then he begins to cry. "There's not going to be a cure, Moira. If there was going to be a cure, it would have come out already. I doubt anyone's even working on it anymore. Things are running down, we're all wearing out. Do you really want to leave Amy and Timmy alone in a world like this?"

"That's crazy talk."

"It's the truth. You and I, we could drop dead in our tracks any day, like Emily, like that friend of yours, Lisa. I've been thinking about this for quite a while now. We have to do something."

Moira's lips are dry. She licks them. "What do you mean?"

"You know what I mean." He tries to twine her fingers in his, but she bats his hand away.

"You mean you want us to kill ourselves," she says icily, "and murder the children."

"The children! The children!" He laughs again through his tears, and then he gets up and crosses the room to the meds drawer. He pulls it open as far as it will go, because the four euthypacks that the law now insists be kept on the premises have been stashed at the very back. "I think we should do it tonight, unless you want a day or two to set our affairs in order, not that our affairs matter any more. But I think it's urgent we go ahead and do Amy and Timmy as soon as possible, just in case, because think what'll happen to them if we drop dead, too. They'd be in the same fix as that Lisa's son you found today."

"You've gone mad," she says.

"No, Moira, I've just stopped fooling myself." But he does seem more than a little manic, shoving the table settings out of his way with a forearm as he sits down, clearing a place where he can get the doses ready. Moira realizes she should have seen this crisis coming, but the children keep her so tired. He breaks open the first euthypack and starts assembling the guaranteed painless applicator, fumbling in his eagerness, but the euthypacks are designed to be forgiving of clumsiness. The first is ready, the second snaps together easily in his hands. "I know it may seem a bit hasty, but think about it, you'll see it's better this way. I mean, half the guys at work are already going downhill, Moy honey, and I don't want to end up like—"

He stops talking then because Moira has come up behind him and sunk one of the steak knives deep into his back. He dies as he hits the floor. Moira falls to her knees beside him, sincerely grieving, but knowing she has done the right thing to protect her children's future.

Weeping softly, she pulls the knife out and turns Jeff onto his back. She smooths his white hair neatly across the liver-spotted dome of his head, bends to kiss his papery cheek. Then, still weeping, but with undamaged hope, she goes to check on her children. Tomorrow is Davey Chang's forty-third birthday, and she needs Amy and Timmy to get a good night's sleep.

# The Fremont Collection

**She explored Loch** Ness, surface to bed and shore to shore, and found nothing but otters and fish. In protective gear designed by herself, she wandered alone across the Mongolian edge of the Gobi, watching vainly for a ripple of deathworms under the dunes. She was stalked by a snow leopard in the Himalayas, but no yeti crossed her path. She braved the Bolivian highlands for the mapinguari, an obscure island in the Philippines for the aswang, the Congolese jungle for the dingonek. Clare Fremont travelled hopefully to these places and many more and left them all empty-handed.

Nevertheless, the Fremont Collection was in no danger of stagnating. Nearly a dozen travel-worn packages with interesting stamps had accumulated during Clare's latest disappointment in Africa, and now their contents were laid out on a worktable that floated on a sea of discarded bubble wrap. Latex-gloved, Clare fingered a mermaid's iridescent scale, about the size and shape of a guitar pick, ordered from Tonga. The baby chupacabra drifted in a pickle jar—Mexican hot peppers, according to the label. The tupperware container beside it held a fine matched set of bunyip fangs, yellow and wicked, allegedly extracted from the mangled flesh of an Australian aborigine in 1872. Less exciting was the horn of a unicorn (the collection already held three) and the baggie of tiny bones said to be the mortal remains of an Icelandic fairy. Alas, the latter looked remarkably birdlike to Clare, except for the tiny skull. She was frowning at it through her hand lens when the butler coughed discreetly at the museum door.

"Miss Clare? Your guest has arrived."

"Already?" She set the lens down on the high-crested skull of what purported to be a juvenile Welsh dragon and glanced at her watch. "Damn, he's early. Show him up, Simmons. Oh, and Simmons?"

The butler turned at the door. "Yes, Miss Clare?"

"Lunch in half an hour, if he lasts that long."

"The usual protocol, then?"

"Of course."

"Very well, Miss Clare."

The visitor's letter was anchored to the table by a large, leathery egg from Central Africa—a mokele-mbembe in embryo, if the accompanying invoice was to be trusted. Clare pulled the letter free for a last scan; it was cheeky and a little cryptic, which annoyed and intrigued her in equal measure. He had a line on something unique, he said, something different and exciting, a discovery that would have every cryptozoologist on the planet salivating into their beer, with particular relevance to herself.

Inelegant phrasing, she thought, even a little insulting to a cryptozoologist with a taste in fine wines. The only reason she had not crumpled the letter into a ball and tossed it on the fire was the fact that it was an actual handwritten letter—not a printout, not an email, not a text message, not even a near-Stone-Age fax. An actual letter, inscribed with pen on actual paper, mailed in a hand-addressed envelope with a stamp in one corner. These days, that was as rare as a bunyip's tooth or a sea-serpent's whisker.

*If* he was being honest, of course. If not, he would be only the latest of many trying to worm their way onto the estate, just to catch a glimpse of the fabled Fremont Collection. Clare was choosy about whom she allowed entrance. Too many would come only to mock or debunk—journalists working up silly-season exposés, hard-nosed skeptics rolling their eyes. Others came with insulting offers to buy this or that treasure for their own collections. Wild-eyed ufologists or conspiracy nutters sought validation for their pathetic fantasies. No, the Fremont Collection was too good for them, too special.

She swept her gaze proudly up the long, cluttered gallery. This was no modern, spartan museum. It was in much the same spirit as in her great-great-great-grandfather's time, only vastly expanded, a Victorian cabinet of curiosities on a majestic scale. A double row of glass and mahogany display cabinets ran down the centre, each exhibit identified with a handwritten tag, some of which were themselves over a century old. One end wall was covered floor-to-ceiling with books bound in fine calfskin covers with spines lettered in gold. A vast array of mahogany specimen drawers and closed shelving filled the long wall, under a sweep of exotic taxidermy. Clement Fremont himself would have felt right at home.

It was he, Clare's great-great-great-grandfather, who began gathering the alleged relics of legendary creatures long before the term "cryptozoology" was even coined. His son, her great-great-grandfather, was a friend of Charles Darwin; their correspondence, carefully curated, filled half a shelf in the temperature-controlled document chest to the left of the main door. Her great-grandfather, grandfather and father carried on the tradition, often in the face of their colleagues' ridicule, which became more pointed as the 20th century came and went. That did not matter to Clare's forebears, and it did not matter to Clare. Nor did the uncertain fates that came with the territory. Her great-grandfather and his elder son, her great-uncle, failed to return from the jungles of Indochina in the 1890s; her father and mother vanished on an expedition into Sasquatch country when Clare was fifteen. Clare, nevertheless, had not hesitated to take up the mantle. Now she was the last of the Fremonts.

"Wow, it's like this whole room's preserved in amber." Her guest lounged in the doorway, wide-eyed, one hand in a pocket of his jeans, the other holding a battered leather satchel. Clare could not tell whether the look on his face reflected awe or mirth, but he was certainly not showing due reverence.

"If you're here to mock, Doctor Chatterjee," she said, "you can turn right around and leave my house."

"Relax, I think it's fabulous. And it's *Mister* Chatterjee. Like you, I never got the union card. But call me Hari." He dropped the satchel and strode across the polished hardwood towards her, hand outstretched—early thirties maybe, a few years younger than she, strongly resembling Indiana Jones with a deep tan. Clare was not made of stone. She put down the fairy skull, stripped off her latex glove, and let her hand be shaken.

"Pygmy marmoset," he said.

"What?"

"That teensy skull there. I bet somebody's trying to sell it to you as a tiny humanoid, right? Did it come out of that baggie of bird bones?"

"*Mister* Chatterjee," Clare began, pulling her hand away, but he stepped past her and surveyed the new acquisitions on the table.

"Cool," he said. "I see a coyote fetus in a hot pickle jar, the skull of a baby hippo, a container of tigerfish teeth, a resin cast of a narwhal tusk—what's the guitar pick supposed to be?"

"*Mister* Chatterjee," she began again, "this is intolerable."

"Why? You knew they were fakes, right? Like this egg—I bet they're trying to pass it off as the egg of a living dinosaur. Whereas you and I know it's fabricated from crocodile leather, one of the Lake Victoria breeds judging by the ridge pattern...look, you can see the stitches."

With dignity, Clare picked up her hand lens and examined the mokele-mbembe egg at the spot indicated. "Of course," she said. "I knew that."

But he was past her already, cruising the nearer display cabinets, face shining with fascination. Clare considered various ways of stopping him, from ringing for Simmons to throwing the dragon/hippo skull at his head, but something held her back. He was right about the fraudulent egg, and possibly right about the rest. In fact, deep in Clare's head was a secret *so very* secret that she barely admitted it to herself: she had long been suppressing doubts of her own about the ancestral monsters. All those grootslangs and bunyips and dingoneks and yetis and sea serpents, all those little mummified claws and nasty things floating in formaldehyde...

"*Mister* Chatterjee," she said for the third time, "I really must insist—"

"Oh, man! Not one, not two, but *three* giant beggarmakers." His shapely nose was all but pressed to the glass of the Java cabinet, as close as it could get to a collection of beetles the size of Clare's fist.

"I'm surprised you take any of our specimens seriously, Mr. Chatterjee. You've been nothing but rude about the Fremont Collection so far."

"Oh, the beggarmakers are real, there's no doubt about that, though they're really just overgrown cockroaches. A friend of mine lost part of his face to them in the Sulawesi highlands." He showed his handsome white teeth in a smile of such charm that Clare completed the unfamiliar process of melting. There were two buttons sunk flush into the side of the worktable: the red button that would summon Simmons and two footmen to escort the visitor off the premises with all necessary force, and the green button that would instruct Simmons to serve aperitifs in the conservatory. Clare pressed the green button.

"Perhaps," she said, "we could finish touring the collection after lunch."

《〉》

Even before aperitifs gave way to appetizers—Hokkaido sea urchin in lobster jelly, topped with beluga caviar—it was clear Hari Chatterjee knew his cryptids. He and Clare quickly found common ground. They had journeyed to some of the same remote pissholes of the Earth, sometimes only months apart; they could share tales of a rotten hostel in Ouagadougou, a surprising little patisserie in Kathmandu. For him, though, the great quest was a matter for holidays and stolen moments. He was a biologist (a real biologist, some would have said) working on contract for a pharmaceutical company with an eye to the bodily fluids of novel amphibians. So far, two new species bore his name: an Amazonian frog (*Phyllobates chatterjeeii*) and an Indonesian newt (*Laotriton chatterjeeii*).

"But you and I would agree," he said to Clare as Simmons cleared away the first course, "that a new species of newt or a jumbo cockroach doesn't really cut it as a cryptid. We're two of a kind, Ms. Fremont. Forget science. We're after something with a bit of glamour, yes? Something out of myth and legend. A true monster."

Clare felt her face stiffen. And just when they were getting on so well! "My family," she said, "has a long tradition of pure research, in the interests of science and truth. Glamour has never been a factor." She paused while Hari helped himself from the platter of duck confit and citrus cannelloni proffered by a stone-faced Simmons. "My great-grandfather, great-uncle, and both my parents were martyrs to that tradition," she continued, "and I have dedicated myself to it as well. Please do not trivialize our...our sacrifice."

Grinning, Hari waved his hand in a gesture that encompassed the linen-swathed silver-laden table in particular and the conservatory in general, as if to say, *some sacrifice*. Rare floral exotica made a living artwork on three sides of the clearing where the table was set; on the fourth, French doors gave onto a small sea of emerald lawn and formal garden. Clare frowned and fumbled with her heavy silver fork. She was starting to wish she had pushed the red button after all.

"Hey," Hari said, reaching across the table to touch her hand, "I'm not belittling the Fremonts, especially not you. I've read every word ever written by your great-great-great-grandfather and all the others, right down to your father, and they were gentleman-adventurers in the classic mold. Great guys, the whole bunch."

"I'm gratified that you approve of them," she said, in a voice so cold that Simmons, hovering, made an instinctive move towards the bell-rope that would summon two burly footmen.

"Approve? Well, not entirely, because they were something else as well that's not quite so admirable. They were true believers, Ms. Fremont." He waved a forkful of duck breast at her, as if admonishing her with a wagging finger.

"Of course they were true believers!" Clare exclaimed. She speared a slippery tube of cannelloni and bit down on it with more force than necessary. "They had to have the courage of their convictions, to carry on the great work..."

"...In the interests of science and truth? Pull the other one, Ms. Fremont. You know as well as I do, they were as gullible as yokels at a fairground freak show. They believed everything, every tall tale, every vague description of something half-seen from a distance at the dead of night or reported fifth-hand by friends of friends of friends of—"

"Is this what you call 'not belittling,' Mr. Chatterjee?" Clare pushed her plate away and signalled to Simmons with a meaningful glance.

"I call it telling the truth. Now you—you're different. I mean that in a good way. The best way possible. And nothing to do with how pretty you are."

Clare hesitated, then shook her head minutely in Simmons's direction. "How could you possibly know anything about me, Mr. Chatterjee? We have only just met."

"Easy. I've read everything you've ever written, as well."

"That's very little to go on," she sniffed. "A couple of monographs, a few notes in obscure journals..."

"It was enough. I'm pretty good at reading between the lines. All those books and monographs written by your forefathers? There's nothing between the lines to read. They are what they are. But you, Ms. Fremont—you have an inner skeptic like other people have an inner child."

"That is complete nonsense," Clare snapped, but she still found herself not signalling Simmons.

"Oh, I think you're just like me, aching to be a true believer. It's what you were raised to be, after all, just as you were raised to take on that great white elephant upstairs, the Fremont Collection. But in your heart of hearts, you're afraid that maybe ninety-nine per cent of legendary cryptids are bogus—it's that pesky one per cent that keeps you going. You think if you can find just one good solid monster, something big and different and glamorous, then it will somehow validate all the rest. And then you can reassure yourself that Daddy and Granddaddy and so on were doing something worthwhile and scientific the whole time."

"And you claim to know all that simply from reading my monographs?"

"Well, you know what they say—it takes one to know one."

Clare regarded him narrowly. He was being unforgivably rude, after such a promising start; a word to Simmons, and he'd be out on the driveway on his backside in under two minutes. He smiled at her, a curiously trusting smile, and returned his attention to the duck.

"Simmons," said Clare, "we'll take our coffee and dessert in the small drawing room in fifteen minutes. Leave us now; you can send Inga in later to clear the table." She waited until Simmons, with an inscrutable backward glance, vanished into the undergrowth in the direction of the door. Then she leaned forward, all business. "Your letter promised a unique cryptid, of interest to me in particular. You have five minutes to tell me about it."

Hari grinned. How very white and straight his teeth looked! "Them, not it," he said.

"Fine. What makes them so special?"

"Well, for one thing," he said, "they exist."

"That remains to be seen." Clare sat back, chin high. "What else?"

Hari leaned back too, lacing his fingers behind his head in a posture so confidently relaxed that it was almost offensive. "What does the phrase 'little green men' make you think of?"

So he was one of those idiots. Clare reminded herself that Fremonts always maintained their dignity, whatever the provocation. She took a deep, calming breath. "It makes me think you have outstayed your welcome, Mr. Chatterjee."

"You thought of aliens, right? Why does everyone always think of aliens? Ms. Fremont, you know that great-grandfather of yours who disappeared in Indochina in 1894, along with one of his sons?"

"Of course."

"Well, that's what he was looking for—little green men. Unfortunately for him, he found them." Hari picked up his wine glass and raised it in a toast.

Lips tight, Clare left her wine glass where it was. "The orang hijau," she said flatly. "You're actually trying to sell me on the orang hijau."

"Yep. Remember what it means in Malay? Green men. And they were definitely on the small side. See? Little green men."

"Mr. Chatterjee, you disappoint me. You had me convinced for a while that you were an honest researcher."

He grinned again. He had a subtle and utterly charming dimple in one cheek which Clare had not noticed before. It infuriated her to notice it now.

"Do you imagine," she grated, "the family did not thoroughly investigate my great-grandfather's disappearance at the time? My great-grandmother's agents borrowed troops from the colonial governor, hired trackers, offered huge rewards, spent months searching for him. No trace was ever found, either of Alfred and Allen Fremont or the orang hijau. The final verdict was that the expedition met with an accident in the jungle, and the orang hijau never existed in the first place. Case closed. And I do think it's time you left." At last, Clare reached for the bell-rope.

"Wait for it." Hari reached under his chair for his satchel, extracted a torn sheet of paper in an acid-free plastic cover, and held it out to her. Glaring, she took it from his hand.

——— «》 ———

The scene: five months and one whirlwind courtship later, nine thousand miles away. Clare had spent her life following in her forebears' footsteps, but never quite so literally. Alfred Fremont himself, her great-grandfather, may have sat by his son Allen's side outside their canvas tent in this same little hollow in the rocky hillside, looking out across the same stretch of rainforest under the same baking sky. That canvas tent was still extant, along with the folding canvas bathtub, chairs, and cots, Alfred's portable writing desk, a pile of Allen's sketchbooks, their evening dress and spare sola topees, all retrieved from their last tragic base camp and preserved in one of the storage basements under Fremont House. State of the art for their time, of course.

The art had changed since their time. Clare's double-walled geodesic domes owed their fabric to the space program, and their form to field tests in Antarctica and the deep Sahara—strong enough to withstand anything from a blizzard to a haboob, light enough to allow a single bearer to schlepp all three modules. Not that Clare had needed bearers yet; her two ATVs were designed for rainforest and mountainside, could float in a flood or across most rivers, and came with solar-powered fridges and satellite arrays. And yet, Clare had the distinct impression that her bridegroom was entertained by her gear, rather than impressed.

Lovely smells emanated from the chef's spacious inflatable cook-tent, the last such meal Clare and Hari would enjoy before the next morning's plunge into the rainforest. Tinned foie gras to start, followed by braised wild-boar cheeks on a bed of polenta and truffles, and mango-curd souffle to finish. It was amazing what one could obtain in freeze-dried form these days. With an effort, Clare pulled her mind away from the prospect of dinner, and back to the facsimile volume of Alfred Fremont's field notes that was open in her lap. The handwriting was blotched and faded, but she preferred it to the typed transcript, which gave no visual cue of Alfred's excitement as he wrote.

*Just over the next hill, or the next, or the next. We are close, that is the primary thing; I could feel it in my bones when we reached the village of Huang two days ago, to where Van Groot tracked the little fellows in '67, and Chauvet succumbed to malaria. The villagers were useless, pointing this way and that way into the jungle—we did not need Sanjit to tell us they were prevaricating. One would almost think they wanted to prevent us from locating the orang hijau. But I have poor Chauvet's sketch map to keep us on the right track, the clue being not what is there, but what is not there: the uncharted spot in the mountain fastnesses where no government surveyor has yet reached.*

What would old Alfred have made of GPS, Clare wondered; what would he have made of the aerial and satellite photos she could access with a tap on her little screen? The small connected valleys that might have been

Alfred Fremont's initial target had been settled since his time, with terraced fields at least a century old advancing up the hillsides and clearly visible from the air. What a pity Chauvet's map and the last notebook had vanished with poor lost Alfred and Allen! And yet, her great-grandfather's principle still held, even in the age of Google Earth. The target species, if it existed, would be found in a place where the surveyors and the godlike eyes of the satellites had not penetrated: an unexciting spur of valley, difficult of access, or a limestone cave which had escaped being turned into a shrine and a tourist attraction. If Hari was right, it was the latter.

For the hundredth time, she drew the scanned copy of that all-important scrap of paper from the back of the facsimile volume and held it beside Alfred's last known page of notes. The spacing of the lines matched, as did the ink, verified by laboratory analysis. The handwriting matched well enough, taking into account the writer's obvious urgency. The left edge of the original was ragged, where the sheet had been ripped from a notebook similar to the ones Alfred left behind in his last base camp. The bottom half had been torn away, taking much of the message with it.

*My dearest Emmeline, I have found the orang hijau and they are a marvel, but they will not let Allen and me go. Poor Sanjit is dead, and most of the bearers with him. Tell Charbonneau he must come in force. Tell him he must follow the third…[end of line missing]…look high on the…[message breaks off]…*

Third what? Third valley, third tributary, third peak? And counting from where? Look high on the what? She and Hari had pored over the satellite photos till their eyes burned, tracing the paths of tributaries and little branching valleys, the lines of summits and saddlebacks in the high hills. Of course it was possible there was nothing left to see—that the orang hijau who apparently wiped out most of her great-grandfather's expedition had in turn been wiped out as the villages spread inexorably into the remoter valleys in the early 20th century. As far as Clare knew, there were very few references to the little green men postdating Alfred's ill-starred foray.

A soft step behind her, a light kiss on the top of her head. Hari pulled the other high-tech camp chair closer to Clare's and propped his feet decoratively on a packing crate. Clare reached out and put her hand on his sleeve.

"Everything ready for the morning?" she asked.

"Ready and raring to go," Hari said. "Ali has the backpacks all squared away, Dev has the field tents packed, Alphonse has the rations sorted out. I've loaded the route into the GPS and emailed the coordinates to Simmons. At least he'll know where to start looking if we don't come out of the jungle. He'd look for you, anyway. I bet he hopes I'll fall into a snakepit."

"Don't be silly, darling." But Clare did not meet Hari's eyes.

"Come on, he's the quintessential old family retainer. He doesn't trust me, believes I married you for your collection, and doesn't think I'm up to the Fremont standard. I think he's skeptical about Alfred's message, too."

"Hari, he's been looking after me all my life, especially after my parents vanished. Naturally he's protective of me."

Hari laughed. "As if the woman who went hunting deathworms in the Gobi Desert would ever need protection. I'll see how Alphonse is doing." But first he reached over and pulled Clare forward for a honeymoon-length kiss. When he was gone, Clare recovered her breath and then returned to frowning at the facsimile of that torn sheet of paper.

Simmons was right about that. Hari's tale of how the fragmentary message came into his hands was more than a little unbelievable. A curio stall in the Russian Market in Phnom Penh (she knew the very stall), stuffed with all the usual tat—and on a dusty shelf near the back, among worn antique coins and tarnished antique oil lamps, lay a dusty photograph album of the late Victorian era. Pasted in the front half were the sorts of photographic views beloved of Victorian travellers in the Far East, the harbours of Hong Kong and Singapore, the temples of Angkor Wat, the stupas of Bangkok. Hari, according to his own account, leafed through it idly and was about to return it to the shelf when a torn half-sheet of paper fluttered from the pages at the back...

What were the odds? Clare often wondered uncomfortably about that. What were the odds that Hari would go to that particular stall, pick up that very album, and be the one person uniquely qualified to recognize the significance of the scrap that floated out? And how would the scrap have ended up in the album to begin with? No wonder Simmons was skeptical. He had extricated her twice before from disastrous entanglements—the self-styled kraken-hunter who couldn't even swim, and the bluff and handsome seller of Sasquatch body parts that all turned out to be molded rubber. But Hari was different, and now he was her husband. Simmons had been right to urge caution, but she was reasonably hopeful he was wide of the mark this time. Idly, she fingered her lucky bracelet and gazed across the canopy of the rainforest spread out below.

There was the notch in the treeline that marked the trailhead they would enter in the morning, insignificant in a sea of achingly green leaves and towering trunks. And there was the footpath down to the forest, too steep even for the ATVs, a clamber through tumbles of limestone boulders leading to a treacherous fan of scree. And there was—something moving.

She sat forward, squinting. Something flitted among the boulders about a hundred yards away, a tiny shape almost invisible in the shadows. She lost it, found it again a little further down the slope. What was a child doing down there? The nearest village was miles away. But there it was, sized like a five-year-old, a too-large head bobbing on a slender neck, shirtless, little arms flailing as it scampered down the steep path. Clare was not fond of children, but she did have a sense of adult responsibility. She stood up, shading her eyes, watching for it to come into the open on the scree. Should she follow, make sure the child was safe? Hesitantly, she started forward.

"Chow's up, Clare. Alphonse sent me to get you." Hari came up beside Clare, peered into her face, followed the direction of her eyes. "What's going on, wife? You look like you've seen a ghost."

"Not a ghost," she said, "a child. Down among the boulders."

Hari laughed. "Are you sure it was a child? Was it green, by any chance?"

"Green? Like the orang hijau? Not that I could see," she said, taking Hari's arm, "but don't you think we should go down and check on it? What if the poor thing's lost?"

"I don't think that'll be necessary. Look down there, the kid's properly supervised."

Clare followed his pointing finger: there were two figures, one significantly taller than the other, partially hidden in one of the shallow gullies that creased the scree like folds in a fan. As she watched, the pair emerged fully at the bottom of the slope and vanished into the treeline.

"See? Nothing to worry about. Let's eat."

There were two thoughts that Clare could not shake as they strolled arm-in-arm towards the elegantly laid table in the dining tent. First, on reflection, maybe there had been a greenish cast to the skins of both distant figures; second, that Alfred and Allen Fremont had customarily dressed for dinner, except in the very depths of the wilderness.

———— «◊» ————

It was a two-day hike to the foot of the range of hills that enfolded the valleys of immediate interest. The going was gently uphill, and not challenging; it was a well-travelled track, with the undergrowth encroaching on but never quite overwhelming the path, and narrow log bridges spanning the network of placid streams oozing down from the hills. Now and then villages were in earshot, invisible in the distance along side-paths splitting off from the main trail. They encountered nobody even then, though Clare often had the impression that eyes in the undergrowth were watching them pass.

Only three bearers marched with Clare and Hari, old hands from one of Hari's previous expeditions. Clare thought of the mob of servants and bearers, forty-odd at least, who usually eased Alfred's journeys into the wild. Her own retinue of chef, drivers, and two camp servants was relatively restrained—but then, Alfred had not had the advantage of all-terrain vehicles to carry the load to the edge of the rainforest. Ironically, Clare would have welcomed a larger entourage in the deep green wilderness. Hari's field hires were silent when she was around, almost to the point of sullenness, though she heard them being chummy enough with Hari when she was not visible. She privately dubbed them the Brothers Grim but did not share the joke with Hari.

Late on the second afternoon, the forest thinned and the slope of the land steepened. Abruptly, not long before sunset, they broke into the open at the lower edge of a great staircase of terraced fields, with a large village a few hundred yards to the north. The partly tamed landscape stretched far past the village, splitting in the distance under three high saddlebacks divided by rocky ridges. Even before she checked her printout of the satellite image, Clare recognized the landforms. Their first candidate for Alfred's target location was a possible cave on the third and highest of the saddlebacks, the only one showing no terracing on its lower flanks. Could it really be so easy?

The village, as they entered its outskirts, was quiet—too quiet. Dusk had fallen by then, but Clare could see no lights shining through the bamboo sides of the houses; could hear no sound of women at their work. And where were the goats, chickens, and children who were always the first responders in any remote village Clare had ever entered? The only indication the village was not deserted was the scent of roasting meat hanging in the air.

"I bet they're all gathered in the centre of town, waiting to greet us," Hari said cheerfully when Clare mentioned her misgivings.

Clare thought it over. "How would they know we're coming?"

"Oh, they'd know. Bush telegraph. I also bet they've got a feast waiting for us—smell that roast pig? We're honoured visitors." They turned a corner between two compounds walled in brushwood. "I told you so," Hari added.

Clare estimated that about a hundred villagers were gathered in the square around a small bonfire, some men in rather flashy sarongs nearest the fire, plus a few women and a large crowd of children keeping to the shadows. The fattest and most broadly smiling of the men, wearing the most outrageously tasteless of the sarongs, moved forward to greet them. Clare presumed that he was the headman of the village.

"I guess we're obliged to stay in town for the night," she whispered.

"Of course we are, lucky us. And they'll give us an excellent dinner. Unfortunately, my love, there will be speeches. Don't worry, I'm pretty good on the local lingo. Just don't drink too much of the local booze."

Clare was savvy enough not to need the warning, but it was easier said than done. The predicted feast, roast goat and piglet and unfamiliar greens, arrived with a small river of potent drink, and continued to arrive long after the brief tropical twilight had vanished into full darkness. There were lengthy and rather drunken speeches from the headman, jangling performances on flutes and drums, more food, more booze…and only when Clare was on the point of falling asleep from boredom, overfeeding, and strong drink did Hari raise any pertinent questions. The headman listened jovially and threw back his head in laughter.

The orang hijau? Yes, Hari translated, the headman knew of them, but they were no more than a story told to naughty children by their grandmas, to discourage them from mischief. The high saddleback hill to the north? Worthless, too rocky and dry to repay the effort of terracing. White-faced visitors in the past? A few colonial officials in the years before independence, but these valleys had only been settled within the headman's father's lifetime. And no, he knew no stories from times before then, no stories of a lordly orang putih with a sola topee on his head and many servants and a little house made out of canvas. Even as Hari finished translating, Clare was already thinking ahead to the next candidate site marked on the satellite map.

———— «» ————

Clare woke late, with a less ferocious headache than she figured she deserved. Sipping a cup of the divine blend of Thai coffee packed by Alphonse, she sat beside Hari outside the tents, which the Brothers Grim had pitched by the remains of the bonfire in the village square. Any memory of the end of the evening was hazy, which did not surprise her. The surprise was the utter silence that again lay over the village, not so much as the morning crow of a rooster, the fussing of a baby, the bleating of a goat.

"Where is everybody? Why is it so quiet?"

"I don't know. Maybe they're in the fields. This is the kind of insanely expensive coffee where the beans are dug out of elephant poop, right?"

"Of course," said Clare. The silence bothered her. She fingered her lucky bracelet, then drained her mug of coffee and poured another. "We should get going soon. Is it really worth checking out that cave on the saddleback? Surely the headman would know if anything significant was there."

"If he was telling the truth. Remember the villagers who tried to throw poor old Alfred off the scent? Maybe these guys know more than they're willing to tell us. Anyway, we're here now, we may as well see what's there."

Another feature of the state-of-the-art field tents was how easy they were to strike. Within fifteen minutes of Clare finishing her coffee, the Brothers Grim were standing ready with their loads on their backs, and Hari was scrutinizing the distant saddleback through Clare's digital binoculars.

"I see the potential cave opening high on the slope," he told Clare, "and I've got a good feeling about this. Let's get going."

Clare grunted. Could it be her low-level hangover that was making her feel uneasy? Or was there something else? And why was the village continuing to deliver such a good impression of a ghost town, dusty and dead? She felt the skin crawl on her back as she shouldered her pack and plodded after the others along the hardpacked dirt of the path. As they passed the last house, she was not reassured to see that the terraced fields were empty of workers—the only moving objects in the suddenly forbidding landscape were her companions and a few vulture-like birds wheeling high over the saddlebacks and catching the rising sun on their wings.

Hari continued to be cheerful, almost irritatingly so. "That's a cave for sure!" he crowed some time later. They were halfway across the lower flanks of the middle saddleback by then, and Clare did not need the binoculars to distinguish a gaping black mouth high on the next hillside. It was partly shielded from above by a rocky outcrop, which might explain why it had not shown up well on the satellite photos. It was only at Hari's insistence that this set of valleys had even been targeted in the survey—the ambiguous blotch of pixels on the satellite photo could have been anything from a transmission glitch to a copse of bushes. But there the cave was, and it looked like a big one. And an hour later, there were also Clare and Hari and the Brothers Grim, staring into the great black hole in the hillside.

It was *big*. Clare estimated that two semis could drive into it abreast, assuming they could get up the steep grade of the saddleback. The overhang beetled above it like an eyebrow, and many paths zigzagged up through the scrubby ground cover to the mouth. Inside was darkness. Without being told, the Brothers Grim produced collapsible LED lanterns and powerful flashlights from their packs.

"After you," said Hari.

The stone floor of the entry was clean—too clean, not so much as a windblown leaf or petal—and polished as if from millennia of shuffling or dancing feet. Clare played her flashlight across the high, rough ceiling and then stabbed it into the dark interior just as the Brothers Grim turned on the LED lanterns. She caught her breath with a gasp. A woman less accustomed to shocks and perils might have shrieked.

The whole village must have been there; hundreds of faces stared back at Clare from the rear of the cave. So many children! But of course, she realized, many of them were not children. They were just very small, and their skins were undeniably tinged with green in the merciless glare from the lanterns. There was a hefty scattering of standard-sized adults as well, including the village headman in his lamentable sarong, plus some actual children. As the crowd began to shift forward to encircle the interlopers, little green faces were lifted toward Clare's like phototropic flowers seeking the sun.

"May I present the orang hijau," Hari said. He had been holding Clare's hand. Now he had a firm grip on her upper arm.

"They're real," Clare breathed. "Alfred was right."

"Yes, Alfred was right. Though I'm not sure you could really call these guys cryptids—there's no doubt that they're one hundred per cent *Homo sapiens*. The chlorotic skin and tiny stature come from some sort of minor mutation involved with protein processing, probably on Chromosome 20, but they can still breed with other humans."

Clare froze as he spoke. "What are you talking about? How do you suddenly know all this?" And why were his fingers so tight on her arm?

Hari shrugged charmingly. "They're a classic example of reproductive isolation—right up until last century, when farmers began to move into the valley, and the two populations meshed quite happily. Of course, people in the wider area knew all along where their little green brothers lived. They'd been trading with them for centuries."

"You've been here before." Clare tried to turn, but now one of the Brothers Grim was holding her other arm with a grip like an iron vise.

Hari relaxed his hold. "I found this place two years ago, while I was looking for something else."

"You've been lying to me all along."

"Well, yes, mostly, but that's irrelevant now. There's more to see." He set off toward the back of the cave, the orang hijau and villagers parting before him, Clare following perforce in the grip of the Brothers Grim. She was less surprised and much less hurt than she had expected to be, in the event that Simmons's worst suspicions were confirmed. She sighed. It was the kraken-hunter and the Sasquatch-salesman all over again.

At the rear of the cavern was a shrine: three bed-sized platforms built of rough masonry, two of them occupied, all of them banked with bunches of frangipani and jasmine. The occupants had been there for a long time, long enough for the stone beds to grow patchy coverlets of moss over them, and vines to take root in the crevices. The skulls were tightly wrapped in leather faces and topped with wisps of pale hair; bony hands emerged from sleeves; lichen-spotted boots pointed to the ceiling. The beards were braided with strips of faded red cloth, and the sola topees laid on the sunken chests were wreathed in more jasmine blossoms. At the feet of each corpse was a mildewed notebook.

The third stone bed looked newly built.

"At least you know now what happened to Alfred and Allen," Hari said. "They became gods." His face was lit with his most charming smile, the seductive dimple deeper than ever. He picked up one of the notebooks, opened it to the last written page, passed it to Clare. The top half of the page was missing, torn out along a jagged line familiar from many perusals of a certain document in an acid-free plastic cover. "Here's the rest of Alfred's distress message, in situ. He never got a chance to send it, unfortunately for him, until I came along more than a century later."

"I did have my doubts about the curio stall in Phnom Penh," Clare said tightly, "and so did Simmons."

"Ah, but you still went ahead and married me. And I want you to know, darling Clare, I honestly have regrets. I've enjoyed being married to you, and I wish we could have had more time together. We have so much in common—all those monsters we've always yearned to find."

"You're a monster."

"True enough. But I'm an apologetic monster."

Clare's lips tightened. "What are you planning to do with me?"

"Nothing. My part is done—bringing you here. The rest is up to the orang hijau. That was the deal. I think they intend to round out their collection of Fremonts, but you'll become a goddess in the process."

"And what do you get out of it?"

Hari looked surprised at the question. "Let's just say I'll take good care of the Fremont Collection. Also the Fremont fortune."

Clare shook her head sadly. That was all she needed to hear. She took a deep breath, headbutted Hari, ducked under the outstretched arm of the nearest Brother Grim, and dove through the crowd of orang hijau. The element of surprise and decades of judo lessons carried her close to the mouth of the cave before the headman tackled her to the ground.

She kicked him expertly in the groin and hurtled into the open air.

Her lucky bracelet was inset with an emerald and a ruby. She pressed the ruby until it clicked, and waited a heartbeat for the beep that would verify the transmitter had done its job. Then, as the orang hijau flooded out of the cave behind her, she turned to hold them off by sheer force of personality until Simmons and the helicopters could arrive.

———— «» ————

The scene: nine thousand miles away, six weeks and one fruitless trip to Tierra del Fuego later. Clare was glad to be home. Simmons met her in the foyer and relieved her of her laptop case; the footmen would take care of the rest of the luggage.

"Welcome home, Miss Clare. Refreshments will be served in the conservatory when you're ready. And may I say, Alphonse has outdone himself in honour of your return."

"Later, Simmons, thank you. Did any interesting specimens come in while I was gone?"

"Eleven acquisitions are laid out for you in the gallery. Three or four look interesting. Also, the DNA results on the orang hijau arrived; Mr. Chatterjee was correct, the mutation was indeed on Chromosome 20."

Clare yawned. "I'll look at all that later, too. And the other matters?"

"Ready for your inspection, Miss Clare."

They passed through two locked doors and a key-coded elevator to reach the Alfred and Allen Fremont Memorial Room, an exclusively private exhibit in a newly renovated corner of the topmost basement. Alfred and Allen had been cleaned and curated, and now reposed in a re-creation of their final base camp using the original camping gear, retrieved from storage. Clare had considered siting them in a mockup of the shrine in the cave, but this arrangement seemed somehow more respectful.

"They do look at peace," Clare said. "You've done well, Simmons. And the other matter?"

The other matter involved two more locked doors and a ride to the lowest basement, passing the taxidermist's laboratory on the way. The lights came on automatically when Simmons opened the last door for Clare.

It was a large room, though low-ceilinged, painted a pale blue that blended well with the grey marble flooring. There was ample space for many more than the three glass-encased dioramas lined up on the room's long axis. In the first, the late kraken-hunter was framed by a mural of ocean waves, and he was dressed in the same vaguely nautical jacket and cap he had affected while alive. The late vendor of fraudulent Sasquatch parts occupied the second, dressed in his jeans and leather jacket and surrounded by his wares, against a mural of mountains and firs. Clare passed them both without a glance and walked on to the third.

"Magnificent, Simmons," she said. "The taxidermy staff deserve a bonus."

"That has already been taken care of, Miss Clare, under my authority. Though, if you will permit me to speak freely, they had excellent material to work with. In my opinion, Mr. Chatterjee was already the most decorative of your husbands."

Clare examined the smile, the intact dimple, the hand resting gracefully on the head of a little green man in a tiny sarong. The latter was a wax figure, of course; the flesh-and-blood orang hijau were in no danger from her. But the jeans and shirt were the same ones that Hari had worn on that final day of their marriage, as was his fetching bush hat. He leaned elegantly against a replica of one of the stone beds, and the back curve of the diorama portrayed to a nicety the rough-hewn wall of the cave.

A few tears were natural; Simmons was ready with a handkerchief. "He made some stupid mistakes, though," said Clare, sniffling, "like trying to mislead you with the wrong GPS coordinates before we left base camp. I assume those were the coordinates where he was going to claim I vanished." She blew her nose.

"Indeed, Miss Clare. An accidental fall into the river, apparently, with his bearers as witnesses. Though, to be fair, he was not being entirely stupid. He could not have known about the tracker in your bracelet. And he had no idea I was even in the country."

"Perhaps." Her lucky, lucky bracelet. If Simmons had not talked her into hedging her bets, the indomitable butler would not have been in the country, and could not have arranged the loan of a few troops from a certain cooperative general of his acquaintance. And if Simmons, bivouacked twenty miles from her base camp, had not observed the bracelet's GPS tracker moving in the wrong direction on his screen, he would not have shifted his troops closer to Clare's actual position. She may well have ended up, after all, heaped with flowers on that hard stone bed.

The operation had been quick and clean—no resistance from the terrified orang hijau or the villagers, and only feeble resistance from Hari and his men, easily overcome. The yield was four prisoners, two Fremont mummies, and some quick DNA swabs taken at Clare's insistence before the helicopters lifted off for the long flight to the capital. Clare did not ask Simmons to specify what he planned for the Brothers Grim. She declined to exchange another word with Hari. Instead, she had a shower and a good night's sleep in the Hilton, and in the morning she took a flight to Tierra del Fuego, where a reliable source had reported a sighting of the legendary ayayema.

The exhibit was perfect. Perfect. Clare leaned in to examine the label in the corner: *Homo domesticus chatterjeeii*. A novel species, she thought; a true and glamorous monster, her own personal cryptid. She turned away. "I'll take that refreshment in the conservatory now, Simmons," she said.

# Condominium

**Annabelle types:** *Consider first the gold-painted cobblestones in the rockery beside the villa—an ultima thule of bad taste, but oh! how they shine! Hidden in plain sight among the mufti stones, ovular, fulvous, like great swollen Easter eggs wrapped in foil; philosopher's stones, self-transmuted—*

Self-transmuted, our ass! It is only The Virgin who remains impressed by the visual memory, sitting there in our grey sweats, with the coffee cup in its own brown ring on the scarred tabletop; poor little Virgin, staring at the screen through Annabelle's eyes, fingers clawform on the keys in correct at-rest position, thinking hard. She is again pondering the First Law of Creative Writing Without Tears: write about what you know. This simple dictum is giving her a great deal of trouble because she knows almost nothing. She does not know what our book is about, does not know where the metaphor is going, does not even know how to finish the sentence about the damned rockery.

The Crone knows too much, so she is saying almost nothing. She sits at the dressing table of our cerebral cortex, constructing the distraction of a sexual fantasy, drawing black silk stockings towards the clips of a lacy black garter belt. Collectively, our feelings about this are mixed—good calves, perhaps, but the matching panties are, at the most charitable, no better than thought-provoking. The Crone would like to pick up some stud, any stud, and have some fun. Any fun. She knows all about the shortness of life. She does not want to sit around staring at a word processor, especially a word processor that is not even processing words. Screw the book, says she.

Then there's The Matron: pragmatist, realist, the only one of us with a lick of genuine sense. She knows we have more urgent things to do than write this stupid book: the dishes, for example. How long before the clean plates run out and the roaches move in? How long, indeed, before the saucepans grow their own tiny legs? The Matron hovers at the windows of our soul, her lips moving in silent calculation as she directs Annabelle to look towards the kitchen nook where the dishes fester. Screw the book, says she.

Annabelle looks across at the dishes piled in the sink. She sighs. Yes, it would be nice to screw the book, too nice. What glows at her from the screen bears little resemblance to what she intended to write, which was something witty, vivid, poignant, and/or lyrical, preferably all at once. A few profoundly lilting phrases to capture our impressions when she saw what those weirdos next door had done with their rockery. I will use that, she'd said to ourself, in my description of the villa. Those gleaming cobbles—that villa where even the humble stones are gilded. There must be something they could symbolize. The dishes catch her eye again.

The doorbell rings. Annabelle pushes back from the table, on the whole not unwilling to be distracted, though we are divided in our reaction. Saved from ourself! Alternatively, foiled again! But whoever may be at the door, The Virgin is professionally obliged to feel she would like them to go away so we can keep working. She thinks over the deletion of *ovular, fulvous* as Annabelle's right eye approaches the peephole; she decides the cut would leave the sentence unbalanced. Beyond the door stands one white male, young, good-looking, bearing a flat white box. The Crone licks her lips. The Matron assumes it's the pizza. Annabelle opens the door.

"Nineteen-thirty including tax," he says. That will be twenty bucks including an embarrassingly modest tip. While Annabelle counts out quarters, The Virgin peeks at his face and takes notes. His eyes are deep grey, of a hue that would lend itself to metallurgical metaphors: iron, steel, silver. His upper lip is long enough to permit a baroque curve on either side. There is a touch of Neanderthal in the brow ridges, but the rest is pure Cro-Magnon. This is a face we might profitably borrow. The Matron, waking up to his character potential, wonders if Annabelle should keep him talking in the interests of research. The Crone wants to keep him talking, period; bugger the research.

Apparently he has other pizzas to deliver. The door closes behind him and leaves Annabelle full of vague yearnings and The Virgin unable to concentrate. The Crone and The Matron are united for once in thinking the pizza is an issue of the highest priority. At a gross investment of twenty dollars, it must provide tonight's dinner plus tomorrow's, and also tomorrow's breakfast and lunch—still an extravagance, but conscionable once the cost is divided among four meals. Furthermore, it can be eaten straight out of its flat white box, thus deferring the moment when a plate must be washed.

We consider, as Annabelle eats, the image of the pizza delivery man. Should the character we make of him be gay? The Crone would find that disappointing, though The Matron thinks it might increase the book's diversity quotient. On the other hand, The Virgin fancies the idea of a romantic figure, recontextualized in a properly postmodernist fogbank. The Crone will go along with that, just so long as he ends up getting the girl. The Matron wonders if he should be co-opted as an extraterrestrial or perhaps a serial killer, in that the goddam villa has been visualized to hell and back by now, but nothing interesting has happened there. She argues that a teeny sideways shift into one of the genres may not be such a bad thing. The Virgin is not convinced that anything interesting is obliged to happen at the villa. The Crone points out that soft porn qualifies as a genre if you're careful to call it erotica. Annabelle finishes off our second slice of pizza.

It is now ten-forty, time to get back to work, but first Annabelle switches on the light because the world outside has gone dark, and the screen-glare in our dim room has exactly the phosphene quality of a migraine headache. She curls our fingers onto the keyboard. The Virgin pecks and ponders, pecks some more.

Annabelle types: *His shoes, soft-soled, make no sound as he cruises the rockery like a shark on a reef. His grey eyes—polished steel by daylight, shiny iron disks by night— travel from bolted shutters to locked doors, from the garden's shattered security camera to the French window ajar on the balcony. His foot slips. He looks down to see dark splashes disfiguring the gilded stones of the rockery and trailing off towards the pagoda. "Fuck," he says aloud, "I'm too late."*

The use of the f-word has been previously debated, voted upon, and unanimously passed. Still, Annabelle's fingers stumble over it, and she pauses. She scrolls up a few pages, then reads down them again. She is not to be distracted from this, not even when The Crone asks whether the pizza boy is the cop or the psycho, nor when The Virgin edits with helpless obsessiveness as we read, nor when The Matron suggests taking a break for some therapeutic dishwashing. When Annabelle reaches the end, she puts our face in our hands and begins to weep.

"I'm wasting my time."

Timidly, The Virgin offers her mantra: *one must suffer...* The Crone snorts, The Matron counts the moments lost and sets them against the moments ahead. Annabelle dries our eyes, blows our nose, and curves our fingers on the keyboard again.

# Red Carpet

**"Perhaps," murmured the** Secretary-General of the United Nations, in his beautiful Oxford-African English, "we should have gone for something less reminiscent of a rock star's arrival."

"They're honored guests, Osei," said the President of the United States. "The red carpet is traditional."

"But I understand they do not perceive colours as we do."

"Sure, but we've explained the symbolism to them. Don't worry, the carpet's great."

The President was not looking at his colleague as he addressed him, nor was he looking at the red carpet. Like twelve billion other pairs of earthly eyes, his were fixed on the Mallart ship, graceful and immense, floating down from the stratosphere as effortlessly as a petal on a breeze. How lucky he was, he thought, to be one of the few tens of thousands privileged to be present at this moment, here at the pivot point of human history. Most of those other twenty-four billion eyes had to be content with watching satellite-fed screens: flat-backed televisions in a billion living rooms, screens the size of parking lots set up in a million town squares, chunky antiquated cathode-ray screens surrounded by entire African or Indian or Amazonian villages...

"But are you certain—"

"It's great, just great," the President repeated patiently. The Secretary-General's last-minute nerves were annoying, but forgivable. First contact? One would rather think it was the Second Coming, judging by the Earth-wide aura of wonder, the species-wide holding of breath. But unlike the Second Coming, this event was not falling upon the human race in the twinkling of an eye, and certainly not as a thief in the night. The incoming Mallart ship had been visible for weeks from most spots on the skin of the planet, a new star in the skies of New York and Mecca, Rio and Timbuktu. And even before it became visible in the telescopes, there had been the eleven years of radio signals angling in towards the ecliptic from the constellation of Cassiopeia. And now it was here. Its curved crystalline belly was no more than half a mile up.

Naturally there were skeptics. They were no longer able to doubt the existence of the Mallarts, but they maintained a dour suspicion of the visitors' intentions. The President bet himself, though, that the nay-sayers were watching along with all the rest of the human race, if only in hopes of seeing the Mallarts reveal themselves as agents of an alien apocalypse. In the President's opinion, those killjoys had watched far too many science fiction movies. Nothing was going to go wrong. How could it? Over and over, the Mallarts had demonstrated their benevolence, their altruism, their nobility of character. Again and again, via their transmissions, they had shared the benefits of their technology: the simple yet clever twiddle of muons that let cold fusion become practicable, the astonishingly useful nanotech blueprints, the elegant recipes for handy, stable elements far beyond the end of the old periodic table. Thanks to the Mallarts, Earth was already cleaner, greener, and better fed, and the tide of human misery was on the ebb.

Somebody was discreetly sniffling behind the President. He glanced back. The Prime Minister of Canada was dabbing at her eyes with a crumpled tissue. As the President watched, the Pope handed her a hankie. The President turned back to the spectacle of the great ship, feeling tears of his own at the corners of his eyes. Yes, this was a moving moment. All around the great paved landing circle, a quarter-mile across, sat the lesser heads of state, the Nobel scientists, the artists, the representatives of every ethnic group and subtle shading of color from Swedish to San !Kung, from Maori to Mi'kmaq. Before him flowed the shimmering scarlet river of the carpet, a handmade labour of love whose creation had involved whole armies of weavers from seventeen sovereign nations and cost upwards of thirty-six million American dollars.

The Mallart ship was low enough now for its details to shift into clarity. The surface was lightly pitted with the dust of interstellar space; pearl and silver played across its flanks. Its upper curve was a golden mirror, haloed and rayed by the sun rising behind it. It was beautiful. Beyond beautiful. Like the Mallarts themselves—or so the President hoped. He pondered this as the shining soap-bubble of the ship sank towards them.

The Mallarts had transmitted no effective pictures of themselves. This was not, the experts assured humanity, related to some sinister agenda. It was because, for evolutionary reasons, their major senses did not involve visible light, and the self-images they transmitted were muddy and hopelessly pixelated, like primitive ultrasounds. The President's consultants, three of whom had Nobel prizes, had explained it to him in eye-glazing detail: the Mallarts "saw" quantum densities, perceived by organs on their faces, weighted and filtered by the Mallarts' powerful brains. The explanation of quantum densities had kited straight over the President's head, but he had hung on to one reassuring detail—the Mallarts had faces.

He was not alone in being relieved. Five years before, when the scientists first presented their projections of the Mallarts' physical makeup, that was the single finding upon which all the media had seized. The Mallarts were humanoid! Bilaterally symmetrical, with a head at the top, two arms, two hands, two legs, two feet—and a face! In fact, much of what was theorized about their appearance was based on linguistic parallels rather than the indecipherable images, building on words that seemed to mean much the same in the Mallart speech as they did in the languages of Earth. Eyes, nose, mouth, all distributed in approximately the same pattern as on a human face: nose in the middle, with an eye on either side, and a mouth centered below. The Mallarts corroborated this in a widely disseminated message. Yes, they said, they did look much like their soul-siblings on Earth, at least in part. And yes, they also had genders, two of them, which corresponded functionally to the modal sexual dimorphism of humankind.

Somehow, this sharing of a physical template marked the beginning of the end of humankind's knee-jerk xenophobia. Forget about the planet-saving technology freely given; people could relate to a humanish face. Artists' conceptions, wise and lovely, flooded the internet within days of the announcement. Biologists wrangled learnedly over hypotheses of panspermia and convergent evolution. Preachers, imams and rabbis discoursed on the clear confirmation of God's image, in which both humans and aliens were created. The New Agers declared themselves not at all surprised by the transcendent oneness of being. But out of these disparate threads, the hundreds of different takes and spins, one great fabric of opinion was woven. The Mallarts were the best thing ever to happen to the human race.

Two hundred feet, a hundred and fifty. The President could make out a blackened scrape just below the ship's equator, no doubt a souvenir of that wildly improbable deep-space clash with a meteoroid some two years back. When the Mallarts had mentioned it rather offhandedly in their next transmission, prayers for their safety had ascended from a million pulpits and shrines all over Earth. And now, safe and sound after their journey of many light-years, here they were. Seventy-five feet, fifty, twenty-five. Prisms of refracted sunlight rippled across upturned faces as the ship rotated to align with the red carpet.

No, nothing could go wrong. Their joint plans had been too careful, their precautions too all-encompassing. Gravity? Not a problem, just a few per cent heavier than that of the Mallart home planet. Air? The oxygen balance was acceptable, though a bit thicker than the Mallarts were used to. They would not even have to wear masks.

Communications? No problem. The first message from the Mallarts, eleven years ago, had been transmitted in twenty-seven major Earth languages and dialects. The plans they had sent for a translation device had even been improved upon by a think tank of terrestrial engineers and linguists, humankind's proud contribution to the technology exchange. And it helped that the Mallarts' voices were resonant and rather musical, much like an oboe in tone.

Novel microbes? That had been a huge concern, whipped to hysteria at one point by the killjoy skeptics: visions of a plague that would trivialize the Black Death and the Spanish Lady and the Coronavirus and the horrendous Texas Chickendance, a plague that would be set into dire motion by one casual out-breath from a Mallart mouth. That was why so much bandwidth over the last four years had been devoted to uploading Earth's entire medical database for the Mallarts' painstaking analysis. The visitors were now immunized against everything Earth could throw at them, and had scrubbed or reengineered any possible microbial hazard on their ship and in their bodies. Within moments, and without fear of contagion, Earthlings and Mallarts could clasp hands in friendship.

There was no jarring of the ground when the ship touched down, just a gentle crackling in air. To the President's left, the Chairman of seven billion Chinese used his cellphone to snap a picture. A flight of videodrones buzzed overhead towards the golden blister of the airlock. On the daises lining the carpet, the thousand members of a specially assembled symphony orchestra held their instruments poised. Twelve notable composers and ethnomusicologists had collaborated on the welcoming theme, fusing Mozart, whom the Mallarts greatly admired, with the most inclusive possible range of world music. Absurdly, the President found himself wondering what the Mallarts would make of the strands of rembetika and gamelan, bluegrass, dhrupad and kapungala, not to mention the massed didgeridoos. Himself, he found it all a bit confusing. Then he caught a deep breath and forgot all about the music, because the blister was...not opening, exactly, but dissolving in a swirl of opalescence, and a rainbow bridge was materializing from its lip to the business end of the red carpet. Three tall figures, robed and hooded in light, took shape in the opening and descended the gangway with a gait that looked utterly human.

Here we go, thought the President. The culmination of years of planning, the fulcrum of a greeting ceremony that represented the greatest single cooperative endeavour in the history of the species. Just don't trip, he told himself. With the Chairman on one side and the Grand Mufti in her silver chador on the other, trailed by the Secretary-General, the Dalai Lama, the Pope, assorted Prime Ministers, and the King of England in his motorized wheelchair, the President waded along the red carpet towards the waiting Mallarts. He was acutely aware of twenty-four billion eyes watching through the lenses of the hovering videodrones, and of the giant versions of himself lumbering across screens around the perimeter of the greeting area. Forty feet, thirty feet, twenty. Now he found himself advancing eagerly with both hands outstretched. Fifteen feet. Ten. The three Mallarts stepped forward to meet him, casting back their hoods of light.

The President stumbled. The Pope stopped dead in the path of the King of England's wheelchair. The Grand Mufti, with a squawk of outrage and disgust, covered her eyes and stumbled off the red carpet. On the dais, the music faltered into cacophony. The Dalai Lama burst into a fit of giggles— but then, he was only twelve years old. Indeed, the President could well imagine all of the several hundred million twelve-year-old boys on the planet collapsing in fits of giggles at that same moment, while several billion mothers were busy covering the eyes of small children and virgin daughters. He recovered from his misstep, and—while the Secretary-General untangled the Pope from the King of England's wheelchair—stepped forward with the Chairman of seven billion Chinese to do the honors on Earth's behalf. For the honors still needed to be done.

He glanced up again at the Mallart leader's face and afterwards tried very hard to keep his eyes out of focus, but the picture was already too clear in his mind. The head: an elegant dome bisected along the crown into two swelling lobes, for all the world like a pair of... but no, he would not go there. The nose: a six-inch cylinder of wrinkled skin with a swollen tip, pierced with a single nostril, drooping between the two dangling sacs of the visual sensory organs.

The mouth: a puckered sphincter that pulsed open and shut as the Mallart leader took his first breaths of earthly air.

Abandoning any thought of his carefully prepared speech, with its full load of what were suddenly double-entendres, the President groped for words, any words. "Welcome," he said finally. "How was…how was your journey?"

"It was long and hard," the Mallart said, echoed by the translation device, "but at last we have come!"

The President winced. Holding the Mallart's slim-fingered hand in his, he turned and began the long, blushing journey back to the podium.

# An Inspector Calls

**He arrived on** a cross-Nile ferry jammed with customers—with bereaved families, I mean, each bearing a shrouded corpse on a board, and wailing loud enough to draw the notice of Osiris himself through many cubits of solid sand. My new employee was easy to spot, being the one who was not weeping, tearing at his garb, or liberally besmirched with ashes and dust.

He was different in other ways, too, ways that did not at first dispose me well towards him. Priests take some pride in being a soft lot, pasty from spending their days in dark sanctuaries and shaded temple courtyards, spreading easily into prestigious paunches by their middle years. Apart from his spotless linen kilt, this one looked more like a field hand or professional warrior; tall, broad, flat-bellied, muscled like a statue, his skin almost Nubian-dark. Over a long, well-shaped nose, he was absorbed in watching the swarms of mourners offloading their dearly deceased onto the shore.

"I suppose that's the new lector priest. Not bad." Nofret was at her post on the quay, ready to direct the mourners towards the tent of purification set up between the canal and the necropolis. She is my kite-mistress, the headwoman of the professional mourners, twenty years in the business and very good at her job. She is also my beloved wife and the mother of several of my junior embalmers and my one dear little daughter, Merbeset, the great joy of my life. Nobody does grief as well as my Nofret, nor has a better eye for what the market will bear when it comes to negotiating fees with the bereaved. Today, as the last corpse came ashore, she assumed a mien of warm sympathy and waddled off to round up our new clients, with Merbeset at her heels. I left her to it and dodged through the crowd towards the lector priest.

He was just stepping onto the bank, moving with a stately grace that I was forced to admire. Perhaps, I began to think, it was no bad thing that he looked so unpriestlike. I could see him going down very well in funeral processions, well enough to add a few grains to the profits of the house. Slap a mask of Anubis over his head, and he might play the god's part far better than our current wine-soaked Overseer of the Secrets and save us a bit on the subcontracting as well. His hands were empty. I looked past him for a porter staggering under baggage, but the priest was alone, and the last off the ferry. No matter, I thought, we could provide him with robes and a sash out of our stocks of linen until his gear arrived.

"You must be Hormaat," I said as I reached him. "I am Anubis, proprietor of this benighted necropolis."

He looked down at me over that slightly too-long nose, not into my eyes but at a spot that was roughly at the centre of my forehead. Amun bless me, he really was the tallest priest I had ever met. After a moment of silence, he shifted his gaze downward to meet my eyes.

"You call yourself Anubis?" he said. "You dare to take the name of the great god himself, he who fetches the dead to the Hall of the Two Truths?"

Self-righteous pious turd, I said to myself—but what a resonant voice! I could imagine the effect of such sonorous tones on our living clientele, that wonderful voice booming funerary spells across an echoing necropolis. But I had to laugh at his gravity. "Anubis is not the name I was born with, my friend, but it's a damned good name for the owner of a mummy factory, wouldn't you say? Come along, Hormaat, I'll—"

He stopped me with a heavy hand on my shoulder. "I am not Hormaat."

"What do you mean?" I cried. "The guild promised he'd arrive this morning. We've got a stack of stiffs to deal with in the Cutting House, plus three or four new ones to wash from this boatload, plus two funerals tomorrow, and I'm seriously short-handed. Why isn't he coming?"

"The one who was called Hormaat in this life cannot come," said the newcomer in his rich voice. "He cannot come because he has begun his own long journey to the Hall of the Two Truths."

Now I was irritated. "You mean he's dead?"

"I was with him when his journey began. His flesh now lies in a tent of purification on the west bank at Thebes, while his ka waits for guidance at the gates of—"

"Save it for the customers," I broke in. "Well, may Set take him and Amemit devour his ka, but I suppose it can't be helped. You'll do just as well. What was your name again?"

"My name is…Saweser." He had paused for a beat before speaking his name, almost as if trying to think up a good one, and I felt a brief touch of suspicion. Was he truly a priest? Had the guild really sent him? But contemplating his grave, impassive face, I decided he just had a naturally measured way of phrasing himself, which would not come amiss when he was reading the spells.

"Saweser?" I repeated. "Son of Osiris? Well, that's another grand name for a necro priest. Have you worked with embalmers before?"

"With embalmers, no," he said, "but I have worked with the dead." He looked into my eyes so strangely that I felt my suspicions stir again. I was, however, extremely short on lector priests.

"Good, so you know some of the basics, and I guess you're not squeamish. Come along, I'll give you the tour and then get you started."

《 》

Our first stop was the washhouse, as we embalmers call it amongst ourselves. To the rest of the world, it is more formally and respectfully known as the Tent of Purification. Mine is a professional yet decorative structure of carven poles hung with rather fine patterned matting, all inwoven with repeating friezes of the signs of life, prosperity, and health. I noticed Saweser nodding with approval at the bright matting, the tall jars of lotus flowers that flanked the opening, the large barrels of Nile water and palm wine for the ritual bathing of the deceased.

"In my experience," I whispered to him, "spending a little extra on this part of the setup is never a waste. Remember, this is just about all the paying customers ever see." He gave me that strange look again but made no comment.

Just inside the entrance, my dear Nofret was already dickering with a pair of principal mourners, an ash-covered farmer in a ritually torn loincloth and his equally disheveled wife. Our sweet Merbeset crouched not far away, the darling, observing but keeping her mouth shut, like a good little apprentice mourner. Nofret was using the wooden models, three little corpse-dolls depicting the likely results of different levels of expenditure. They graded from lifelike down to a bony horror with bared teeth, a reminder to the customer that you get what you pay for when it comes to embalming. Nofret had them talked up to the second model already. The deceased, a handsome boy of about ten, lay naked on one of the pallets, ready to be washed once the price was settled. Saweser surprised me by kneeling beside the dead child and gently patting its hand.

"Sentimental, are you?" I whispered to him. "I thought you'd worked with stiffs before."

He rose to follow me out, but he did not look at me this time.

——— «◇» ———

We followed the same path the corpses take after their bath, to the large courtyard enclosing the Houses of Purification and Beauty—or the Cutting House and the Stuffing House, as we like to say. Unlike some necro bosses, I prefer to keep a little distance between the mourners and the processing department. Therefore, my main operation is in a separate compound on the desert edge of the necropolis proper, a good long walk from the washhouse, surrounded by a shoulder-high mud wall topped with acacia thorns. The thorns are not to keep people out; the smell, I've always thought, makes a more effective barrier in that regard, rot and incense, sewage and resin, like a combination latrine, abattoir, and perfumery. No, the thorns are placed in hopes of keeping out desert scavengers, who seem to like the smell.

I pointed out the sights to Saweser. Just inside the gate were the huge dumps of natron, glistening like powdered silver. Ahead of us was the House of Beauty, a large flat-roofed mudbrick structure with few windows. To the right of that was the smaller, and much smellier, House of Purification. And all over the extensive courtyard lay the dead, ranged in tidy rows, each one visible only as a natron-covered mound with a wooden toe tag at one end. This is where our deceased clients spend up to forty days, slowly pickling and drying in the natron salt and the sun, until they're ready for wrapping and planting. I took Saweser's arm and strolled over to the far corner of the courtyard, in front of the House of Purification, where some very junior embalmers were at work.

"We had a little trouble with the jackals last night," I said.

His head jerked up. "Jackals? What kind of trouble?"

"The usual kind. A pack broke in and made a meal of some of our customers. We're dealing with it."

In truth, it was a very minor attack. The jackals had come over the wall at the corner, despite the thorns; they had disinterred no more than a dozen corpses from the natron piles, and not eaten much of any of them. My juniors were collecting the strewn body parts into large baskets, pawing through the scattered natron with salt-inflamed hands to retrieve the toe tags.

"Whatever will you do? How will you make sure that each departed one is correctly assembled?"

This time, it was I who gave him a strange look. What an idiot. "Why bother? We've got the toe tags. Everything gets wrapped up nicely anyway."

"I understand," Saweser said, so coldly that I began to be irritated. Who in the names of all the Ennead did he think he was? All the customers needed to see was the correct name on a bandaged mummy of roughly the right shape and size. Trying not to show my annoyance, I took his arm and led him towards the House of Purification—and then changed tracks toward the House of Beauty. Foolish, perhaps, but I did not want this long-nosed disapproving bastard son of Set to see how we were cutting corners in the Cutting House this week, being so short-handed and all. Normally I like my cutting crews to do a reasonably professional job—the careful slit in the abdomen, a hand slipped inside to draw out the innards for separate processing—but not when we've got a backlog. Faster to stick a funnel up the arse, flood the gut with cedar oil, and move on to the next stiff; after a week you pull the plug out and just pour the innards away, with the families none the wiser.

Since the Stuffing House also holds our storerooms of linen and spices, of incense, cassia and myrrh, it is the best-smelling corner of my little empire. I led Saweser through the front doors, which are flung wide during the day to keep a good draft blowing through, and down the central hallway, flanked on both sides by the fragrant storerooms. From a workshop at the end floated the competing voices of several lector priests attending on different corpses, and the effect was, I thought, pleasantly busy and professional. I looked up at Saweser—gracious Isis, he seemed even taller than before—and saw that this place, at least, had managed to impress him more favorably. We stopped on the threshold of the workroom.

The embalming crews, which included three of my sons, were not doing a bad job. With Saweser at my heels, I walked around inspecting the several mummies currently in process: two adults and a child recently pulled from the natron piles, four or five adults at various stages of bandaging, two adult-sized packages of linen ready to be boxed up for burial. Several lector priests were hurrying from table to table as needed, mumbling from their scripts or supervising the placement of amulets within the linen wrappings, but the Overseer of the Mysteries was not present. This, I thought, was probably just as well.

We stopped at the worktable where Penanap, my second son, was stuffing a dead child's belly cavity with balled-up linen scraps and handfuls of sand, along with some token sprinkles of myrrh. I saw the disapproving look creep back onto Saweser's face. What, did he think other mummy factories did not make similar economies? My son greeted me cheerfully, with a curious glance at my companion.

"Another funeral for Merbeset to shine in," he said to me, indicating the blackened mummy of the child—a little girl, I saw, of about Merbeset's age. Yes, our precious Merbeset was much in demand as a mourner at kiddy funerals. Natural talent, I was proud to say, though there was also Nofret's excellent training in weeping, writhing, and tearing at the hair without doing actual damage. Someday, I hoped, Merbeset might be kite-mistress here in her mother's place. I clapped my son on his shoulder and turned to introduce him to the new priest.

But Saweser was paying us no attention. He was examining the dead girl-child with a little smile on his face, like a fond uncle, and he reached out to brush her tough, blackened cheek with his fingertips. Penanap rolled his eyes.

"Are you quite sure," I asked Saweser, "you've worked with stiffs before?"

He looked down at me with his brows drawn together, but then his gaze slid right over my head. I whirled to see what he was looking at, because I fervently hoped the instant fury flooding his face had a target that was not me. And it did.

Khaemwese had just staggered through the door to join an invocation in progress: our resident Overseer of the Mysteries, the living incarnation of the great god Anubis while he wore the jackal mask. Seeing him for a moment through a newcomer's eyes, I could halfway understand Saweser's rage. The mask was overdue for replacement, worn and scabbed where gold leaf and lapis-blue paint had flaked away. The tips of both ears were broken. When set on Khaemwese's fat shoulders, balanced over his wobbling belly and breasts, the mask was actually comical. And Khaemwese was drunk as usual, swaying between two young sweepers, slurring the invocation shamefully when his turn came to speak. I gave him a filthy glare myself.

"Is that," Saweser hissed, "what you consider to be a fitting incarnation of the great Son of Osiris?"

"Well, not really," I said, "but he works on a very small commission."

Saweser growled—yes, actually growled like a dog—deep in his throat, and swung his furious eyes and great snout of a nose around to me. The crews were watching us, the lector priests had fallen silent and were standing there with their silly mouths hanging open, and even that damned Khaemwese was paying a vague and dribbling attention. Very bad for discipline, I thought, as well as for our tight schedule. Time to put the snotty bugger in his place.

"Priest," I said coldly, drawing myself up, "remember who is boss around here. I am, and you are my employee. So either you take your big nose and your oily hide back to the east bank on the very next boat, or you grab a script and start gabbling over the stiffs, along with the others. But I warn you, I am sick to death of your attitude."

An odd change came over his face. He looked almost amused. "Sick to death? Not yet."

"What do you mean? I gave you an order!"

But he was already heading for the workroom door, reaching it in three paces of his very long legs. He paused to look back at me. "I serve a different master," he said, "and came to this place on other business. But I will remember you," he added, "when your heart is weighed in the court of my father Osiris, in the Hall of the Two Truths." And he was gone.

Damn it, I thought after a shocked moment, he was an imposter! A spy from one of my competitors? Or maybe (and my heart misgave me, as we say) an inspector for some dratted nosy commission from the Great House, checking into business practices in the mummy factories? As if any of the other necro bosses did things any differently! As if Osiris himself would care! But I could not risk letting that lying conniver report back to his masters, whoever they were.

"Catch him!" I cried. "He can't have gone far!"

But he was not in the corridor when we flooded out of the workroom to give chase, and even those long legs could not have reached the outer doors in that short a time. "Check the storerooms!" And so we did, all of us, embalmers, lector priests, sweepers, right down to fat Khaemwese puffing along under the Anubis mask. Saweser was nowhere.

I left the others doing a frantic second search, sweeping bales of linen off the shelves, checking inside the coffins, thrusting lamps into the darkest corners. Meantime, sweating and quaking with disquiet—no, of course I was not feeling guilty—I took myself to the gate of the compound and surveyed the track that led along the edge of the necropolis, back towards the riverside and the Tent of Purification.

There was no sign of Saweser, unless he was hiding himself among the heaps of natron or skulking among the tombs in the necropolis. But then my dear Nofret appeared far off along the track in a cloud of her own dust, cradling a bundle in her arms. Even at that great distance, I could hear her wailing in that wonderfully trained voice of hers. As I have said, nobody does grief like my Nofret.

It seemed, though, like an odd time for a rehearsal, and if it was a demonstration for Merbeset's benefit, it was wasted. Where was the child, anyway? I took a few steps along the track beyond the gate, intending to meet Nofret and warn her about the false lector priest. Then I saw what she was carrying and began to run.

# The Scrolls of Bishop Eubulus

**Great-grandfather's moth-eaten souvenirs** from his years in Singapore. Great-great-grandmother's watercolours of Venice from her Grand Tour. Crazy great-uncle's SS helmet from a battlefield in the Ardennes. A packet of Edwardian postcards, a scrapbook of Victorian-era clippings from the *London Illustrated News*. You cannot easily dispose of them, not even in the most determined of downsizings. It is hard to put them on eBay because you have no idea of their worth, and you fear being cheated if they are valuable, or scorned if they are dross. Anyway, if they are proper heirlooms imbued with the sacredness of named ancestors, they are yours to store for your lifetime or until you can pass them on to the garages or attics or basements of the next generation.

And if you are an archaeologist, as I am, you are further hampered by your knee-jerk instinct not to pitch any relics of the past on the dust-heap, no matter how burdensome they are.

My newest burden was an ugly wooden chest about the size of an old-fashioned microwave oven, the kind that could take a whole turkey, reposing in the dustiest corner of my late grandmother's attic. It was brassbound and locked and there was no key, but it was not particularly heavy—no chance of pirate treasure, alas. When I wiped the dust away, *Hervey* and an address in Whitby, Yorkshire, were revealed in bold black letters on the lid. Propped against it was a framed portrait in oils, about eighteen inches square, of an elderly bearded gentleman in mid-Victorian garb. That the artist had been an amateur was painfully obvious.

"Why me?" I asked.

"You're the archaeologist in the family," my mother said. "Your granny made it very clear they should both go to you. On account of your interest in history, I suppose."

"They're not exactly in my field of expertise," I pointed out. They were almost two millennia outside my field, in fact, since I doubted the contents of the chest had any relevance to second-century sociopolitical dynamics on the imperial Roman frontiers.

"Don't you want them, Helen?" My mother's voice took on an overtone of tears. "Granny would be hurt. She was so proud of you and your career, you know. She didn't even ask me if you'd ever get married. She thought you'd be pleased the chest was going to you. She didn't know what was in it, but she was sure it was old."

The guilt card trumps all others. One cannot argue with a dead granny, nor a live mother on the point of weeping. I lugged the chest and painting down from the attic and into my car, along with a threadbare Persian carpet which had also fallen to my lot. As I slid the painting into the car, the sunlight revealed a faded inscription on the back, dated July 1855: *Arthur Aloysius Garbutt, by his loving daughter Amelia.* The names rang a bell.

When I returned to my late grandmother's kitchen, clapping the dust off my sweater, my mother was mournfully packing up saucepans and mixing bowls and other detritus destined for the charity shops. "Who was this Arthur Garbutt, anyway?" I asked.

"Your great-something-grandmother Julia Winslow was born a Garbutt," she said, adding, "I remember this potato masher from my childhood. They don't make them like this anymore."

"So Arthur's an ancestor?"

"Probably." She turned a decrepit saucepan thoughtfully in her hands. "Don't ask me, ask your Auntie Freda. You know she knows everything."

Every clan has an Auntie Freda with instant recall of whole generations of the family tree—the one who can explain the difference between a first cousin twice removed, and a second cousin once removed, and will do so at length at family reunions. I wondered bitterly why Granny had not left the sea chest to her.

"What about Hervey, the name on the chest?"

"Not a clue," my mother said. I gathered hopefully from this that the Hervey chest, whatever it contained, might carry no ancestral sacredness, and could have some eBay potential. Granny would never know. I was stuck, though, with the dire ancestral portrait. I hung it up in the spare bedroom as soon as I got home, just to get it out of the way.

—— «» ——

If the chest had not been locked, I would probably have dealt with it that same day as well. As it was, the new term had just begun, and I was carrying a full teaching load and working rather desultorily on my monograph about markers of ethnic variability in the Roman cemeteries near Winchester. The Hervey chest stood unregarded for three months in a corner of my study, gradually vanishing under a positively archaeological deposit of papers and books, remembered only on the occasions when I stubbed a toe on its brassbound corners. But at the end of the semester, when I had marked the exams and recovered from the faculty Christmas party, I sat down at last to work on my long-neglected monograph. I stared for some minutes at my notes. I poured myself a glass of wine. I rearranged the pens and paper clips on my desk. I stared at my notes again—and then somehow I found myself gazing with gratitude at the corner where the Hervey chest reposed.

After deciding the chest was not in itself an object of value or historical interest, I broke the lock with a screwdriver and swung back the lid on its tarnished hinges. The top layer was a removable inset shelf filled with something that immediately quickened my scholarly interest: a hefty manuscript, yellowed by time but otherwise in good condition, closely written in a sloping copperplate hand. Taking up the rest of the shelf was a pair of long, thick, hardbound books which I took to be Victorian photograph albums.

Turning first to the manuscript, I found the writing too cramped to decipher without concentrated effort and a better light, though odd words leapt out and waved for my attention as I riffled through the pages. *Nubia. Ismail Pasha. Halfa.* Suddenly it looked as if the contents of the trunk might be within my research area after all—there was no more fascinating frontier than Roman Egypt's southern border with Nubia. Already apologizing to my late grandmother for doubting her, I replaced the pages on the pile and picked up the first of the albums.

It was not an album, but a sketchbook, battered but in reasonably good condition, dated 1820 on the flyleaf. What came next was extraordinary: thirty-seven pages crammed to the margins with skilled botanical or anatomical drawings of flowers and twigs, beetles, birds, snakes, and scorpions, scribbled all around with notes and measurements and each signed with a minute *JSH*. Could this be the Hervey whose name was painted so boldly on the lid of the sea chest? It was a reasonable inference. There followed a number of blank pages, and then a separate series of drawings began— drawings that made me catch my breath and take a good, solid gulp of wine.

This second section was devoted to landscapes—level desert punctuated with pyramidal or flat-topped hills, a low-banked river scattered with boulders and backed with cliffs. Even better, some of the landscapes featured ruins. Skylines of columns emerged from tumbles of broken masonry; squat mudbrick dwellings flocked around the façades of grand temples, like midgets clinging to the skirts of giants. I recognized Qasr Ibrim, a crag crowned with a jagged fortress, viewed from the riverbank far below. The mammoth stone face of Ramesses the Great peered in quadruplicate through the dunes of Abu Simbel. A lumpen tower of eroded mudbrick looming above a party on camelback had to be the Western Deffufa at Kerma, a primeval Nubian capital. And in the final sketch of many, a group of steep-sided pyramids backdropped by a high massif stood out in sharp relief against a sky roiling with clouds. The royal cemetery at Jebel Barkal, deep in Upper Nubia, or I was a Dutchman.

Now, I had never done fieldwork in Nubia, the Nile Valley south of Aswan in what is now southern Egypt and the northern Sudan, but the area figured in several chapters of my doctoral dissertation. I thought I knew all the early European travellers to that part of the Nile—Bruce, Burckhardt, Cailliaud, Linant de Bellefonds, the detestable treasure-hunter Ferlini—but Hervey was new to me. A quick Google search yielded nothing. The sketchbook suggested that, like the Frenchman Cailliaud, he had been one of the handful of European experts accompanying Ismail Pasha's armies on Egypt's brutal invasion of the Sudan in 1820; unlike the other early travellers, Hervey had not published his observations, and so was forgotten. I could already see, though, there was going to be a nice fat book in this for me. The sketchbook alone was of huge historical value. What narrative wonders would I find in the manuscript?

The other sketchbook was missing most of its spine and looked much more fragile, not just battered but also heavily charred, as if rescued from some long-ago fire. Further, it was held shut by a thick strip of some tough grey-black leather about an inch wide, which had been coiled haphazardly a couple of times around the book's middle and finished with a lumpy knot. As I gingerly lifted the book, flakes of burnt paper rained from the bottom edge.

Well, that was the end of that, for the moment. I yearned to grab a knife from the kitchen, slice through the leather strip, and fling the book open, but archaeologists are trained *not* to behave like Indiana Jones. The precious sketchbook looked ready to fall to pieces. Stabilizing it was a job for Sigrid Holmvang, the conservator at the university museum, who had just flown home to Norway for Christmas. Muttering darkly, I resigned myself to being inhumanly patient for at least a couple of weeks until she flew back again. Meantime, I did what I could—set up a good light, laid a ruler alongside the sketchbook for scale, and took multiple pictures of the front and back covers, the leather strip, the knot, the charred edges. I photographed the 1820 sketchbook as well.

Then I turned back to the sea chest and found a surprise previously concealed under the sketchbooks—a letter scrawled on a wrinkled sheet of paper with the letterhead of the Hotel des Anglais, Cairo. This was already intriguing; it was the hostelry that later became the famous Shepheard's Hotel, home away from home for generations of Egyptologists and European travellers. I scanned the letter eagerly and then—I am not embarrassed to say—flung back my head and hooted with triumph. (There are advantages to living alone.) Here in my hand was the missing link between the ancestral Arthur Garbutt and the mysterious Hervey.

———— 《》 ————

*Hotel des Anglais, Cairo*
*12 April 1843*
*My dear Garbutt,*
*I have abandoned the Excavations in the Korosko Reach and have returned to Cairo with no Treasure but the Scrolls themselves. There is not time to explain—this is written in Urgency and Dread, for I greatly fear they have tracked me, and that is the Long and Short of it. Ha! A grim Jest.*
*Now I must hasten to engage with the shipping agent about the Chest. It will follow soon after this Letter. Keep it safe, but DO NOT OPEN IT. If God permits me to see Whitby again, we shall examine the Scrolls together; if God wills otherwise, I implore you to burn the Chest unopened, along with our Correspondence and my other papers left in your keeping, and scatter the ashes off the Whitby Cliffs. Forgive me, old friend, for the Burden I am transferring to your shoulders. I hope it will be but a Brief Time ere I relieve you of it.*
*Once again, DO NOT OPEN THE CHEST.*
*In haste, your devoted Jas. Hervey*

———— 《》 ————

I slipped the letter into an archival document sleeve and poured myself another glass of wine. What price the Winchester necropolis? This was Christmas come early—indeed, the next ten Christmases all tied up with a huge red bow and sprinkled with glitter. It seemed Mr. James Hervey, whoever he might be, had carried out hitherto forgotten excavations in the early 1840s, in a most intriguing area—the Korosko Bend of the Nile, the permeable membrane between Nubia and Roman Egypt for centuries. The Korosko Road also began there, an immemorial caravan route that bypassed the great loop of the Nile by cutting straight south through some exceptionally unattractive desert, with very little water or shelter on the way. The archaeological implications could be immense.

Maybe. As I calmed down, I began to doubt that the site of Hervey's excavation would be completely unknown to modern scholarship. In the 1960s, before the raising of the Aswan High Dam, hordes of archaeologists had combed Lower Nubia like it was a cat with fleas. Hundreds of sites spanning thousands of years had been surveyed, recorded, excavated, before the waters of Lake Nasser rose behind the dam to drown them forever. Some major architectural treasures were raised to higher ground, or even moved stone by stone to Khartoum, Leiden, New York. It was an international salvage campaign of historic proportions. Hervey's excavation—which, honestly, in the 1840s, probably meant a reckless, destructive hunt for museum pieces—would have little or no archaeological value except for one thing: Hervey's mention of scrolls.

Ah, scrolls! What price the bejewelled golden baubles of the pharaohs? Archaeologists will salivate at many types of artifact, from sherds to turds, but the prospect of ancient written records is quite intoxicating. No wonder the sea chest was so light! Papyrus scrolls would weigh next to nothing, but they could be of more historical value than a whole trunkful of gold. Shaking with excitement, I grabbed the leather loops at each end of the inset shelf and lifted it clear of the chest...and then uttered a few heartfelt words that my sainted granny would not have liked at all.

The chest was empty.

But not completely empty—fine-textured pale sand was scattered across the bottom, mixed with darker flecks and a few glints of mica, embedding a motley assortment of small items. I pulled on a pair of latex gloves and carefully extracted them: a long white woollen sock, very soiled, with a hole in the toe; a well-preserved white linen handkerchief monogrammed "JH" in one corner; a pair of old-fashioned gold-rimmed spectacles with cracked lenses; the desiccated corpses of three scarab beetles; and a half-dozen thin-walled potsherds that looked Nubian Christian in style. And then the prize: a tiny ivory figurine, about the size of my thumb, though it was not one of the mad horde of deities worshipped along the ancient Nile. Perhaps Greek? The shape was hard to pin down, but it reminded me of the tentacled sea creatures on Minoan and Mycenaean pottery from a much earlier time. I laid my finds on a tray and sat back to take stock.

Without the scrolls promised in Hervey's letter, it was a pathetic trove, though I could still count a few blessings. Hervey's own manuscripts and notes were a treasure in themselves, if only for his account of travelling with Ismail Pasha's 1820 invasion force. The Winchester necropolis could return to the back burner—this Christmas break, and all spare time in the foreseeable future, would be the exclusive property of Mr. James Hervey.

———— «» ————

Eager though I was to attack the manuscript, the next day belonged to my clan's annual Christmas potluck extravaganza. I love some of my extended family, am quite fond of others, tolerate most, and cannot stand a few. En masse, they fill me with an urge to flee. The one I regard with most ambivalence is Auntie Freda, my mother's eldest sister, who is pushing seventy with a persistence that makes you yearn for seventy to push back. With her single-minded devotion to genealogy, she can be a bore. On the other hand, given my own obsessive interest in the past, I feel a certain kinship with her. In another life, she might have been a detective or a forensic anthropologist, not a bank manager. Normally I do everything I can to avoid a tête-à-tête with her, but this time I sought her out between Auntie Janet's Christmas tree and the potluck buffet, led her to a chair, and sat her firmly down.

"Arthur Aloysius Garbutt," I said.

"Your great-great-great-grandfather," she answered promptly. "Born 1794, died 1858. Father of Julia Garbutt Winslow, born..."

I cut her off before she could unwind the entire ancestral line. "What do you know about Arthur Garbutt?"

"Quite a bit. I made a point of visiting Whitby a few years back while I was researching the Yorkshire connection." She brightened. "You inherited Amelia's portrait of him, didn't you? I wouldn't mind a copy of it when you have a chance."

"It's yours," I said.

"I wouldn't dream of taking it after Mother left it to you. A photocopy will be fine."

Damn it. "Arthur?" I prompted.

"Yes, Arthur. Let me see." And she was off. I will not attempt to reproduce the sideways leaps and circuitous wanderings of her narrative. Her face took on a look I often see on colleagues and in the mirror, the exhilaration that comes from galloping a hobbyhorse through a forest of fascinating minutiae. I could relate to that.

The Garbutts were shipowners in Whitby, Yorkshire, and very well off. Arthur Garbutt himself was a scholar, Cambridge-educated, rich enough to indulge his passion for ancient languages and general antiquarian pursuits without having to pay much mind to business. With the estimable Hannah, née Holmes, he fathered four sons and two daughters, including the artistic Amelia, who never married, and my ancestress Julia, who did. When not occupied with his masterwork on Yorkshire barrows, he walked the moors and picked things up, and then wrote dull pamphlets about them. He helped to found the Whitby Museum and filled several cases with his flints and bones and medieval oddments. ("Maybe that's where you get it from, dear.") Some of his donations were still on display nearly two hundred years later—Auntie Freda had seen Arthur's name as donor on the labels.

I cut her off again before she could ramble into the byways of Yorkshire antiquity. "Did Arthur ever go to Egypt?"

Auntie Freda frowned at the Christmas tree. "As far as I know, he never went further abroad than Venice. But it's interesting you should ask. He did give the museum several Egyptian artifacts, which one of his Cambridge friends brought back for him."

"Scrolls?" I croaked from a throat suddenly dry.

"No, not scrolls. Some of those servant figurines they put in tombs, a few faience amulets, a mummified cat, things like that."

"Do you…" I cleared my throat and tried again. "Do you remember the friend's name?"

"I don't think I ever knew. Oh look, it's time for Secret Santa!" She rose and started to move towards the action, but paused to add, "Poor Arthur. He was an invalid for the last fifteen or so years of his life—a stroke when he was about fifty, I recall. Great-great-aunt Amelia Garbutt looked after him. Come to think of it, there were some letters between her and Julia in the Whitby archives, and I've got a volume of Amelia's self-published pamphlets. I'll dig out my notes, if you like…yes, dear, I'm coming."

And she was gone. For the first time in my life, Auntie Freda had left me wanting more.

———— «◊» ————

Artist, antiquarian, natural historian—rebel. That was the picture I formed of James Scott Hervey from hints and allusions dropped throughout his manuscript, scattered among animated descriptions of Cairo, the titanic temples at Luxor, the desolate moonscape of the eastern desert, the journey into Nubia with Ismail Pasha. The first clue was his fervent self-congratulation at *not* being the vicar of Nether Pottsby, North Yorkshire, the awful destiny intended by his parents and Cambridge tutors. Instead, he had travelled. His manuscript name-dropped Shelley in Italy and Byron in Greece, mentioned rooting about in Pompeii and cataloguing beetles in Spain, joining excavations in Sardinia, and braving the Ottomans to sketch castles in Syria and Turkey. What took him to Egypt in 1819 was employment with the forward-looking ruler, Mohammed Ali Pasha, to help compile a library of the best of European science and literature for Cairo's edification.

By a lucky chance his exquisite anatomical drawings of scarab beetles came to the great Pasha's particular attention. If a man could draw such lovely pictures of bugs, so the Pasha's thinking ran, he could draw anything, and the Pasha was keen to have as much scientific information as possible about the soon-to-be-conquered territories south of Egypt. Thus it was that James Scott Hervey was hired to join the little band of European experts accompanying Mohammed

Ali's expeditionary force to the Sudan under one of his junior sons, Ismail Pasha, a position which Hervey accepted with enormous anticipation. He was twenty-seven by then, a seasoned traveller in difficult places, and this was an opportunity not to be missed.

In the event, he did not march down the west bank of the Nile with Ismail Pasha's armies. The expedition included a large fleet of sailing boats that carried supplies, arms, ammunition, the European physicians, and a handful of the scientific experts, including James Hervey. His remit was to sketch and sketch and sketch again: bugs and herbage, mainly, but the Pasha had also instructed him to watch out for ancient sites that might hold a promise of interest or profit.

I will waste little time at present on the details of his trip up the Nile. Those interested must wait until my book comes out. But I will say he was a vivid and engaging writer, with an artist's eye for detail. He describes Mohammed Ali's Turkish and Albanian troops, picturesque in their layered jackets and ballooning trousers, and the wild camel-mounted Ababda tribesmen of the Eastern Desert; there are pages larded with tiny sketches of this most colourful invading force. He was darkly amusing about faring up the Nile through the perilous cataracts, a process that sounded rather like white-water rafting with a bathtub for a boat, leaving behind a string of wrecks and corpses. He waxed lyrical about the beauties of the islands and broad cultivations between the cataracts, the richness of the fertile strip running along the river through the limitless desert, the majestic procession of ruins. Only one incident from this phase of the manuscript needs to be recounted here in full.

Hervey had joined the boats just above Aswan, along with a few of the other "Frankish" recruits, hoping to start his catalogue of Nile curiosities before meeting Ismail Pasha and the main body of the army at Wadi Halfa. The journey was relatively smooth until the flotilla sailed into the Korosko Reach, that tricky S-bend in the Nile where contrary winds could make upriver navigation difficult, sometimes requiring the boats to be beached until more obliging winds arose, or even to be dragged by teams on the shore. It was there where his portion of the flotilla paused under the promontory crowned by the ancient fortress of Qasr Ibrim, allowing him more time than usual to sketch and to wander about on the bank. And it was there, on the evening of the same day, where he recorded a story that later took on great significance.

Hervey had formed the habit of spending his evenings on the afterdeck of the riverboat, not with his fellow Europeans, but with the rather motley Egyptian crew quartered there. His particular informant was Abu Saleh, a wrinkled little ex-fisherman from one of the villages close to Korosko, notably garrulous and not always reliable. Hervey, whose mastery of Arabic was improving daily, enjoyed drawing the little man out about the ruins visible from the river, ruins which Abu Saleh embroidered with the most fantastic folklore. Who built them? The Anag, the giants of ancient times. How old were they? As old as the Nile itself. Did they conceal ancient treasures? A slightly shifty "no." Were there any ruins from the time of the Christians, the Nasrin? (Though he had escaped a life as a Yorkshire country parson, Hervey retained an interest in the primitive forms of his earlier faith.) And yes, said Abu Saleh, there were many places where the Nasrin had once ruled, which were now haunted by unquiet spirits and unusual foxes, including a place they would pass tomorrow if God willed it—probably Faras was meant. There was even one place where the Nasrin still ruled, though no man who feared God and loved his life would go near it, lest the swimmers take his head...

At this point, Hervey noted an uneasiness among the company gathered on the deck under the stars, particularly among the deckhands drawn from the local area. Where was this place of the Christians, Hervey asked. Just downstream, Abu Saleh replied, far up a winding side-channel, or *khor*, whose mouth they had passed only the previous day near the town of Korosko. It was said that there was a village in that khor, large and rich, and a Christian mosque with ungodly paintings on the walls, and a Christian imam with terrible powers, and swimmers that even the crocodiles feared—

But here the mate gruffly intervened and sent Abu Saleh ashore to do some obscure nautical task, and nobody else offered to take up the tale, nor any other tale. Neither was Hervey able to continue questioning Abu Saleh himself, as the talkative sailor was shifted next morning to a different boat and Hervey never saw him again. Hervey was interested by the story, but not really inclined to believe it, given that the Christian kingdoms of Nubia had crumbled centuries before. All the same, he thought, it would be intriguing to follow that khor and see what unprepossessing cluster of hovels had given rise to such grandiose tales—and then he put it out of his mind until later. Much later.

Again, the details of Ismail Pasha's pacification of the amenable Nile tribes and the defeat of the mighty Shaqiya are outside the scope of this narrative, though Hervey was a great admirer of the young pasha and described their conversations and the early progress of the campaign in detail. Most of the horrors that later defined the invasion were still in the future at the time Hervey left Ismail Pasha's entourage—Ismail's ghastly death by treachery and fire in Shendi, the hideous retribution that followed, the devastation, the torture and massacre of whole villages. Long before then, Hervey was back in Cairo with a different kind of horror behind him.

His undoing was such a small thing: he tripped. The day after sketching the pyramids at Jebel Barkal, he lost his footing on the gangplank and tumbled into the muddy water near the bank, slicing his trousers and the flesh of his calf on a nail on the way down. Though he cleaned and dressed the wound himself that evening, it was still sore in the morning, hot and red by the next day, and suppurating by the day after that. Indeed, he was lucky not to die of that simple scratch. There followed a four-week gap in his journal, during which he was carried upstream in a fever as the boats fought their way through the Fourth Cataract. When at last he came back to himself, he was lying naked on a native-style cot under a ceiling of straw matting, while a gaunt European distinguished only by an immense ginger beard swabbed him down with cool water. He had been left behind in the town of Abu Hamed, to recover or not, while the young pasha and his armies continued their triumphant march south to Berber and thence to Sennar. Hervey's part in the invasion was over.

Abandoned in the desert! Well, that was not quite true, but he filled a page with his bitterness at the fate that tore him from the pasha's entourage and left him lying, limp with weakness, in a dismal clutter of mud hovels on the bank of the Nile. On the other hand, he was safe with the garrison Ismail had left behind, now engaged in building a gimcrack fort in the strategic town at the south end of the Korosko Road. His companion was a Scottish surveyor named Lachlan MacLeod, also lately in the pasha's service, who had been too ill with dysentery to travel onward to Berber. The young pasha had left the surveyor with a bag of piastres, Hervey's release from his commission should he survive his injury, and a string of extravagant regards and regrets that did not comfort Hervey at all.

So it was that, almost three weeks after Hervey regained himself, he and Lachlan MacLeod joined a group of traders bound north along the desert road to Korosko, from where they could easily find passage to Aswan and eventually to Cairo. In Hervey's account regarding the time in Abu Hamed, MacLeod comes across as a pleasant Scot in his late thirties, who had learned the surveyor's trade in Wellington's army and went east to seek his fortune when Waterloo ended the wars. He was not well educated, at least in the eyes of a Cambridge man, but he was competent in his trade, kind enough to nurse Hervey in his illness, and honest enough to hand over Hervey's share of the piastres. A caricature of him in Hervey's manuscript consists mostly of beard and eyebrows. Like Hervey, he appears in no other account of the invasion. Perhaps this is not surprising, considering the circumstances of his death.

———— «» ————

It was at this point in my transcription of Hervey's manuscript that Sigrid, the museum conservator, returned from her Christmas in Norway. We were still a few days from the beginning of term, and she had time to spare for what was essentially a private favour rather than official university work. She was excited, in her dour Norwegian way, as I laid the damaged sketchbook on the worktable in her lab and briefly recounted its provenance and backstory, and then she forgot all about me. As she examined the leather strip holding the book closed, the lumpy knot, the charred edges, I decided to leave her to her abstruse technical mutterings and get back to Hervey's story. I waved at her from the door, and that was the last time I saw her alive.

———— «» ————

The Korosko Road was not a pleasure trip. Some forty years after Hervey's journey, an experienced British traveller described it as the worst place on Earth, worse than the Khyber Pass or the dismal traverses of Abyssinia. It was a route where the only respite from slogging across the sand was picking a painful way along knife-edged ridges and strews of ironstone rocks, where the track was lined with camel cadavers in every posture of agonized extremis, where the only water at that time of year was the sulfurous sludge from the wells of Murad at the midpoint of this tour through hell.

Hervey, still weak from his illness, did not have the energy to be eloquent in his descriptions. His manuscript included a few half-hearted sketches of bizarre rock formations, odd conical hills like the teeth of immense dragons thrusting up through the sand; he wrote of the russet, gold, and violet dunes that lapped up against the black ridges, the desolate flatlands strewn like an old battlefield with ironstone concretions resembling round-shot from cannons, the shimmering mirages of the "false sea," the dazzling shield of stars overhead as they trudged through the bitter cold of the nights. But mainly he complained. His illness made him querulous, his disappointment at the premature ending of his venture made him irritable. Poor, patient Lachlan MacLeod became the butt of his ill humour. His camel suffered too, though never in silence.

And on the sixth morning of the desert crossing, when Hervey fancied he could smell the Nile at last and the traders assured him Korosko was only a day or so away, the wind rose to a scream and the hills to the west vanished under a moving, billowing mountain range of sand. It was MacLeod who grabbed Hervey's reins and wrestled his camel to the ground, MacLeod who shoved Hervey into the lee of the beast, MacLeod who spooned up against Hervey and held him steady while the haboob winds turned the air into sand, and the sand into a screeching, pummelling, smothering legion of demons—Hervey's words, not mine. When at last the onslaught ceased, it was MacLeod who shifted frantically and broke through the dune that had built up over them and pulled Hervey out into the seething afternoon air.

Macleod's camel was gone. Hervey's camel staggered to her feet when MacLeod beat her, sand deluging from her sides. Of the traders, there was no sign. They were on their own.

Which way? Hervey favoured a sharp turn to the west, where they could not fail to stumble on the Nile eventually. But MacLeod, who had participated in charting the river on the way south, had a better grasp of how the land lay. The river's course would be angling southwestwards away from them at this point, whereas Korosko was almost due north and certainly closer. This was an important consideration, as most of their supplies and all MacLeod's baggage had vanished into the sandstorm along with the rest of the little caravan. They had one camel, a small bag of dates tucked in among the paintboxes and notebooks in Hervey's saddlebags, a little sack of currently useless piastres, and a few mouthfuls of water in a nearly empty waterskin, and that was all that stood between them and death. So MacLeod prevailed, and the two of them—Hervey on the camel, MacLeod trudging alongside—headed due north.

Do not imagine their path lay along an obliging stretch of flat desert in this last leg of the Korosko Road. They had reached the expanse of rocky highlands east of the river, dissected by the khors, the great fractal cracks that deepened into meandering ravines and eventually reached the river as side-channels. Twice they were forced to make lengthy detours in order to keep to their northward course. When they stopped to rest in the late afternoon, Hervey recorded his increasing frustration in his diary—these ravines were sure to run down into the Nile eventually, so why not use one of them to make a dash for the river? But he lacked the strength to argue the point with MacLeod.

They rode on by moonlight, revived by a few dates and the last of the water. Hervey slipped in and out of half-sleep as the saddle rocked under him—he was in Cambridge again, dream-strolling through King's on a winter's night, with a strangely unharmonic evensong drifting from the Chapel and across the quadrangle—and then he jerked awake. The camel had halted, and the moon was full, high, and bright. Hervey looked down at MacLeod, who looked back up at him, head cocked, finger on his lips. They were at the inlet to another khor, a shadowy rift zig-zagging westward across the moonlit silver wastes. The music—distant, faint, and not remotely resembling the King's College Chapel choir—was not a dream, and it was coming from the direction of the rift.

"We should gang on as we were," said MacLeod, reaching up for the reins.

But Hervey replied, "Where there's singing, there's people; where there's people, there's water," and he kicked the camel in the side and urged her forward into the ravine. After a moment he heard MacLeod trotting along after him, muttering. The khor began as a broad, gentle declivity that rapidly narrowed and steepened as the rock walls rose on either side; soon they found themselves stumbling along a narrow stony path in near darkness where the moonlight could not reach, with nothing but a slice of starry sky above them to mark the edges of the defile. The singing ceased, but there was only one way forward.

They came upon it suddenly—a meagre glow reflecting off the rock walls of another dogleg turning ahead of them. Even the camel perked up. There was a smell, too, a tantalizing composite of vegetation, rot, and the scent of slightly brackish water. They stumbled along to the turning and emerged with startling suddenness into a slim valley surrounded by sheer cliffs, where the moon made a path across a lagoon of still water fringed by palm trees. But that was the least of it. Hervey briefly forgot his thirst and weakness in the simple, urgent desire to have a paintbrush and a canvas and a full set of oils in his hands, because a sketchbook and a pencil could do no justice to the beauty that faced him.

More than five thousand years ago, the Egyptians were capable of fashioning alabaster vessels with walls so thin they would seem to luminesce if a flame were set within them. The ruins lining the far side of the lagoon gleamed in the moonlight with precisely that shimmering translucence. Hervey noted a temple façade lined with columns, flanked by the remains of a maze of walls; he saw the glimmer of a monumental statue on the edge of the lagoon, though he could not make sense of the shape. Of the phantom choir that led them there, there was no sign.

His camel saw only the lagoon. For once, Hervey had no trouble making her move.

The water was indeed somewhat brackish, and yet more delicious than the finest wine, the sweetest honey. The camel and the two men waded into the shallows and drank, drank, drank. The normally sober and earnest MacLeod splashed Hervey playfully. Hervey splashed him back, feeling the dust and sand of the Korosko Road sluicing off his skin. Then MacLeod collapsed on his back into the water and swam a dozen strokes out into the lagoon, beckoning Hervey to follow—but Hervey hesitated. An odd ripple that was not of MacLeod's making had caught his eye, arrowing towards the Scotsman.

*Crocodile* was Hervey's first thought. He cried out a warning, but MacLeod, now treading water and peering curiously into the depths, did not react. "Damned strange, James," he called back, and Hervey shouted again as something slender and sinuous emerged from the water behind MacLeod's back, waved its tapered end above his head for a moment, and then curled around his neck. It was hard to make sense of Hervey's account of the next seconds: a choked cry from MacLeod as he seemed to rise waist-high out of the water, a snapping sound, a wet ripping sound, and then a confusing moment when MacLeod's neck appeared to elongate even as his body fell away and slipped under the surface. His head remained perched a yard or more above the water on that impossibly long neck—until the neck shifted and became something like the forepart of a huge rearing snake and dropped MacLeod's head into the water with a gentle splash.

Time slowed. Hervey watched frozen while a dark hump broke the surface and closed around the floating ball that was MacLeod's head and then fell away underwater again, pulling the snake-thing behind it. It was the sight of a ripple moving rapidly in his direction that shocked him at last into scrambling clear of the shallows and dragging the camel after him onto the shore. He did his best to climb the camel as if she were a rockface, throwing himself up her side as she bucked and protested, crashing painfully to the sand, hurling himself upwards again, falling again. Then one thrashing hoof caught him square in the belly and knocked him headfirst against an ironstone boulder.

———— «» ————

It was just after I finished transcribing that passage in Hervey's manuscript that a ghastly coincidence took place. We were a few days into the new term, undergoing the normal chaos of the shakedown phase, and I was looking forward to going home to a restorative glass of wine after the last class of the afternoon. As I sorted through the papers on my desk, one of the Inca specialists, Elise, poked her head round the door. From her flushed face and shaking hands, I deduced she was excited, and not pleasantly.

"Did you hear about Sigrid Holmvang?" she asked in an unsteady voice.

Being not immediately excitable, I continued packing the day's mail—a couple of new journals and a conference invitation—into my backpack. "What about her?"

"Helen, she's dead."

"What?" A journal slipped out of my hands and tumbled to the floor.

"At the museum, murdered in her own lab. She—" Elise gulped, looked behind her, and beat a strategic retreat. The door immediately filled to capacity with two men in dark suits overlaid by brown overcoats.

"Dr. Thomas? Dr. Helen Thomas?"

"That would be me." I bent down to pick up the journal. I had never seen plain-clothes detectives in the flesh before, but there was no mistaking what they were. They were courteous but firm, reserved and yet informative. Yes, regrettably, Dr. Holmvang had been the victim of an attack in her laboratory; no, they were unable to give me any more information at the moment. But they did have some questions.

Apparently she had been working on my little side project around the time of the fatal attack. The notes on her worktable were headed *Thomas/Hervey Sketchbook*, along with my university phone number and email address. Various tools and fixatives were laid out, which a colleague in the conservation department confirmed were used for stabilizing documents or other paper materials.

"What about the sketchbook? Is it safe?" I asked, and then blushed at my own question. Poor Sigrid had not been a close friend, but I had liked and respected her, and it felt monstrously tactless to be worried about the Hervey volume in the face of her death. But Mason, the taller detective, treated it as an important question.

"We wondered about that, too. We're still working on the inventory, but we haven't found anything like a sketchbook in the lab or Dr. Holmvang's office, just the notes. Is it something of value?"

"It's a family heirloom," I said miserably, "and certainly of historical interest. I have no idea of its monetary value, if any."

"Could someone have murdered her for it?" His bluntness sounded deliberate, as if he were trying to startle me into a damaging revelation.

"I can't imagine why anyone would," I answered, unfazed, "or even how anyone would know it was there. Until it came to me a few months ago, it spent decades in a chest in my grandmother's attic. I gave it to Sigrid for conservation less than a week ago and I hadn't mentioned it to anyone else. And no, Mr. Mason, I don't think the album could possibly be of interest to a thief or murderer."

"It seems to have disappeared. That makes it of interest."

I thought about it. "It was in pretty bad shape, which is why I handed it over to Sigrid. Did you check for a relaxing chamber?"

"A...what?"

"A relaxing chamber."

"Some kind of spa thing?"

"Not quite," I said. Which is how, within the hour, I found myself in plastic booties and a baggy white full-body condom, being conducted into Sigrid's lab with strict instructions not to touch anything and to walk only where I was told. I was relieved that Sigrid herself had been taken away by then—she would have hated a bunch of strangers poking about in her meticulously ordered lab. She could never abide a mess. If she were not dead, she would already have tidied up the shattered flasks, overturned stools, and scattered papers left behind by the death-struggle with her murderer.

She would have started, though, with the blood. I could not believe how much of it was spread around the lab, even spattered on the ceiling and painted in a great stippled swath across the windows, a pointillist version of a bloodstain. Mason touched my arm.

"Dr. Thomas, let's get this over with. A relaxing chamber...what exactly are we looking for?"

"No need to search, it's over there." I had spotted it right away. A large rectangular plastic bin of the sort designed for under-bed storage was sitting unobtrusively on a desk against the far wall of the lab, its lid askew. I was surprised the forensics team had not looked at it already, but it was a fair distance from the contorted chalk outline and pooled blood I was trying to unsee. After the photographer was called over and did his business with the relaxing chamber, Mason carefully removed the lid—and there it was, the precious Hervey sketchbook, reposing safe and sound in a smaller plastic bin that was lidless and nested inside the first. An inch or so of water remained in the outer bin.

"That's all?" said Mason. "That's a relaxing chamber?"

"You were expecting something more high-tech? The pages were brittle. Sigrid was gradually rehydrating them so they wouldn't crumble when she tried to stabilize the edges. This system works pretty well, though it may be significant that the outer lid was loose."

"Why significant?"

"Because the lid has to remain sealed so humidity will build up inside the chamber. Sigrid wouldn't have removed it until she was ready to take the book out. So that could be what she was starting to do around the time she was attacked."

Mason's eyes were thoughtful above his mask. "Possibly."

"There's another thing." I peered down into the relaxing chamber again. "Where's the leather strip?"

"What leather strip?" His voice sharpened.

"There was a leather strip holding the album closed. Sigrid probably hoped it would relax enough so she could unravel the knot without having to cut it to get it off. Did any of your bunch happen to see it?"

"Describe it."

"Dark grey, bumpy-textured, about an inch across, wound a couple of times around the book. Big lumpy knot. That's about it."

"Wait here. Don't touch anything. Don't move." He joined a cluster of forensics technicians across the lab, near the location of that grotesque chalk outline. The conversation looked intense, but the voices were low. Then he came back, trailed by two of the technicians, identical in their masks and white scene suits and clearly in a state of tension. "The leather strip," Mason said. "Tell me again."

I repeated myself, for what it was worth, and added without much hope of an answer, "Why are you asking? What's so exciting about a strip of old leather?"

Mason hesitated. "I'm going to tell you something in the strictest confidence, but only because I think you might have some light to shed."

"Okay."

"Dr. Holmvang was strangled. The ligature marks are... peculiar."

"Strangled?" I stared at him. "How would strangulation leave all this blood? It's like a slaughterhouse in here."

He hesitated again, exchanged glances with the technicians, drew a deep breath. "This is not to be shared with anyone. The proximate cause of death was almost certainly strangulation, but the ligature was pulled tight. Very tight. So tight it came close to decapitating Dr. Holmvang."

"Well," I said after a careful pause, "that would explain the bloodstains. Also, your interest in the leather strip. And perhaps I should leave now, before I throw up all over your crime scene."

That was about the end of it. They gave me a card and promised to keep in touch, I promised to send them all my photos of the sketchbook and the leather strip, and I made it to the Ladies' before losing my lunch.

———— «» ————

I had little appetite for anything that night, neither food nor James Hervey's manuscript. I sipped wine and watched some not-funny comedy on Netflix and a flat-earth debate on YouTube, which was very funny indeed, and then made the mistake of getting into bed. Behind my closed eyelids, Hervey's caricature of Lachlan MacLeod's bushy-bearded face morphed into and out of Sigrid's fine but rather austere Scandinavian visage. Almost decapitated. What did that even mean? Halfway through the neck? Three quarters? Hanging on by a thread of skin? As for the elderly leather strip being used as a garotte, I had my doubts. Sure, it was well preserved, but even after a few days in a relaxing chamber it would remain brittle and delicate and require separate conservation. Lachlan MacLeod's head plopping into a moonlit Nile lagoon two centuries ago had nothing to do with poor Sigrid Holmvang's open neck fire-hosing the pristine windows of her lab. A grisly coincidence, that was all.

I gave up trying to sleep, got up, trudged into my office, and adjusted the reading light over Hervey's manuscript.

———— «» ————

Hervey awoke on a hard bed of sand under full blinding sunlight, perhaps thirty feet from the shore of the lagoon. His camel, still loaded with his saddlebags, was serenely cropping a tamarisk thicket nearby. Though the surface of the lagoon was as smooth and glimmering as a piece of polished pharaonic lapis, Hervey scrambled to double his distance from its edge. Only then did he look around.

The camel was the sole thing moving. Even the tamarisks, the acacias, and the tall dom palms edging the lagoon, were still. The array of walls and pillars across the water had lost the aethereal alabaster glow given to them by the moonlight, turning greyish and stony in the late morning sun. They seemed more ruinous by daylight and were deserted as far as Hervey could see. No smoke rose from cooking fires; no voices, no birds, no insects disturbed the louring silence. Hervey raised himself up on his aching bones and grabbed the camel's rein before she could object, then began to work his way carefully around the lagoon towards the ruins. As he went, he scanned the shore fruitlessly for any trace of Lachlan MacLeod's remains.

He paused to puzzle over the monumental statue towering over the head of the lagoon: dark granite blasted by weather and time, perched on a featureless black cube of granite higher than his head. The form was like nothing he had ever seen in Egypt or anywhere else, but it most resembled a sea monster from some obscure primeval legend, mysteriously stranded in the parched desert: a swollen octopus-man hybrid with a suggestion of a beaked head, and tentacles writhing around the markedly obscene orifice of the mouth. Where the eyes should be, globules grouped like clusters of diseased grapes spilled down the sides of the head, conveying in stone an impression of rot and deliquescence. It was hideous, repellent, and above all confusing, resisting any effort of Hervey's eyes to make full sense of the shape. Why, he wondered, would the superbly talented Egyptians have wasted so much fine granite on such an abominable eyesore?

The ruins were, at a distance, more comfortingly familiar. All over Egypt and Nubia, Hervey had seen the palimpsests of the great temples—pharaonic substrates dating back thousands of years, overlaid with the grand pastiches of the Ptolemies, the iconoclasm of the Christians, the long slow erosion of the Muslim era, all enfolded by accretions of humble habitations. Superficially this looked like a rock-cut shrine of the New Kingdom period with some later additions, a colonnade of lotus-form columns fronting a cave entrance carved straight into the native rock of the cliff; but as he got closer, everything turned subtly wrong. The proportions were off, with none of the perfectly balanced architectural grace Hervey had come to expect of the Egyptians. The columns were too spindly, overburdened by the strangely bloated lotus capitals. On the cliff wall behind the colonnade were none of the usual reliefs, no parades of gods, no striding pharaoh, no sprawling fields of hieroglyphs; the entrance was a squat, plain rectangle that was wider than it was high, creating an effect that was both abnormal and aesthetically unpleasing. Altogether, Hervey thought, the facade was like a clumsy parody of itself, convincing only from a distance.

He tethered the camel to a column, dug out his diary, stepped through the cave entrance, and halted to gape in shock and wonder. Light poured down from holes in the distant ceiling, illuminating a broad cavern with a small, perfect Christian church standing free in the centre. The structure was in good repair, not at all ruinous; he could even swear that a faint fragrance of incense still hung around it, with an underscent of something not so pleasant. Its outer façade was smoothly plastered and covered with texts in what Hervey recognized as the Coptic script.

Fortunately, he stopped to record some of these before entering the little church. The copy takes up half a page of his manuscript, meticulously transcribed though Hervey did not himself read Coptic. Unfortunately, they are gibberish. My own painstaking transliterations yielded a string of nonsense syllables—*gnaiigof'nn ng fhalgof'nn ot kuthulhu ilyaa nogephaii ot f' gnaiih ph'nglui fahf mglw'nafh wgah'nagl…ehyeeog y'or'nahh mgep f' mgepfhtagn…hai ahornah h' nogephaii l' lllln'gha shuggog*—which bore no resemblance to any of the ancient languages I could compare it to, and was certainly not Coptic or Old Nubian. On the same page were over a dozen little sketches of particularly repulsive tentacled sea beasts, nightmarish arachnoids, and even one that disturbingly resembled an ape-like creature with a goatish head and tentacles swarming out of its belly. None of these sketches was annotated, but I assumed they were copies of images on the façade.

Then Hervey entered the church.

What happened next, Hervey himself regarded as powerfully influenced by his state of hunger and fear, the lingering effects of his illness, the shock of MacLeod's terrible death, even the bump on his head from being kicked into a rock by the camel. The account in his manuscript, written some days later in the cabin of an Aswan-bound felucca, took on a light, self-deprecating tone. How silly and missish, he wrote, to be so affected by the silence and the bizarre frescoes on the walls, like a schoolboy shivering at a ghost tale. Surely his eyes and ears had deceived him. Laughing at his own wild fancies was the only sensible course.

He passed under the lintel of the main entrance and into a corridor that traversed the length of the little church, white-plastered and columned on each side, but roofless and lit by the same ambient light from above as the rest of the cavern. Thus he had a reasonable view of the images painted on the columns and the walls of the side-chapels—not Nubian, not Egyptian, not Coptic, barely (he wrote) attributable to anything created on a sane planet travelling through a rational cosmos: oddly angled figures with a distressing resemblance to men made in God's image, other figures resembling nothing that God himself could envisage, all cast in a drama of carnage hardly conceivable to a Cambridge scholar once destined for the clergy. At first, Hervey was more sickened than frightened.

Then his eyes were caught by a brighter glow at the end of the corridor, a mere slit of light, which he deduced would be passing between the leaves of a double door leading into the apse. He shuttered his attention to the escalating horror on the walls and columns, quick-marched to the end of the corridor, and pushed open the doors.

Unlike the rest of the church, the apse was roofed and dark. The glow came from dozens of lamps set out on a plain stone altar, wicks floating in simple saucers filled with aromatic oil. It did not occur to him at first to wonder about the lamps, so overpowering was the visual impact of the frescoes rioting on the walls in the flickering lamplight, vignettes of violence and fire even more loathsome than those in the outer chambers; but dominating the apsoidal rear wall was a larger-than-life portrait of a man in the large-eyed Coptic style, enthroned and clutching an armful of scrolls. Inscribed above it in Greek, which Hervey could read, was *Eubulus Episkopos*, or Bishop Eubulus. And even more overwhelming, driving Hervey's heart straight up into his throat, was the physical presence of the portrait's model—arguably the cadaver of Bishop Eubulus himself, mummified, richly dressed in a gold-figured robe and a golden coronet, hunched on a gold-leafed throne just below his own painted image. In his arms were real scrolls.

In that breathless moment, Hervey forgot everything, including himself and his dire situation, in the wondrousness of it all. The well-preserved mummy of a Christian Nubian bishop! Gold! Scrolls! Astonishing frescoes! Even with their hideous subject matter, the frescoes were artistic marvels, and this was a discovery of the highest order. Hervey rounded the altar in a couple of bounds and eagerly stretched out his hand for the bishop's scrolls.

One of the lamps flared and died. Then another. Which had the curious effect of reminding Hervey of a critical question he should have asked himself when he first pushed his way into the apse: who lit the lamps? He whirled and peered into the shadowed corners where the lamplight did not reach—nothing moved, but the ambience now earnestly suggested to Hervey that wisdom lay in simply grabbing what he could hold and getting himself on camelback and out of this cursed valley within the fewest possible seconds. He whirled again and darted out his hand to snatch for the scrolls, but found himself gazing straight into the pale, unblinking, unmistakably hostile eyes of the late Bishop Eubulus.

Had the eyes been open before? Though Hervey could not settle that question to his own satisfaction later, he was in no doubt in that moment that a presumed mummy had just shown signs of both life and terrifying malice. While Hervey struggled to speak (to apologize or to plead, he was not sure of his own intentions) the mummy's blackened jaw fell open and a mass of grey worms writhed into the lamplight—and grew, and grew, thickening into tentacles as they lengthened, reaching blindly towards Hervey's face.

Hervey turned and ran.

How fortunate that both he and the camel had drunk their fill the night before. He tore the rein free from the column, and this time managed to scramble onto the camel's back, kick her mercilessly in the ribs, and race away from the ruins. To his left, the smooth waters of the lagoon began to bubble and stir. He closed his eyes and kicked the camel again. The sun assaulted him from above. Where to go? Not along the edge of the lagoon; the Nile and the rational human world might well be only a few steps beyond the lagoon's mouth, but who knew what might be slithering from the water, even now, to block his way? He did not look back. He angled away from the lagoon, past the granite-mounted monstrosity, past the palms and tamarisks, and pointed his camel's head towards the gap in the cliff where he and MacLeod had penetrated the valley, not ten hours before. Atypically, the camel entered into the spirit of Hervey's panicked retreat. Within seconds they were through the gap and thundering uphill along the defile towards the high desert. Nothing followed them. Barely two hours later, after an easy ride north, Hervey was amazed and profoundly relieved to find himself in a busy little fishing village on the bank of the Nile, just downstream from Korosko. His manuscript was completed, as I said, on board a felucca bound for Aswan a few days later. It ends with Hervey's regret that his own panicked folly had prevented him from seizing even one of the scrolls of Bishop Eubulus.

———— «»  ————

A week passed with no progress in tracking down the murderer of Sigrid Holmvang, except for identifying the murder weapon. The forensics lab did this based largely on photos I had taken of the infamous, and now vanished, leather strip that had been coiled around Hervey's album. It turned out the texture of the leather was distinctive and rather nasty, resembling under magnification a dense terrain of tiny indented hillocks reminiscent of weeping boils. The species could not be identified, but the texture was a perfect match for marks left on poor Sigrid's neck, face, and left arm. Therefore, I was interviewed several times by Detective Mason, not as a suspect, but in hopes of pulling out every iota of information I had regarding the Hervey volume and the leather strip. It was a waste of my time and his. I had already told him everything I knew, including the contents of the companion volume from 1820, and had put all my photographs and notes at his disposal. Meanwhile, the sketchbook from the relaxing chamber was impounded as possible evidence, with no word of when it would be returned to me, if ever.

I was at a loose end. Teaching became a chore to be endured, and not happily. The Winchester necropolis monograph could not lure me; I shoved it aside again after a terrible evening spent staring blindly at my screen. All I could think about was Hervey's bizarre narrative, with its tantalizing conclusion. Clearly, on the evidence of the Cairo letter addressed to Arthur Garbutt, he had returned to the Korosko Reach some twenty years later, but I could not proceed with his story without seeing the contents of the later volume. Despairing, I dug out the few items sifted from the sand lining the bottom of Hervey's chest, and the ivory figurine suddenly made sense—it was a tiny, stylized rendering of the massive statue described by Hervey on the bank of the lagoon, mouth-tentacles and all. Now my fascination with Hervey's story officially became an obsession. There was only one thing I could do.

I phoned Auntie Freda.

———— «» ————

"My notes on Julia Garbutt Winslow's correspondence? Of course, dear. I can do better than that, though, if you're interested."

"You've got copies?"

"Digital photos."

Of course she had copies. This was Auntie Freda. "Anything of interest?"

"Depends on what you call interesting. Most of them are pretty boring, even for me. But I also have a bound collection of pamphlets written by Julia's sister Amelia Garbutt, the one who never married—did I tell you Amelia wrote as well as painted? Short stories and poetry, published privately and handed out to friends and relatives. One of her brothers had a few bound copies made up after she died, and I found one online. Would you like to see that as well?"

I hesitated. "Are the stories any good?"

"Does that matter? They're relics of a collateral ancestor," she said, rather sharply. "Although," and her voice warmed, "I do remember quite an entertaining horror story. The book's worth a look."

Having seen Amelia's dismal portrait of her father Arthur Garbutt, I was not too hopeful about her literary talents. But I thirsted for anything new bearing on James Hervey, and some nuggets of information might conceivably be buried in the sisters' correspondence—an account of a visit from dear Papa's old Cambridge friend, say, or the passing mention of a mysterious sea chest arriving from Egypt. The chest had surely been landed in Whitby, because here it was in my own study, but had Hervey himself landed? I could think of nowhere else to look for confirmation but in the words of one sister or the other.

The bag Auntie Freda dropped off a couple of days later contained a flash drive of the digital photos of Julia's letters, some handwritten notes which proved only minimally helpful, and a slim blue calfbound volume with *Lilies from a Lady's Garden, by A.M. Garbutt* embossed in gold Ruskinesque letters on the ornately tooled cover. I shuddered at the title and put it aside.

The twenty-seven letters on the flash drive were dated between 1840, when Julia moved to London with her new husband Hubert Winslow, and 1846, when the Winslows (supplemented by their first three children) returned to live in Whitby. Only Julia's side of the correspondence survived, and Auntie Freda was not wrong about its tedious nature: household trivia, delicately worded obstetrics, colic, problems with the parlourmaid, teething, problems with the cook, more colic, more teething—to be honest, my ancestress was something of a whiner.

I scanned through the first few letters for any mention of James Hervey or Egypt, then turned impatiently to early 1843, the approximate time when Hervey would have ventured towards his investigations in the Korosko Reach. Maddeningly, there was a gap of seven full months between mid-April and late October of that year, after which Julia's letters invariably enquired after or commiserated over the state of "Poor Papa." Auntie Freda had inferred from this that Arthur Garbutt suffered his permanently incapacitating illness in the summer of 1843, an inference that made good sense. I could not help observing, as well, that Poor Papa's illness began thought-provokingly close to the time when Hervey and his scrolls were due to arrive in Whitby. Could there be a link? Alas, after ruining my eyes for several nights over Julia's cramped handwriting, I had to accept that I would not find my answers in that direction. For my purposes, Julia's correspondence was a bust.

——— «» ———

Other things happened. After Sigrid Holmvang's terrible death, the university museum began to acquire the reputation among students, and even some of the staff, of being haunted. Slithers and thumps were heard in the walls and ductwork, flickers of movement were half-glimpsed in dark corners; an undergraduate had a nervous breakdown after sketching alone in the classical sculpture section. It was all due to the power of suggestion, according to the skeptically minded, though that explanation lost favour after the second murder.

That happened while I was still struggling with Julia's letters, about a month after Sigrid's death. The victim was a janitor checking the furnace in the basement, and the official story was that he had been strangled, though no details were released. Back came Detective Mason to my doorstep—was there nothing else I could remember about the sketchbook, or the strip of leather, or anything else that might be even remotely relevant? My answer was no. This time he did not favour me with any inside information about the murder; all my hints and eventually my blunt questions about whether poor Mr. Sorenson had been decapitated in the process of being strangled went unanswered. I began to sleep with the light on and a meat hammer under my pillow.

———— «» ————

*Lilies from a Lady's Garden, by A.M. Garbutt.* Notwithstanding the ghastly title, it was the last resource currently available to me with any chance of a Hervey connection, so I gritted my teeth and cracked the cover. There was a frontispiece, a line-drawn portrait of a lady in early Victorian dress, so dismally executed that I wondered if it was poor Amelia's self-portrait. Next came an introduction by one Daniel Garbutt, Amelia's older brother, essentially a eulogy for a sister who had passed her life in loving duty to family and God before slipping away prematurely to her eternal reward. Daniel went on to describe his sister's laudable devotion to the arts, the private publications of her literary works in pamphlet form, and his own tribute to her memory in the form of this collection of said pamphlets. He also noted that one story was never published in her lifetime but was found among her papers after her death in 1863 at the age of only forty, after a lingering illness.

I did not expect to find much of value to my own quest, but now I felt driven to read the whole thing anyway, out of a newborn sense of pity for my collateral ancestress Amelia. No doubt it was good of Daniel Garbutt to collect his sister's writings, but the tone of his introduction was insufferably patronizing. To 21st-century sensibilities, the woman he described was the spinster sister helplessly forced into lifelong servitude to an invalid parent, a woman who never had a chance at a life or marriage of her own, who enjoyed barely five years of freedom after her tour of duty ended with her father's death. Poor Amelia! I felt obliged to give her effusions a full and sympathetic reading.

The poetry was dire, but the same can be said of much Victorian verse. To be honest, though, her stories were not bad—derivative, with overtones of Austen and the Brontes, Dickens, Thackeray, and Mrs. Gaskell, but competently written and with a certain imagination and even wit. Of course they were all inescapably moral, with virtue rewarded and vice coming to a fair range of terrible fates; even so, I found myself liking Amelia more and more. Then I turned the page to the final story in the volume, the one not published in her lifetime, and knocked over my wineglass in shock.

The story was entitled *The Scrolls of Bishop Eubulus*.

———— «◊» ————

Some women are born with a thirst for adventure, but into a milieu where adventure is considered unwomanly. This was the plight of Amelia Garbutt's heroine, Alicia Greenwood—note the initials. Alicia, sheltered, pretty, well-bred, sublimated her cravings for the exotic by reading all the memoirs of exploration and travel she could lay her hands on, from Haklyut's *Voyages* to the works of Marco Polo and Mungo Park. But nothing enthralled her more than the multitude of letters her father received through the years from his old Cambridge friend, Joseph Harcourt—note the initials.

The letters came from everywhere and anywhere. One year, the daring Mr. Harcourt might be trekking through the snow-laden passes of the Himalayas and wandering in disguise across the Tibetan plateau; the next might see him sailing among the lush islands of the South Pacific, or consulting ancient manuscripts in the libraries of Baghdad, or questing on camelback into the Empty Quarter of Arabia Felix. He ranged the Yucatán with the artist and explorer Frederick Catherwood. An oilcloth-wrapped package of papers was forwarded from Halifax, describing a journey around the northern tip of Labrador to cliffbound and ill-reputed Akpatok Island, where even the hardened whalers Harcourt was sailing with were reluctant to land. A letter from Patagonia told of months spent with other whalers at the opposite end of the world, and a tantalizing glimpse of the icy coast of Terra Australis Incognita, the landmass we now call Antarctica. In short, Harcourt's letters showed him to be a man who could journey to Timbuctoo or Fiji as readily as Alicia's father might jaunt to Harrogate for the day. He was Alicia's *beau ideal* of the intrepid gentleman voyager.

Therefore, she was disconcerted to discover at about age twelve that her own father was paying all of Harcourt's travelling expenses, and a stipend besides. The copious letters were not simply a correspondence between friends and fellow antiquarians, but also reports on where the money was going. This revelation briefly diminished Joseph Harcourt in her regard, but she soon realized that even the intrepid must eat. Furthermore, it occurred to her that her father, as trapped as she was herself in upper-middle-class conventionality, might also be living vicariously through Harcourt's travels, and so she was able to justify and forgive them both.

By fifteen, she became aware that her feelings for Harcourt, a man thirty years older than she, whom she had never even met, had warmed to an intense romantic passion. Hold that thought.

In her nineteenth year, an even more intriguing realization came upon Alicia. Housebound with a "female complaint" and unable to take part in a family excursion to York, she seized the opportunity to seek out a long-suspected cache of Harcourt's letters which her father had withheld from the family. What she gathered from this furtive reading was that Joseph Harcourt was not travelling to all those perilous hells on Earth for any of the commonly accepted reasons: not pleasure, not profit, not evangelism, not a desire to benefit the glorious British Empire, nor even a straightforward wanderlust, like her own. He was on a quest. But a quest for what?

Alicia knew already that Harcourt had been indelibly affected by a mysterious experience in Egypt a little before her own birth in 1823, but even the most assiduous eavesdropping on her parents' conversations had failed to turn up more specific information. The hidden letters did, however, give Alicia a rough idea of what Joseph was looking for. Apparently there was a god of sorts, a very ancient and quite deplorable one, whose cult echoed across the dark side of any number of vanished civilizations and lingered on in the most barren, remote, degraded corners of the mid-19th-century world. The genesis of the quest was an inscription hastily copied by Harcourt during that life-changing Egyptian incident and translated for him two years later by an aged

Buddhist monk in Mongolia, who also taught him to read the mysterious ancient language in which it was written, which he called Ri-lye-khian. Here is the inscription, as reported by Amelia/Alicia:

*Sons and daughters of Kuh-thool-hoo await the return of their father in this dead home. Many years have they waited. Now may he return to devour the world.*

It appeared to Alicia that Harcourt's subsequent travels must have been in search of other traces of this mysterious and terrible Kuh-thool-hoo and his (or its) scattered cult places. The secret correspondence described some of these: shattered blocks of granite tracing vast, oddly angled foundations on a forgotten plateau in the Andes, a kind of Machu Picchu on steroids; a blackstone tower thrusting a hundred feet above the central wastes of the Arabian desert, where Harcourt scaled steps that were surely not built for human limbs, up to a trapezoidal platform open to the sky; a coral lagoon built on tumbled cyclopean masonry off a dead volcano in the South Pacific; and more, and more, each discovery more outlandish than the one before it. Even the besotted Alicia wondered now and then whether Mr. Harcourt might be exaggerating his explorations to some degree.

And then, with little warning, the legendary hero of Alicia Greenwood's young life was made flesh. That is, Joseph Harcourt sent a terse note to Alicia's father, announcing his imminent arrival in the (fictional) town of Wisby in the autumn of 1842. All Alicia's romantic fancies were soon put to the test, and survived. The explorer was strikingly handsome in a hollow-eyed, haunted style, his weather-beaten brown skin and lean frame making a dazzling contrast to her father's soft paunch and beef-fed complexion. Alicia was naturally unable to let Mr. Harcourt know of her secret passion, and he barely noticed her existence except as her father's de facto housekeeper, her mother having died the previous winter. Bringing afternoon tea or evening whiskey to the men in their deliberations, however, gave her many opportunities to exercise her skill at eavesdropping, and what she heard thrilled her, but also terrified her on her beloved's behalf.

Harcourt had hit an impasse in his research. He had located, mapped, and sketched a score of ancient sites around the world related to the enigmatic Kuh-thool-hoo, and was convinced that the god's epicentric temple lay in the frozen lands near the South Pole, but he suffered from a lack of solid textual material. Most of the inscriptions in his files were fragmentary, severely eroded, and often beyond his competence to decipher, sufficient to tantalize but not to shed much light on the cult of the ancient deity. It was time, he told his friend and patron, to return to Egypt and acquire the scrolls of Bishop Eubulus by any means possible, from purchase to theft, and even to *force majeure* backed up by violence. As for the deadly cultists or "children of Kuh-thool-hoo" perhaps infesting the lagoon, Harcourt planned to travel with a detachment of well-armed Egyptian soldiers as bodyguards, and as labourers in any excavations he might undertake. What could go wrong?

Alicia, not liking the sound of the "children of Kuh-thool-hoo," began to fear for the life of her hero. As a chaste young woman still under her father's roof, she could hardly express her tender feelings to Mr. Harcourt, but she found an opportunity before his departure to gift him with a half-dozen linen handkerchiefs embroidered with his initials by her own fair hands, and a silver shirt-pin topped with a cloisonné forget-me-not. What more could a maiden do to make her devotion clear?

Harcourt accepted the shirt-pin and the handkerchiefs, but not the hint. He took ship for Egypt; letters began to arrive for Mr. Greenwood and were clandestinely devoured by his daughter. From Cairo, Harcourt wrote that he had obtained the services of twenty armed Egyptian soldiers through the good offices of the British consul and a hefty bribe to an unspecified Egyptian bureaucrat (receipt enclosed), plus an experienced dragoman named Yusuf, a cook, and a suffragi for general domestic duties in camp. From Aswan, he wrote of the difficulties, eventually overcome, of procuring a boat to go upriver. From Korosko, he wrote of buying camels for himself and the baggage (the others could walk), and the imbecile reluctance of the local people to guide him to the fabled ruins on the lagoon where the Nasrin apparently still ruled, which he was certain was the site he had visited so many years before. That letter was written in early February and arrived a month later; the next did not arrive until mid-May, and sounded suspiciously similar to the letter I found in the chest, written from the Hotel des Anglais in Cairo in April. The sea chest, by some fluke of the shipping lines, arrived the day after that letter. And then—nothing.

Joseph Harcourt's chest reposed untouched for many weeks in Mr. Greenwood's study, as James Hervey's chest had reposed in mine, with this difference: Joseph Harcourt was expected to arrive at any moment. Then came a day in late June when Mr. Greenwood received a disturbing package by messenger from London, the contents of which he shared with Alicia only after several days had passed. The package contained a shocking report from the British consul in Cairo: a headless, decomposed body recovered from the Nile had been identified as an Englishman by the name of Joseph Harcourt, whom the consul knew to be an associate of Mr. Greenwood. The consul had taken the liberty of forwarding to him the few effects found on the body of the deceased, deeming Mr. Greenwood to be Mr. Harcourt's heir for lack of other contacts. If Mr. Greenwood knew of relatives or other legal heirs, the consul begged him to inform them of this tragic event, and of Mr. Harcourt's burial in Cairo. Further, should Mr. Greenwood have any knowledge of the whereabouts of a missing detachment of Egyptian soldiers last seen in Mr. Harcourt's temporary employ, the consul would be most grateful to be informed, and would otherwise consider his own duties to be discharged. The effects included two monogrammed handkerchiefs and a silver shirt-pin decorated with a cloisonné forget-me-not.

Screw it. At this point, I shall give up on the fictions of Alicia and Joseph. This narrative was the autobiography of Amelia Garbutt, and her hopeless devotion was for James Hervey. The writing style differed from that of Amelia's other prose: simpler and more direct, with little adornment, few Victorian circumlocutions, no echoes of Dickens *et alia*. Her heartbreak when she heard of James Hervey's death rang true, unlike the formulaic vapourings of the Sophias and Charlottes of her previous tales. Naturally, Amelia felt obliged to hide the extent of her sorrow, just as she had hidden her passion, but she may as well have rent her garments and heaped ashes upon her head for all the notice her father took. In fact, Arthur Garbutt seemed more distracted than sorrowful at first.

On a sunny July afternoon about ten days after the consul's packet arrived, Amelia was passing the door of her father's study, which was usually closed. This time it was open, and Hervey's chest was visible in the middle of the room with its lid flung back. Wild with curiosity, but also shocked—she vividly remembered Hervey's instructions to burn the chest unopened—she stepped into the room, and then pulled up, startled. Arthur Garbutt was there, sitting in his library chair by the window with a large hardbound volume in his lap.

"Go away," he said. His voice was flat, his face set and ashen. Amelia did not remember him ever looking so deathly pale, even during her mother's final illness a year before.

"Dear Papa," she said, "will you not burn the chest now, as Mr. Hervey's letter required?"

"Go away," he repeated, and this time she turned on her heel and left, closing the door softly behind her. That evening at dinner he did not mention the incident, but was hectically jovial even before he started on the port, and positively maudlin by the brandy. Amelia was disturbed; the louder he laughed, the more fear she saw in his eyes. She did not sleep well.

The next morning was worse. Arthur returned from his daily constitutional—climbing up and down the famous 199 steps leading to the ruined abbey on the Whitby cliffs— with a pale face and shaking hands. He startled Amelia by slamming the door shut, locking it, and collapsing into a chair in the front hall. Intrigued, Amelia brought him a sherry and then peered out through a chink in the parlour curtains. The only two figures in the street had already passed the Garbutt mansion, a tall gentleman in a long cape leaning on the arm of a much shorter man wearing a fez and a dark suit of a subtly foreign cut. A retired sea captain and his manservant from abroad, Amelia surmised. Whitby swarmed with such characters. She shook her head and went to tend to her father.

Arthur Garbutt did not stir from his room the next morning. Amelia went out on her usual round of errands and then set off on her own daily constitutional, along the river and out to the lighthouse at the end of the west pier. There had never been a better place in Whitby to watch the ships setting off for foreign parts, and to imagine herself standing on one of those decks bound for Tangier or Vladivostok or Constantinople, but she found herself cured of that now. Hervey's murder had tainted those dreams; in her grief, the very thought of faraway places nauseated her. She swore to herself as she stood at the base of the lighthouse, staring at the waves with tearless eyes, that she would never stand in that spot again. Based on what happened next, I think she may have kept that oath.

She turned to leave, and there they were, almost within touching distance, shoulder to shoulder between her and the lighthouse. Amelia recognized them at once. How wrong she had been—these grotesques could never be a retired sea captain and his manservant. Was there a circus visiting the town? Wrapped in a hooded cape, the towering old man was the very image of a comic stage villain; the companion was a long-armed gargoyle in a fez. But there was nothing comical about the black silk scarves wound mask-like about their jaws, nor the pale, cold disks of their eyes, which were fixed on hers in a shocking disregard of manners. Repulsed, but also affronted by their rudeness, she drew herself up reprovingly.

"I beg your pardon, gentlemen," she said, in the sharp tone taught to her by her old governess for just such occasions.

Neither replied. But the elder lifted a long, thin hand to his scarf and began slowly to unwrap it from his face, still watching Amelia with a silent intensity that began to frighten her. It came to her that she was alone at the end of the pier with these two unnerving madmen; it came to her forcefully that she would rather jump off the pier than see whatever was under the scarf the old man was unwinding. The rush of fear and disgust gave her strength. Pulling her mantelet tight around her body, she shoved her way between them and ran for the shore.

——— «» ———

That night, after her maid had dressed her for bed and retired to the attic along with the other servants, Amelia wrapped herself in her dressing gown and tiptoed down the hallway to her father's study. The time was almost midnight. Her father had vanished into his bedroom with a decanter of whiskey for company immediately after a silent dinner, and the only brother still living at home was in America on business. Effectively, she had the house to herself. She took the door key from atop the lintel and found the key to James Hervey's chest in the second drawer of her father's desk.

The contents of the inset shelf were much as when I opened the same chest myself, nearly two centuries later: papers and a large hardbound album. The papers appeared to be largely accounts and receipts. Amelia lifted the shelf and saw the body of the chest was filled with papyrus scrolls, perhaps a dozen of them, each secured with a thin strip of leather around its middle. She did not like the feel of the scrolls; her hand felt unclean from picking up the first, and she dropped the thing back into the chest immediately and wiped her fingers on her dressing gown. In the most melodramatically Victorian phrase of the story, she wrote that "a chill of evil crept up Alicia's arm from the mere touch of that ancient, accursed papyrus." Shuddering, she turned back to the inset shelf and picked up the album.

The flyleaf was marked "Korosko Reach, 1843." What followed was part sketchbook, part journal. Amelia skimmed it quickly, listening with half an ear for her father's tread in the hall.

Hervey's expedition had marched into the Valley of the Nasrin, the Christians, to find it deserted. Nothing moved in the townsite nor made ripples in the lagoon. There was no indication that oil lamps had been lit in the little church in the cavern for some time, and the bishop's throne was empty. Hervey set up his work tent near the temple façade, and the main camp some distance away, closer to the shore, then set his soldiers to combing the ruins for signs of life or treasure. They found nothing significant.

On the third day, Hervey began his formal operations in the church, copying the grisly scenes on the walls and transcribing the inscriptions. Amelia described the sketches in his notebook as "unspeakable." Meantime, under Hervey's direction, a team of soldiers began hacking through the floor of the apse into a suspected vault beneath the altar, where the flagstones rang hollow.

On the fourth morning, two soldiers were missing from the encampment and were presumed to have absconded. Yusuf, the dragoman, reported that the remaining soldiers were uneasy. The cook and suffragi were sullen. The work continued.

On the fifth day, the soldiers broke through into the vault under the altar and recovered a cache of papyrus scrolls, several pounds of silver and lapis jewellery, a golden coronet of rather crude workmanship, and seven tiny figurines of a peculiarly repellent nature in gold or ivory. On the same day, murmurs in the camp about a pair of elusive phantoms haunting the farther reaches of the ruins came to Hervey's ears. Hervey discounted these reports as the results of superstition and cowardice. He despatched a soldier on camelback to Korosko that night to forward a report to Arthur Garbutt regarding the scrolls and treasure, but he purposely did not mention the nonsense of the spectral visitors. There is no evidence that letter ever reached Whitby.

On the sixth morning, another soldier was missing from his bedroll. Strange drag marks were observed on the sandy margin of the lagoon. The soldiers' mutterings became more fearful; the ghostly figures, *et-Tawil wa el-Qasir*, the Tall and the Short, were seen in every shadow, behind every crumbling wall. The soldiers kept their rifles close as they dug into the mounds of sand lapping up against the most promising of the structures surrounding the temple-cavern, while Hervey continued his copying in the church.

On the seventh morning, another soldier was missing from the camp.

On the eighth day, Hervey decided reluctantly to cut the expedition short and return to civilization. The few artifacts and Christian-era pottery turned up by the workers outside the cavern were not very compelling, and morale was abysmal. He had the scrolls in his possession already, the textual material that was his true object, plus the treasures that had been concealed with them under the floor of the sanctuary. That was enough for him. The soldiers cheered when he made his announcement, and cheered again when he assured them they would receive their full two-month salary anyway, courtesy of Arthur Garbutt. Departure was set for late the next afternoon after the full heat of day had dissipated.

But that night, while the soldiers slept and Hervey was in his work tent sketching one of the ivory figurines, odd music wafted across the valley, softly in the beginning. Hervey thought he was hearing the wind at first, mimicking the sound of chanting voices as it soughed through the ruins. Then he thought perhaps the soldiers were singing in the camp, celebrating their last night in the valley; then he remembered a night long ago, also a night with a full moon, when the chanting of an unearthly choir lured him to the valley, and Lachlan MacLeod to his death. This time, though, thanks to the tutoring of the Tibetan monk, he could understand the words.

*The children of Kuh-thool-hoo and Yog-sothoth call to their forebears. They will come, they will come, they will come to eat the stars.*

Hervey's nerves had been tested many times in the past twenty years, and they did not fail him now. He checked that the rifle leaning against his worktable was loaded and ready, and then calmly copied the words of the song into his sketchbook. When that was done, and he was rising from the table to shout for Yusuf, a single shot sounded from the direction of the lagoon. Good—the soldiers were doing their job. Then a scream, cut short, and another shot, followed after a few seconds by a fusillade, and then a rising chorus of shrieks. The chanting continued in counterpoint to the screams, but now Hervey wasted no time in parsing it. Twenty years of danger had also taught him when to run.

He threw open the chest, emptied it of his clothes, and tossed in as many of the scrolls as would fit, plus the ivory figurine from the table; he replaced the inset shelf holding his papers, threw in his sketchbook, and slammed the box shut. The treasure and other artifacts, he swept into a canvas bag. Then Yusuf burst into the tent, gibbering of beasts and demons oozing up out of the lagoon—Hervey shook him by the shoulders and ordered him to carry the chest and bag out to the camels, which were hobbled close to the tent.

Then Hervey abandoned his men. There is no kinder way to express it, and even Amelia found it hard to accept or forgive at the time. How could this be the action of a hero, *her* hero? He did not even consider grabbing his rifle and running to investigate the shrieks emanating from the soldiers' camp. Instead, he scrambled aboard his kneeling camel, grabbed the chest from Yusuf's arms, and brought the camel lurching to her feet. He looked back to see the dragoman, still clutching the canvas bag, hurl himself onto one of the baggage camels. The weird chant cut off, but a chilling cacophony of hoots and squawks and roars mingled with the screams from the camp.

Without mercy, Hervey kicked his mount forward. When he glanced back, Yusuf's camel was surrounded by a tide of capering, misshapen figures, and Yusuf was no longer in the saddle. The camel bellowed, a terrible sound, and then the tide of dark figures rolled over her and pulled her down. Grimly, Hervey yanked at the rein and aimed his mount across the valley towards the gap into the khor, exactly as he had done twenty-two years before.

As he approached the great statue on its black granite plinth, two dark-robed figures stepped from its moon-shadow into his path. One was tall, the other short. Hervey did not hesitate. He plunged straight towards them, straight through them, blessedly past them; then he looked back and saw that both figures were still on their feet and had turned to face him. Though the moon was behind them, he saw the glow of large, pale eyes under the dark hoods. One of them called out to him in a shrill voice. Hervey turned his face forward and applied his heels to the camel's sides, and never looked back again. Nobody and nothing followed him out of the valley.

That was the last entry in Hervey's album, written the next night in the relative safety of Korosko. Amelia laid the album back in the inset shelf, closed and locked the chest, replaced the key, and crept fearfully back to her bed. It was all horrific, but there was one detail that had haunted Hervey in his final journal entry, and now haunted her, echoing in the memorable nightmare that troubled her in the only hour of sleep she managed that night: the shrill voice in the valley had called out to Hervey in English.

"Give them back!"

—— «» ——

It was the smell of smoke that woke her. She grabbed her dressing gown, flung herself out of her room, and raced down the hallway toward the light flooding from her father's open study door. Why build such a fire on a warm summer night? The question was answered as soon as she halted, panting, on the threshold. Her father was crouched on the hearth, feeding the flames with handfuls of the papers scattered like a snowdrift around him. His face was scarlet and pouring sweat. Amelia cried out when she saw him tossing packets of Hervey's letters into the fire, along with loose sketches, maps, tables of strange runes and disquieting pictographs. All that was left of James Hervey's legacy and life was vanishing into ashes.

"Why, Father?"

Arthur Garbutt glared up at her and rooted among the surviving letters, pulled a sheet free, balled it up, threw it at her, then returned to feeding the hungry fire. Amelia smoothed the paper out—it was Hervey's final letter, written from Cairo, and as she scanned it she at last understood his somewhat obscure jest. *I greatly fear they have tracked me, and that is the Long and Short of it. Ha!* Ha indeed, she thought grimly. It seemed the fiends had followed Hervey to Cairo, and the chest to England, and her father to this house. Very well, then.

She dropped the letter on the table and surveyed the room. There was an arrangement of exotic weaponry over the mantelpiece, sent to her father over the years by the late James Hervey himself. Crossed spears, artistically arranged arrows fletched with bright tropical feathers, longbows, blowpipes, throwing sticks—a kris. She ran to the mantelpiece, kicking papers out of her way; she wrenched the kris off its bracket, slid the snake-shaped blade out of the sheath, tested the shining iron edge. It was hearteningly sharp.

What next? A glance at the window showed an empty moonlit street, but that meant nothing. The hall outside the study seemed full of soft creaks, footfalls, sighs. They were perfectly innocent sounds, she had no doubt, but she found herself regretting every Gothic novel and ghost story she had ever read. "Papa," she said, as loudly as she dared, "I'm going to the attic to rouse the servants, just in case of trouble. Papa?" He paid her no mind—the drift of papers was falling fast, and the fire was being smothered in its own ashes. Clutching the kris, Amelia hurried to the door and into the dark hallway.

Real footfalls on the stair, not imagined. Backlit by the moon shining through the open street door, two silhouettes were steps from the top. Four round eyes shone into hers with their own pale light. Amelia half-turned to bolt for the back staircase, but they were already too close. She threw herself back into the study, slammed the door, and fumbled for the key; it was not in the lock. She braced herself against the door, feeling a soft thump on the other side. "The key, Papa, quickly!"

Her father was kneeling beside the open chest, filling his arms with scrolls. He looked up without comprehension. "They've come!" she shouted. "Give me the key!" The door handle, pressed against her hip, jiggled and turned; she shifted to grab it with her free hand, bracing the door with her shoulder. A powerful thud shook the door, then another, and then it crashed open and pinned her behind it against the wall. Thus hidden, she heard her father cry out, and then a few words in a shrill *wrong* voice, as if a serpent had been granted the power of speech: "Give them back."

Amelia peered around the edge of the door. She could see her father, transfixed, and the tall man in profile unwrapping the scarf that covered his lower face. Her father screamed as the scarf fell away; something long and tapered writhed from the tall man's mouth and wrapped itself around her father's neck. Amelia did not scream—she was no shrinking violet, my great-something aunt. She roared, and leapt from behind the door, and brought the kris down on the tentacle-thing with all her strength. Her father fell away with the severed tentacle still around his neck. The tall man slowly turned his head.

Amelia backed away, holding the kris in front of her like a crucifix. Now she was inclined to scream, but she lacked the breath. The tall man had no mouth, only a tangle of tentacles where any proper Christian's mouth would be, one of them truncated and dripping. He seemed to suck in the waving horrors as she watched, and now there was indeed a mouth, narrow lips curved in a smile more chilling than anything Amelia or her Gothic novelists could ever have imagined. That reptilian voice spoke words she did not recognize; she realized the voice came from the little man, who was gathering up the scrolls, not with arms, but with tentacles emanating from his bared belly. He smiled at her too, exposing a mouthful of sharp black teeth. Amelia raised the kris higher, and a single tentacle whipped out between the tall man's lips and flicked it out of her hand. The little man laughed—and then they turned their backs on her, the little one still laughing, and were gone. She heard their footsteps in the hall, on the stairs, the soft closing of the street door.

She ran to her father and dropped to her knees beside him. His spectacles were gone and there was a bright band of blood around his throat, but he was breathing. She loosened his shirt and put a cushion under his head, then ran to the back stairs and shouted for the manservants.

What now? The fiends were gone; the scrolls were gone. Good riddance to both, she thought, but perhaps she could preserve what little remained of James Hervey's legacy. The Korosko Reach sketchbook was already in the dying fire, scorched but not alight; she dragged it out of the embers onto the hearthstones. Some papers remained on the table—Hervey's last letter, a thick manuscript in his familiar handwriting, another sketchbook. Amelia fit the shelf into the now-empty trunk, and threw in the letter and the manuscript. She was bending to pick up the sketchbook from the hearth when a dark snake slithered out of the shadows and wound around her wrist.

This time she did scream.

She pounded her wrist against the bricks of the fireplace, and the thing fell away into a coil on the hearthstones. A dark ichor dripped from the thicker end—how could she have forgotten the severed tentacle? And how was it still moving? It twitched, and she battered it with the sketchbook; it responded by winding around the scorched cover, the undamaged end waving in the air as if challenging her. She picked up the sketchbook with the fireplace tongs, tentacle and all, and dropped it into the chest, smashed the other sketchbook on top of it, and slammed the lid shut. Only then could she breathe again. Faint stirrings inside the chest roused her to one last burst of effort. She found the key, locked the chest, and opened the window to throw the key far across the deserted street.

———— «» ————

That was the end of Amelia's story, but I can infer the rest. Arthur Garbutt never recovered from his near-strangulation and the stroke that accompanied it, and Amelia spent her next fifteen years as the dutiful daughter attending his sickbed. The chest? It would have been stored in the Whitby attic, no doubt, along with Amelia's portrait of her father, until both items attained the sacred status of heirlooms and migrated to the New World as part of the Winslow impedimenta. And eventually came to me.

Naturally, I have widened my research while preparing James Hervey's Nubian manuscript for publication. I have found no trace of Kuh-thool-hoo or the associated cult in archaeological literature, though there are some intriguing traditions related to areas in Hervey's letters as cited by Amelia, including the deep desert of Saudi Arabia and a legend-cursed island off the coast of Baffin Bay. There is no record of a Bishop Eubulus in Christian Nubia, though

Eubulus is a perfectly respectable early Christian name, a companion of the Apostle Paul, so a bishop called Eubulus is credible. But what of the Valley of the Nasrin?

I have done a deep dive into the records of the expeditions responsible for the area around Korosko in the Aswan salvage campaign. An intriguing reference is made to a site far up one of the khors, the ruins of a townsite with traces of every period from the Neolithic through the Pharaonic to the Christian, but so comprehensively shattered that the archaeologists suspected a deliberate destruction had taken place. If there ever was a cave there, its entrance was irrecoverably blocked. Link that to historical records of the first uses of dynamite in the Nile Valley in the early 1870s, experiments by Egyptian and foreign sappers carried out in remote locations in southern Egypt and northern Nubia. Link it also to folklore collected by ethnographers involved in the salvage campaign—stories of a place near Korosko so evil that soldiers came at last to destroy it, stories of the corpses of rotting demon-spawn the size of large crocodiles or small fishing boats washing up on the shores of the Nile villages for days afterwards. If those linkages are valid, then the domain of Bishop Eubulus was destroyed a century and a half ago, and later drowned under a hundred feet of Lake Nasser. In Amelia's own words, good riddance.

But what do I make of it all? I hardly know. Was the valley truly a surviving outpost of an abominable ancient cult, taking on the protective colouration of a whole series of Nubian and Egyptian cultures through the millennia as its celebrants awaited the return of their dread god Kuhthool-hoo? Was Bishop Eubulus no more than the latest guise assumed by the high priest of that literally unearthly congregation? The physical evidence from the sea chest is vanishingly thin but is not inconsistent with Hervey and Amelia's narratives; consider James Hervey's dirty sock and clean hankie, Arthur Garbutt's broken spectacles, a tiny ivory figurine with tentacles swarming out of its mouth....

And then, there are the murders at the museum.

The murderer has never been caught; nor has the presumed murder weapon, the leather strip, been found. I took a great interest, however, in the sightings of a peculiar greyish snake of unknown species glimpsed around campus in the spring, which greatly excited the herpetologists in the Biology Department. Perhaps fortunately for the herpetologists, it never fell into any of their traps. Do I honestly believe it was a deathless offcut from the tentacle of a monstrous demigod, revivified in poor Sigrid Holmvang's relaxing chamber? I'm not crazy. Officially and for the purposes of my book-in-progress, the answer is no. Unofficially, whenever I walk around campus I carry a pocket-knife and keep a cautious eye on the shrubbery.

# Small World

## Prologue

**Once upon a** time, four point seven seconds and seven time zones apart, two human female infants initiated unpredictable sequences of contingent events—that is to say, they were born. Alice's birthplace was Leeds, on the island known as Great Britain. Melissa was born in Edmonton in the Canadian province of Alberta.

Separating them spatially at this vital moment were an ocean and most of a continent, or, on a more direct route, several thousand miles of hot mantle and relatively cool crustal rock. On the face of it, Alice and Melissa were mutually irrelevant phenomena, total and irrevocable strangers, and we should be clear from the outset that they never met each other. But this is a small world.

## Connections I

Alice and Melissa rose from the same corner of the gene pool and shared innumerable forgotten links at uncountable ancestral levels. Most recently, in the early years of the last century, Melissa's paternal grandfather emigrated from Harrogate, Yorkshire, to western Canada, leaving behind a large extended family who did not grieve to see him go. Among these were fifth and third cousins of his, themselves not directly related, who married in Bradford and produced the baby girl who would later become Alice's mother. Further back, in the latter 19th century, the youngest sister of Alice's paternal great-grandmother bore a child destined to marry a cousin of Melissa's maternal grandmother. Both Alice and Melissa could count themselves first cousins six times removed to a gentleman vicar living outside Huddersfield at the time of Victoria's coronation. And so forth. And as the generations recede, the connections become more fibrous and finely interwoven, until by a certain point in the distant past, Alice and Melissa's joint ancestors comprised the entire human species of that time.

# Connections II

While still in their childhood and teenage years, Alice and Melissa had several common friends of friends. Melissa's neighbour and earliest playmate in Edmonton was a large-headed English boy with pale eyebrows, whose dimly remembered contemporary first cousin in London attended the same girls' school as Alice. Furthermore, the headmistress of that school, briefly worshipped by young Alice, eventually died in the same mid-air collision as Melissa, although the elder lady was a passenger in the other plane. Melissa's first lover was a second cousin twice removed of Alice's, through a great-grandfather killed in the Boer War. And so forth. Melissa and Alice's tertiary and quaternary links defied counting, and at the eighth remove their separate spheres of acquaintance effectively merged into one.

# Encounter I

Shortly after Alice and Melissa's eighteenth birthday, both happened to travel from their homes to the city of Toronto; Alice to study for a year as an exchange student in the Conservatory of Music, Melissa to attend the marriage of her brother in the nearby city of Peterborough. Briefly, in the following manner, their paths crossed.

Alice was boarding in a large, elderly house outside central Toronto. On the morning of Melissa's arrival by air from the west, Alice took the subway into the city centre to visit the Royal Ontario Museum. Melissa, en route from the airport to the Central Station via the subway link, happened to be travelling in the car next to that boarded by Alice, and caught a glimpse of Alice's red plastic raincoat as the train braked into her station. That glimpse did not register in Melissa's conscious mind. Alice was looking at her watch when Melissa's face flashed past a few feet away, and she did not see Melissa at all.

# Encounter II

Some years later, when Melissa began advanced orientalist studies in Oxford, Alice had already become a music student in London. Of the interim, little needs to be said, except that Alice bought an Oxfam sweater cast off by Melissa's professor's wife, and regularly patronized a Camden Town butcher who was Melissa's mitochondrial-DNA twin and third cousin once removed. Meanwhile, Melissa was handed a leaflet by the student of theology who would in due course conduct Alice's funeral service.

One day, Alice met a friend for an early drink at the pub across from the British Museum, and ordered a vermouth that she drank while sitting on a stool at the end of the bar. Afterwards, she browsed the shelves of Foyle's, then caught a homebound train at Tottenham Court Road. Not three minutes after she left the pub, Melissa entered it and sat on the stool that was still warm from Alice's rear, and ordered a martini, the vermouth for which came from the same bottle as Alice's drink. But this, although notable, was not the end of it—for when Melissa finished her business at the museum later that afternoon, she too walked to Tottenham Court Road and bought a *Guardian* at the same newsstand where Alice had bought her *Times*.

# Connections III

By a striking coincidence, Alice and Melissa married within an hour of each other, though Alice's wedding took place on a rainy morning in London, and Melissa's on a bright Beirut afternoon. Alice's husband was a Russian violinist who had gone to some trouble to disengage himself from his homeland to join her, after a frenziedly romantic encounter in a Prague hotel. Staying in the same hotel the following week was Melissa's uncle from Calgary, whose business involved the buying and selling of Czech steel.

Melissa's husband was a Palestinian Christian whose most recent genetic links with either woman dated to the 13th century of this era, but who had lived for several months only two streets from Alice in Camden Town. Alice's marriage to her violinist, sadly, lasted barely seven months, whereas Melissa's ended with her death two years later.

# Encounter III

After her divorce, Alice rented a cottage in Berkshire, not far from Heathrow Airport, where she taught and wrote music. One grey day, she sat at the piano listening to the rain over the ticking of the metronome. At the same moment, Melissa sat on a plane at the airport, bound for Beirut to join her husband. Alice got up to fill the kettle; Melissa, feeling the usual brief lightening of body as the jet lifted its nose off the runway, watched Heathrow fall away below.

Not many seconds later, Alice switched on the kettle and a plane arriving from Majorca came down into the same airspace as the Beirut-bound jet. There was an explosion of great force, Melissa ceased to exist as a discrete entity, and the ground below was barraged with the debris of both jets and their passengers. One large chunk of fuselage, to which clung some carbon-based molecules most recently pertaining to Melissa (but the use of which could be traced back through a regression of entities, human and nonhuman, vegetable, saurian, invertebrate, to the primal ooze from which life rose, and beyond that to the atom-factories of numerous distant stars) chanced to fall on Alice's cottage. Alice died of her injuries the next day.

# Epilogue

Melissa's husband flew from Beirut for the memorial service dedicated to victims of the air disaster, though there was no body as such for him to bury. Afterwards he wandered around the churchyard with a fistful of roses, examining the obelisks and angels, the crosses, the tablets, the stone Bibles, the moss-ridden indecipherable slabs. Few living people remained in the churchyard by then—but at a newly raised mound still carpeted with wreaths, he came upon an elderly woman dressed in black, whose face bore the tracks of recent tears. This was Alice's mother. Although she was a stranger, he traded with her the mutual recognition of the freshly bereaved. And, although Alice was also a stranger, he stooped and laid the roses on her grave.

# Operation
# HAND OF GOD

**"The generals are** here, Mr. President."

"Show them in, sugar, show them in."

They troop in a little resentfully, followed by a selection of aides, specialists, other ranks, and one technician, who assumes his place at the single wired-for-absolutely-everything computer console. The generals would prefer this historic event to take place in their natural habitat, the Pentagon, all polished tables and power chairs and video screens fit for a sports bar, the specialists and technicians at stations lining the perimeter, the air thrumming with military potence. But what this Commander in Chief wants, this Commander in Chief gets, and what he wants is to watch the culmination of Operation HAND OF GOD on his own White House turf. For one thing, he and the technician are the only ones who get to sit down until it's over.

HAND OF GOD is his own inspiration—the name, not the operation. The operation is one he has inherited from three and a half previous administrations, though it has taken that long for the technology to catch up with the brilliance of the concept. Phase One is complete: the arming and deployment of the drones over the strongholds of the terror organizations, the hideouts of the highly placed imams, torturers, executioners, and commanders of the armies of Allah. An array of twelve large screens, four across and three down, shows drone images floating above Kabul and Raqqa and a palace in Umm Farha; three supposedly secret training camps deep in the Iraqi desert; two sand-coloured fastnesses in Afghanistan; a Roman-era border fortress far east of Aleppo; a mud-walled compound in a Libyan oasis; an unassuming village in the Pakistani highlands; and the mouth of a sandstone cave, where one armed and bearded figure keeps watch.

"Go," says the president. General Brewster nods to the technician.

The technician hits a few keys and pushes a button.

A few tense moments later, all the images descend to ground level. The screens afford excellent close-ups of sand, camel dung, litter, the edge of a water tank, a surface of cracked mud, a shining tiled courtyard, a rough adobe wall. All images simultaneously blur after thirty-odd seconds, as if the same tide of quicksilver has flowed across each lens. Then all images refocus and drift upwards, coming to hover at about twice the height of a tall man.

"It's done," says General Brewster. "Phase Two is underway."

"That's it?" says the president.

"Watch," says General Brewster.

The technician hits a few keys and pushes a button.

The drones dip as one, to focus on the ground below. In the centre of each image, a silver puddle grows and divides and grows and divides again in a rapid shimmering mitosis. One appears to throw out a series of luminous tentacles; another expands in a lopsided star shape; a third fans off towards the edge of the screen. The drones begin to rise slowly, showing silver tides dispersing across the sand or the mud or the tiles, slipping into the water tanks, oozing up adobe walls to open windows...

"Screen Four," says the general. The technician fiddles with a joystick. One image expands—the Libyan compound. A black-swathed woman ambles across the courtyard, water jug on head, bare feet slogging through sand where the silver streams have so recently flowed. The generals watch her anxiously until she passes out of the drone camera's range. Several of them visibly suppress sighs of relief.

"Nothing happened," says the president.

General Brewster patiently clears his throat. "That's right, Mr. President. In this case, that's what was supposed to happen. And thank God for it."

"Okay," says the president, "but—"

"Screen Eight," the general interrupts. "Watch this, Mr. President."

Screen Eight is the sandstone cave mouth, known by many of those present to conceal a bunker complex dating from the rule of Saddam Hussein. The guard is almost invisible in the shadows just inside the cave, a charcoal silhouette of man and gun—until he staggers into the open, tearing at his chest. Two steps, three steps, the start of a fourth—he collapses onto his belly, twitches a bit, flips half over, lies still with his wide-open eyes staring almost directly at the drone.

"Fuck me," says the president. "It works. That's a beautiful thing."

"Equalize the screens," says the general.

The technician pushes a button.

Action has begun on eight of the twelve screens. A bearded man lurches into the Libyan courtyard. Other bearded men boil out of tents in the desert camps, ripping at their t-shirts. Afghan guards tumble out of cunningly hidden guard posts, Syrian guards plummet from Roman ramparts. Several women flee across the shining tiles of Umm Farha, not looking back.

"Shit," says the president, "I wish we could get sound on these things. You can't tell if they're screaming or cheering behind those fucking veils." Then he grins his trademark grin and pumps his fist in the air. "That's it, motherfuckers! The war on terror is fucking finished! We've won like nobody in history has ever won before!"

Cheers and applause, reminiscent of Houston Mission Control after a successful launch; handshakes, backslaps, high-fives, and a grateful drift towards the champagne and seafood buffet newly revealed in one corner. General Brewster, however, pauses to whisper to the technician. The technician hits a few keys and pushes a button. All twelve images flare and die.

"What did you do that for?" demands the president. "I was watching that!"

"Mr. President, it's all in the summary I sent you. It's how Phase Two finishes. As soon as the nanobots are deployed and we have visual confirmation of the effects, the drones are told to self-destruct. We can't risk even one of them being captured."

"Come off it, they're almost invisible."

"Nevertheless, sir, the point of the operation is to look like the hand of God, as you yourself so aptly put it. It's got to look like Allah withdrawing his stamp of approval and reaching out to stop the hearts of the most radical leaders and their minions. In Phase Three, all the tame imams in the western democracies will be riding that horse hard in their sermons. It's all in the summary."

The president waves General Brewster into the empty armchair beside him and signals for two glasses of champagne. "Yeah, the summary. I kinda read it. Enough for me to tell you to stop pissing around and just get the little fuckers on the ground already."

General Brewster takes a deep breath. "In fact, Mr. President, we would have liked a few days longer to assess the nanobots before—"

"Bullshit," says the president. "BioCross was late delivering. We couldn't risk that goatfucker slipping away from Umm Farha before we dropped the bugs."

"Very true, sir, but we were a little worried about the nanobots being as—well, as selective as BioCross promised they would be."

"You're a bunch of old women, you generals, you know that? All we have to do is point the bugs at the murdering terrorist ragheads and set them loose, am I right?"

"It's a little more complicated than that, Mr. President." The general takes a hefty gulp of champagne. "BioCross engineered the 'bots to look for a combination of visible flags—male, bearded, armed—along with chemical markers indicating weapons use, and certain hormonal markers suggested by the Gitmo project. For some of the priority targets, we fortunately had DNA samples as well. And I know you favoured the exploding heads scenario, sir, but the mass heart attacks were more practical to engineer."

"I thought they couldn't work out how to do the exploding heads."

"Technically, they could. BioCross could have programmed the 'bots with any number of recognition and attack algorithms, sir, but they were constrained by the size of the drones. You have to deliver a critical mass of the 'bots before the reproduction function will kick in. All this was in the report, Mr. President."

"Fine, we'll save the exploding-heads thing for the Chinese." The president heaves himself out of the armchair but stops and frowns when a severe-looking woman in a power suit sidles up and touches him on the arm. "What is it now? This is a party."

"FBI, sir. He says it's urgent."

The president's face reddens dangerously. "FBI? So what do the Fucking Bullshit Instigators want this time?"

"I really don't know, Mr. President, but it sounds important. He says it's relevant to Operation HAND OF GOD."

"Then it better be goddam important. Stay, Brewster."

The dark-suited man, sweat shining on his smooth black forehead, threads his way to the president through the crowd of generals and holds out a thick sheaf of printouts stapled together. The president grabs it, drops back into his chair, and scans the first page, three columns closely printed in a small font. He passes it to General Brewster and glares up at the agent.

"Big deal. A list of screwball organizations."

The agent opens his mouth, but General Brewster gets there first. He is as ashen as the president is flushed, and the hands leafing through the papers are having trouble keeping steady. "If this really is relevant to HAND OF GOD," he says, "it means we're in trouble."

"It's just a goddamn list."

The agent and the general trade looks. The general raises his eyebrows and mouths a single word. The agent nods. The general turns paler still. "Mr. President," he says, "all along,

BioCross has been assuring us that we, the United States military, are their only customer. That they are working only for us. That nobody else will be getting access to the nanobot technology, that it will stay under our control. God knows we paid them well enough. But this…"

"Spit it out!" roars the president.

The general stares at him with doom-laden eyes. "This is apparently a list of their *other* customers."

The president grabs the papers back. A small clearing of stillness begins to grow around the two armchairs, as more of the revellers take notice. "Okay," says the president, "tell me about them. What are the Heirs of Almighty Thor?"

"White supremacists, sir," says the agent.

"Nubia Nova?"

"Black supremacists."

"The Nation of Jehovah?"

"Black supremacists. Antisemitic."

"The Sons of the Fiery Nexus?"

"Basically nihilists, sir. They hate everybody, but especially the rich."

The president continues down the list—heirs of this, sons of that, sisters of the other thing—committees and collectives and cooperatives and free states and fronts and brigades and peoples' armies…and every one of them, it seems, has it in for somebody or other. Whites. Blacks. Asians. Gays. Gender-non-binaries. Boomers. Millennials. Journalists. Christians. Non-Christians. Jews. Non-Jews. Hindus. Non-Hindus. Muslims. Non-Muslims. There are the Buddhist Saviours with a unique and terrifying vision of peace on Earth, the Neo-Ghost Dancers, the militant Marxists who wish to rid the world of capitalists, the Randite Objectivist Squadron who wish to rid the world of moochers. Over five thousand organizations are on the list, on every continent, in every nation. Even the president is pale under his makeup by the end of page five.

"But," he sputters, "how could all these crazies afford to hire BioCross? *We* could barely afford them."

"Mr. President, a good many of them are, in fact, quite wealthy. We understand some of the others were offered attractive discounts. As for the rest, there is reason to suspect we were accidentally subsidizing them ourselves, along with the Chinese and the Russians. That is, some of the trillions we paid to BioCross was diverted into customizing products for other organizations."

"Products? What fucking products?"

"Nanobots, I'd guess," says General Brewster levelly, "engineered to target the chosen enemies of each client. Different recognition criteria, of course. Different delivery systems: airborne, waterborne, food contaminants, maybe insect vectors. Different morbidity modes—you know how many we looked at before we settled on heart attacks. And if all these groups are Biocross customers, and if all of them let their particular strain of nanobots loose..." He stops and gazes with suspicion at his empty champagne glass.

"But why?" the president bellows. "Why would BioCross do that?"

The agent flips to the last page. "They were originally known as the Gaia Firsters, sir. Members of an eco-terrorist organization that we presumed had gone extinct in 1979."

"Some fucking hippies did this?"

"Hippies of a sort, Mr. President. Their philosophy was essentially that humans are cancer, and the only way to cure the planet is to wipe out the entire species. Except perhaps themselves." He clears his throat and finishes with visible embarrassment, "We thought they blew themselves up decades ago. It seems they went to grad school instead."

The president's colour returns to the choleric. "You better be able to tell me you've stopped the bastards."

"Unfortunately, Mr. President, it appears they got the shipments off to all their other customers at the same time as we took delivery of HAND OF GOD." The agent wipes his forehead again with an already sodden sleeve.

"Where did they ship to?" General Brewster shoots to his feet, waves for one of his aides. "If we act fast, we can head off the shipments, or at least isolate the effects."

"It's too late, General. The deliveries were well coordinated, and the distribution was global. DHL, mainly. Express delivery."

The general drops back into his armchair.

Unbidden, the technician hits a few keys and pushes a button.

The screens light up again, this time with a shifting array of news stations—CNN, BBC, Al-Jazeera, Fox, Russia Today, China Global, many others, a rainbow of anchorpersons, a gallery of BREAKING NEWS! banners in a babel of scripts. The common factor is the sort of gravity usually reserved for a terrorist attack or the death of a movie star. Less commonly, the pretty Japanese newsreader grabs her throat and slides out of sight under the news desk. The handsome Turk projectile-vomits blood at the camera. Live on CNN, the anchor's face melts.

"Oh, fuck," says the president.

"Absolutely correct, sir," says the agent. Behind them there is a gurgle, a thud, the drumming of heels on the floor. "That's Colonel Goldstein," General Brewster says, looking back, "and there goes General Wayne."

The president takes no notice. "Where are these BioCross bastards now? You better fucking know."

The agent jerks at his tie and dabs ineffectually at the sweat pouring down his cheeks. He detaches the last page of the sheaf, hands it to the technician, and points to a line near the top. The technician hits a few keys. All the screens amalgamate into one; a satellite image zooms deep into the folds of a mountain range far to the west, a tiny bright circle in the exact centre expanding into a larger circle, into a circle made up of tiny hexagons, into a dome.

"It looks like they mean to inherit the Earth, sir," says the agent. "They..." He grimaces, clutches at his belly, crashes to the floor. Three generals are down now, plus six more colonels, the president's aide, and the waitress at the buffet. The president, rubbing his temples with both hands, glares at the graceful dome with its fringe of pines.

"Fucking tree-huggers," he growls, "don't deserve to win."

General Brewster replies with an efflux of black blood.

Groping in his breast pocket, the president staggers out of his chair to the computer station. He stabs a bright red key-card into a port on the console.

"Nuke 'em," he says.

His head explodes.

The technician hits a few keys and pushes a button.

# The Shrieking Sand

**Fourteen days of** blistering sand, of sand-seasoned rations, of sand in the teeth, sand in the gullet, sand that rasped the insides of the eyelids like coarse jeweller's paper; fourteen days of marching down a tunnel in a mountain of whirling sand, three-fourths blinded, peering through the shifting yellow curtain for the vital trail of cairns; sand, sand, sand.

The cousin of the Jezir date trader went sand-mad on the seventh day, raving bareheaded into the wind, and spent the next three days bound and gagged on top of a load of prime dates. On the ninth day, the fat young mercer, Irshek, also went mad—or so it was assumed, when he disappeared from the slow, shuffling serpent of the caravan with one donkey and no water. This was Irshek's first journey, and his last. Any effort to find him would only have led to more losses.

It fell to the drover Shumal to deal with the vanished mercer's remaining animals, two camels and four donkeys buried alive under bales of linen and dyed wool. Like Shumal, the animals were peevish with thirst and grit. None of them, including Shumal, had any liking for the sand where they had been born and where they would probably die. None of them had any love for Taskrisht, bitch-goddess of the Windy Swathe. The animals cursed Shumal, who cursed them back; each of them, in their own way, cursed the desert.

Shumal also found time to curse fat little Irshek for wandering off, and the trainmaster, Chief Kalef, for being the brother of Irshek's wife, and therefore adamant that the mercer's load must be safeguarded and the profits returned to the widow's family, which included Chief Kalef. Shumal regarded this, not without precedent, as a kind of theft from Shumal's own rights of pilferage.

He thwacked the big black-headed camel on its tough neck and dropped back to check the next beast in the late mercer's string. Eight long years he had worked as a drover for Chief Kalef, six miserable caravans per year, four dozen sand-eating desert journeys from Kishti to Iklankish and back again, with a few days to call his own at each end. He received six leadweight palots per journey, plus food, plus the odd item discreetly levied from a load under his care and sold to an acquaintance in the Oxmarket. It was the latter perquisite that made the job worth his while; that, and the time spent in the Fourth Circuit of Iklankish.

Under the folds of headcloth that muffled his face, Shumal licked his paper lips with a tongue like a dry sponge. One day more, and they would be out of the Windy Swathe, and the sand would go back to staying on the ground, where it belonged. The weathered granite spikes of the Sentinels would rise around them like a concourse of giant needles, the line of cairns would meander through the jumbles of the ironstone plateau, the Tooth of Raksh would loom in the distance—and then the Hub itself would appear, rearing out of the massive masonry onion skins of the circuit walls. Another day would be allotted to his duties in the caravan market, to receiving his halfwages from Chief Kalef and to filching his dues from the merchants; then he'd be off to the Fourth Circuit, an adequately rich man for a few hours, to the cool and comfortable tupping den on the Fishtail near the Oxmarket. Thinking about it, trying to remember the name of the huge-bosomed whore with the little yellow tassels and only three teeth, he fondly stroked the flank of the late mercer's spotted donkey. With such paps, with such tassels, the lady had no need of teeth.

He narrowed his eyes to teary slits and peered ahead along the caravan. The haunches of the black-headed camel swayed with sulky dignity under the hill of bales on its back. Beyond it was the grain merchant's big she-camel, her outline dimmed by the sand. Shumal could just make out the delicate backs of her legs and the swing of her white hindquarters, which again called to mind the yellow-tasselled harlot. Eshaant—the harlot's name was Eshaant.

Though she needed a name about as much as she needed teeth.

A bulky white shadow took shape in the ochre void beside the grain merchant's she-camel and pushed through veil after veil of sand. At length Shumal could see it was a man, wrapped like himself in many folds of headcloth and cloak. By the colour of the headcloth, a washed-out splash of yellow, Shumal deduced that his visitor was Chief Kalef.

The trainmaster waved his arms. The folds over his mouth waggled as he shouted, but the words were jerked away by the wind. He came close enough to Shumal to embrace him—not that he would do so, since both of them smelled like a donkey's crotch after twelve days in the Windy Swathe—and screamed into Shumal's ear.

"We're making decent time, Shumal. We'll bypass the last shelter and push on to the edge of the Swathe. So keep the bloody beasts moving, eh?"

Shumal shrugged. It was all one to him. Anyway, it would be that much closer to the tasselled whore, to rough rakk and smooth beer, to harsh nosefuls of ashkiri vapour and the greedy bustle of the Oxmarket. The animals would not like pushing on past the gate-cairn, but no one was about to ask their opinion. Shumal swatted the mercer's donkey on the rump, as if to forestall argument. Chief Kalef began to shove by him, to continue down the line.

The wind explored the tucks of Chief Kalef's cloak, found a weakness, delved into it, shook the folds loose with a squall of triumph. The cloak whipped away like wings from his shoulders, and the front of his robe bellied and parted over his leathery chest. Chief Kalef deftly caught the edges and put himself to rights, wrapping the cloak more securely around him. Then he passed Shumal and was eclipsed by the blasts of sand towards the rear of the caravan. The drover turned once to watch him, but there was nothing more to see.

Shumal fell back a bit and whacked the mercer's other camel. It was a token gesture; Shumal was deep in thought. Under Chief Kalef's robe, exposed by the questing fingers of the wind, he had glimpsed a thick chain that looped as far down as his employer's breastbone, dulled by the wan sandlight, but undeniably of gold. And it was a chain of unusual design, double links alternating with single, worth in itself a good few trips across the desert. Shumal had only once before seen its like: six days previously, around the neck of Irshek, the presumably late and officially lamented mercer.

—— «» ——

The Windy Swathe was almost never calm. By some trick of topography and wind—or simply by the will of the bitch-goddess Taskrisht—this desert shifted its sands eastward for much of one half of the year, and westward for much of the other, a barrier of near-ceaseless turbulence lying across the central wastes of Sher between Iklankish and the coastal province of Kisht. Many merchants preferred the long trek or heavily taxed sea journey around the coast, but Chief Kalef drew his business from those impatient souls prepared to brave the cairnway through the deep desert for a shorter trip and a quicker profit. He should have been a wealthy man by now; even so, Shumal had never seen a golden chain of such impressive dimensions on the chief's windbeaten chest. It would take someone like a hereditary mercer, say, to afford such a costly bauble as that.

—— «» ——

Just after dawn struggled through the curtains of sand, the caravan reached the borderlands of the Swathe. Shumal knew the signs. First he could see the grain merchant's she-camel in her elegant swaying entirety; then the grain merchant himself, lolloping along in the middle of his string on a fine white donkey; then the camel ahead of that. One by one, the screaming veils lifted, the sand devils eased their fury, the beasts ahead of him in the caravan took shape in the sickly yellow gloom. Another outward trip was nearly completed, another miserable handful of leadweight palots was headed for Shumal's pocket.

Chief Kalef called a halt at last, when the Swathe was a dirty smudge on the horizon behind them, and the track wound through the wind-torn granite spires of the Sentinels, at the edge of the badlands. Here they would rest under a searing sky until evening and the final push to Iklankish. Shumal curled up in the shade of the black-headed camel, but sleep eluded him for some time. He was thinking again. He was musing on the short life and sad fate of the young mercer Irshek.

Little plump Irshek had been one of those vanishingly rare creatures, a rich, eligible, and unencumbered orphan with a trusting nature. He was sole heir to a dynasty of successful mercers, with no sisters to endow, no brothers or cousins to share his fortune, no aged mother or aunts or grannies to rule his wife's household. Indeed, when he expanded his business into Kishti and built a fine warehouse in the centre of the city, he had no wife. Chief Kalef soon remedied that.

Chief Kalef had much experience in marrying off his sister, a thrice-widowed beauty of about twenty-five, whose buxom charms were enhanced by her share of her late husbands' estates. Shumal had thought of marrying her himself, not long after her latest bereavement. Chief Kalef, whom he approached on the matter, had laughed. And then, still laughing, had pulled out his long, curved knife and waved it in the neighbourhood of Shumal's most precious organs, though saying nothing in words. Shumal inferred that his suit was unwelcome.

Mercer Irshek, by contrast, was made most welcome. He set up his Kishti warehouse in the Month of Seven; met Chief Kalef halfway through the first week, and the enchanting widow two days after that; though reputedly shy around women, he found himself betrothed within a dizzying fortnight. Scant weeks after that, Shumal went to the wedding feast without regrets or ill will, to consume most of an adult goat and three skins of wine in the bridegroom's honour.

And after the month of honey—during which lucky little Irshek was scarcely seen outside his own bedchamber— what could be more natural than the mercer joining his new brother-in-law's caravan for the harsh but profitable journey to Iklankish? Perhaps Kalef was not the best, nor the most trustworthy, nor even the swiftest of the caravan chiefs to be plying the Windy Swathe crossing, but he was family now. Surely he could be relied upon to take care of his own sister's bridegroom.

Shumal, as a lowly drover in Chief Kalef's employ, was not called upon to express an opinion. He did not even have an opinion then: not when the caravan set out along the hard-packed road through the groves around Kishti, nor when it paused for the omens at the southern temple of Taskrisht; nor when it reached the shrieking yellow hell of the Windy Swathe proper, nor even when Mercer Irshek vanished without trace into the deadly curtains of sand a few days later. Shumal's opinion was only formed when he saw that distinctive golden chain around the neck of Chief Kalef—and it was Shumal's sober and considered opinion that Chief Kalef's lovely sister would soon be on the market again.

——— «◊» ———

Iklankish was just as Iklankish always was, squalid, crowded, stinking, and full of perilous delights. Shumal lived for these brief days. He drank rakk and sniffed ashkiri. He ate dangerous messes of rich oily food and paid his ardent respects to Eshaant, the yellow-tasselled whore. He visited his old friend in the Oxmarket, to his modest profit— Shumal was a reasonable man, never appropriating more from under the packsheets of the caravan than he felt the merchants had allowed for. He had taken nothing at all from the unfortunate mercer's load, however. Chief Kalef's wrath was not to be risked.

Towards the end of the week, very early in the morning on which they were to start their return journey, Shumal half-woke from happy dreams with a smile on his face. "Eshaant," he murmured, nestling deeper into her softness, though a little surprised that her perfume was so pungent. He reached out to fondle the famous paps and snapped out of his dream—instead of warm flesh and silken tassels, his fingers had buried themselves in short, bristly fur. Shumal sat up and groaned, thankful he had explored no further. He was not in Eshaant's brothel. He was wrapped in his blanket in one of the courts of the caravanserai, surrounded by snoring beasts and fellow drovers. Beside him, the mercer's brindled donkey nickered in her sleep.

Shumal peered up at the black star-strewn sky. No sign yet of dawn, so he could probably snatch at least another hour of sleep. Oddly, however, he could hear voices, not just snores, coming from just beyond the pickets, where Chief Kalef's tent glowed faintly with candlelight through the rough weave of its sides. Shumal contemplated going back to sleep for a moment, with longing, and then he contemplated Chief Kalef. Who would the chief be entertaining at this hour, on the morning of an early start? Shumal swayed a little as he thought. Then he stepped quietly over the dreaming donkey and crept across the line of the pickets to the blind side of the tent.

Low voices, yes: Chief Kalef and one other. Something about wool and warehouses. Also a muted clinking, as of something being counted, perhaps coins. Shumal pursed his lips when he heard the magnitude of the numbers. Leadweight palots? He thought not. He knew all too well the hollow clinking of leadweights, whereas this sound had the rich, dense thunk of gold. Then there was a chorus of cascading chinks, as if a pile of coins were being swept into a soft bag, and a moment later the flap of the tent was thrown open. Shumal shrank back into the shadows. A cloaked figure emerged, carrying a small bag in his hand. He stopped and turned on the threshold.

"Brother Kalef," he said, "I commiserate with you and your dear sister on your grievous loss."

"Ah, Brother Lissk," replied Chief Kalef inside the tent, "I weep to think of my sister, widowed again so soon. And my poor brother-in-law, so young, so happy..."

"So rich," the other cut in. After a pause, he laughed out loud and shook the bag in his hand so that the contents clinked and jingled. The chief joined in, slapping his friend companionably on the back. Shocked, Shumal shook his head in the darkness.

"Take heart," the visitor went on, in a voice that sounded distinctly mirthful. "Perhaps he will rejoin you on your homeward journey."

Silence from inside the tent. Then Chief Kalef's voice again, this time sober.

"That, Brother Lissk, is no matter for jesting. May Taskrisht be deaf to your prayer. May the poor sod's bones rest quietly, and his spirit as well."

The man named Lissk became correspondingly grave. "I spoke out of turn, Brother. I wish the dear mercer to rest in peace, and yourself to journey in peace." Then he chuckled again. "And may your lovely sister not long be a widow, and soon a bride again!"

He was gone in seconds, melting into the farther reaches of the caravanserai. Well, well, thought Shumal. So that was the famous—or infamous—Merchant Lissk, perhaps the longest-tentacled and fattest-pursed property broker in all of the Fourth Circuit. Shumal clicked his tongue. Well, well, and bloody well. Had it not been Lissk himself who furnished the unfortunate Mercer Irshek with a letter of introduction to Chief Kalef? And the bridegroom before Irshek, as well, that ill-fated young importer of Omelian silks, who had succumbed suddenly, or so Chief Kalef said, to the effects of a bad oyster? Well, well, well, Shumal repeated to himself.

He shook his head grimly. It was a bad business, this one, with overtones of conspiracy and murder and outright theft. But who would believe him? The golden chain around Chief Kalef's hairy neck was not sufficient proof of anything. Chief Kalef could simply claim it was a present from the mercer to himself, as a new and beloved member of the mercer's family. In Shumal's mind, this overheard conversation was proof enough of dark doings—but who would take the word of a poor drover against the word of a rich and well-connected caravan chief? And how long would he last afterwards, with the dreaded Lissk as an enemy? Anyway, what was in it for Shumal? Let the hounds of fortune run down their own quarry. And as for Lissk's tactless jest—the fool! He should have known better. Everybody knew it was bad luck to speak of the unburied dead rejoining the living. Indeed, it was the next thing to issuing an invitation...

Shumal stopped. He pondered. He thought of the golden chain that graced the hairy and undeserving chest of Chief

Kalef. He thought of the poor plump mercer in his fine grey cloak, so young, so trusting, so rich. He thought of the few miserable leadweight palots in his battered purse, all that was left of the cheese-paring halfwage which that flint-skinned Kalef had tossed to him. He also thought, licking his lips, of the Chief's beauteous widowed sister.

And finally he thought, noting the continued darkness of the sky, that he had time for just one small errand in the Fourth Circuit before the hour came to feed and water the pack animals before departure. Cautiously, but with haste, he crept past the pickets and made for the caravan gate.

«»

Iklankish, that grim jewel set in jade and iron, had diminished to a distant spiky silhouette against the northern horizon by the late afternoon. To one side, a blood-coloured sun was sinking towards the flank of the Tooth of Raksh. To the other, a near-full moon had just risen from the sea. At the point where the road turned inland towards the ironstone plateau and the Sentinels, the caravan halted by the plain grey cube of the northern temple of Taskrisht, to let the priest on duty read the omens for the journey. And though he was supposed to stay back with the late mercer's animals, Shumal crept forward to where he could see and hear the proceedings.

"Hurry it up, you greedy fool," Chief Kalef was saying as Shumal took up a discreet position behind a camel-load of iron pots. "I want to make the first shelter in the Swathe before daybreak. Just cut the tupping beast's throat, will you?"

"Patience," said the priest serenely as he anointed the head of a small, skittish goat. "You know, Trainmaster, it is bad luck to rush the decision of the ineffably irritable Taskrisht."

"It's also bad luck to delay a trainmaster," Chief Kalef hissed.

Shumal listened breathlessly. He wanted the omens to be bad enough to make Chief Kalef nervous, but not bad enough to make him delay the crossing. He watched the quick slice across the goat's throat, the expert handling of the bloodbowl, the casting of dread powders and ashes of unnamed substances onto the sluggish crimson surface. Three times the priest stirred the contents of the bloodbowl, his frown deepening over the half-veil that covered his mouth. Chief Kalef shifted impatiently from sandal to sandal, glancing now and then at the sun's position over the Tooth of Raksh.

The priest shook his head, still frowning. He snapped his fingers. The acolyte held out a second, rather larger knife, with a wicked double point and a line of faded glyphs along the ivory haft. With one casual swipe, the priest cut an opening about a handwidth long in the dead animal's belly, then expertly snagged a loop of gut with the twin tips of the knife. A smooth tug, and the dark coils slid through the rent and hung halfway to the ground. Thoughtfully, the priest set the coils to swinging back and forth, watching the motion with an expert critical eye.

"Tut, tut," he said, shaking his head. "Oh, dear me."

Shumal peered anxiously around the side of the camel. This was only the third time he had seen an augury so unpropitious that the priest had to confirm the omens by cutting the belly; on two of those occasions, Chief Kalef had been worried enough to defer the journey until the omens improved. What if he should do that on this journey? Would Shumal be able to keep his nerve up in the face of a delay? He did not think so. Already his bowels were water at the mere thought of what he planned to do, and too many more days of thinking might destroy his resolution altogether. He held his breath, and let it out slowly when he saw the trainmaster, scowling and grumbling, begin counting leadweights into the acolyte's palm to pay for some lucky chants from the priest.

Shumal sighed again with relief and vanished circumspectly back to where he was supposed to be. He did not hurry, however. Behind him, he could hear the priest's voice lifting in an invocation to Taskrisht and the Hounds of Fate, which was long and complex. It would probably prevent them from reaching the first shelter in the Swathe until long after the rising sun began blasting through the shrieking yellow miasma of sand that lay not far ahead of them. Any other time, this would have filled Shumal with resentment and depression, but on this occasion he did not mind at all. It was enough to know that the caravan would depart as planned. He smiled to himself and patted the black-headed camel on the rump as he passed it.

———— «» ————

Sand, sand, sand.

Shumal always found the return journey to Kishti more trying than the outward journey. On the outward journey, he had his days in Iklankish to look forward to, tassels and rakk and ashkiri and all that; homeward, he had no prospects but a cheerless pallet in his cousin's attic, and far too much critical attention from a pack of strong-minded female relatives. Raksh willing, it would be different this time. For the first few days and nights of the crossing, he was content to trudge along in the lee of the mercer's animals, dreaming bright dreams while laying dark plans.

Two hours past dawn of the fifth day, the gate-cairn and solid walls of the fifth shelter loomed none too soon through the howling yellow hells of sand, just as one of the mercer's camels seemed on the point of collapse. The tired train of the caravan threaded through the narrow gateway; inside, though the sand hurled itself over the roofless walls to dance in the enclosure, the main fury of the wind was broken, and its diminished roar sounded, by comparison, like peace to Shumal's ears. He tended to the animals first, as required, and then joined the knot of merchants and drovers in the covered resthouse in the corner of the enclosure. Even there, the sand forced itself in billows through the crevices in the walls, but it was possible to loosen one's headcloth without taking a faceful of grit. Gratefully, Shumal pulled the cloth away from his nose and mouth.

Chief Kalef was there, measuring out the caravan's wine ration with a parsimonious hand. Shumal waited until the very end for his turn, and then, while Chief Kalef was tying off the end of the wineskin, Shumal pulled at his sleeve.

"What is it, Shumal? Watch the skin, you idiot!"

Shumal allowed an earnest expression to show through the gap in his headcloth. "Chief Kalef," he said as softly as he could while still being heard over the wind that battered the stone walls of the resthouse, "how many souls are we on this crossing?"

Chief Kalef looked at him, two dark suspicious glitters showing between his eyelids. "Seventeen, at last count. Raksh save you, Shumal, don't tell me we've lost someone already."

Shumal carefully hesitated. "Would that be seventeen including you?" he asked.

"What? Yes, of course including me, you halfwit. Tell me—who's missing, who have we lost?"

Shumal said, "No one is missing, Chief. It's just that…"

"Speak up, fool."

Shumal stood on his toes so he could bring his lips right to the bit of headcloth covering Chief Kalef's ear. "Well, you see, Chief—I make us eighteen."

"What?"

"Eighteen, Chief."

Chief Kalef shot his eyes around the dim chamber, counting. Then he made a disgusted noise with his tongue. "Idiot, the pack donkeys can count better than you can. We left Iklankish as seventeen, and we may arrive in Kishti as seventeen or less, but never as more. Who would be mad enough to be wandering on his own in the Windy Swathe?"

"Oh, there's seventeen in here," said Shumal with great sincerity. "The other is outside, by the gate. Or he was a moment ago."

Chief Kalef growled and began to turn away.

"Shortish fellow in a grey cloak," Shumal said conversationally, as he too began to turn away. "But if you're quite sure…"

Behind him, he heard Chief Kalef draw in a startled breath, but Shumal forced himself to walk on, to greet one of the other drovers and agree to a game of stones in the corner before a good day's sleep. The first small seed had been planted. Now and then he glanced up from the game, to see Chief Kalef rolled up in his cloak against the wall opposite the entrance, watching warily every time the wind strained the door against its catches.

—— «◇» ——

The sixth dawn, and they were slogging wearily the last few hundred paces to the sixth shelter. Shumal was more than satisfied with the last night of travel. He had been careful, every time Chief Kalef passed him, to be caught peering out into the swirls of sand at the edges of the lantern light, off into the screeching curtains, as if at something dimly glimpsed at the very limit of visibility. The first time, Chief Kalef had glanced at him and then hurried past, down the caravan. The second time, going up the caravan again, he had fallen into step beside Shumal and grabbed him by the shoulder.

"Hoy, dog!" he shouted into Shumal's ear. "I pay you to watch the animals, not the damned desert. What are you looking at? There's nothing to see out there, is there?"

"Of course not, Chief," Shumal shouted back, but he bobbed his head sidewise to look past the Chief's shoulder. Kalef whirled to look in the same direction, then back to Shumal. His eyes gleamed through the slit in his yellow headcloth.

"Name of a whore, stupid. What are you looking at?"

"Nothing, Chief. Well, maybe nothing. Nothing at all, really. It's just that I keep thinking I see something— someone—out of the end of my eye, but when I look, there's nothing there. Chief, sir," he added respectfully.

"Of course there's nothing there," Chief Kalef bellowed. He paced alongside the drover in silence for a few moments. Then he leaned closer to Shumal and shouted into his ear, "What does it look like?"

"What does what look like, Chief? The thing that isn't there?"

"Yes, you arse."

"Well, Chief," shouted Shumal, "if it really was there, which of course it isn't, it would be something grey and about the size of a man, not a very tall one, and it would be keeping almost out of sight. But of course," he added, "there's nothing there, just like you said."

Long silence from Chief Kalef, while Shumal noticed a packrope coming loose on the load of the black-headed camel and dutifully moved forward to secure it. When he looked back, Chief Kalef was standing in the same place with his head cocked, disappearing fast behind the veils of sand as the caravan continued to move past him. Shumal could just make out that his employer's yellow-wrapped head was turned towards the high desert; then, when he had diminished to a vague dark yellow smudge, like a figure muffled behind translucent drapery, Chief Kalef suddenly leapt forward and ran up the caravan, passing Shumal without a word or a glance. Shumal turned to watch him go. Under his headcloth, he grinned.

——— «◇» ———

It was in the shelter they were approaching, the sixth counting from Iklankish, where Shumal remembered seeing Mercer Irshek for the last time, trudging towards the resthouse with his grey cloak wrapped around him, moving like a man at the very extremity of fatigue. Shumal had been helping the grain broker with his white camel at the time. He remembered glancing up as the doomed mercer passed by a few feet away, and he remembered a vague impression that another cloak-muffled form had joined Irshek's before the door of the resthouse.

That was all Shumal could remember of the mercer's final hours. Late that afternoon, after sleeping away the worst fury of the day, he had awoken to the mutter of grave voices by the resthouse door, the sight of sad head-shakings and shrugged shoulders. Obviously it was pointless to institute a search. What a tragedy! Such a pleasant young man, such a bright future, and newly married to a lovely bride as well! Alas! May Taskrisht greet him with less than her usual severity! And that was the extent of the lamentations for Mercer Irshek, because it was necessary then to gulp down a hurried supper and tend to the packbeasts, or else risk being caught too far from the next shelter when the sun was high again.

The sixth shelter. Shumal had given much deep thought to this, and to how, exactly, Chief Kalef may have murdered his brother-in-law. He did not for a moment believe the mercer's body would be found in the enclosure. Shumal knew every dirty sand-bedevilled handwidth of it—it was practically square, and just large enough to hold two average-sized caravans at a pinch, though this rarely happened. Aside from the gate in the leeward wall and the resthouse in one corner, it was featureless and well-trodden, and other caravans may have used it since Kalef's train passed through on the outward journey. Furthermore, the maintenance crews from Iklankish came through at irregular intervals when the winds were down, to shore up the shelters and clear sand from the cairnway, and Kalef would not have risked one of them finding the body. The Princes in Iklankish took a dim view of any murders they did not arrange themselves.

No, Shumal was fairly sure the bodies of the mercer and the missing donkey would be far out on the high desert, irretrievable, invisible, probably forming the foundation of a new dune of windblown sand by now. He was acquainted with the donkey that disappeared at the same time as Irshek; curiously enough, it had been one of Chief Kalef's own, a donkey that Shumal himself had cursed frequently for its irrepressible stupidity, its inability to comprehend even the most explanatory of wallops. This was a beast that would, by preference, head in exactly the wrong direction for its own comfort and safety—a donkey that, once set on a course, no matter how disastrous, would follow it single-mindedly until it either dropped or was beaten and dragged back into line with its fellows. Many was the stick Shumal had broken on that same donkey's neck. He believed he knew why Irshek had disappeared in its company.

No other donkey in Shumal's long experience would voluntarily leave a shelter in the Windy Swathe, except as part of a caravan. But that donkey! Shumal could see the scene in his mind's eye: the tall form with the yellow headcloth and the shorter grey-cloaked figure, out under the molten flow of sun-scorched sand in the enclosure while the rest of the caravan slept. Then the sudden blow, the collapse of the grey figure, its furtive loading onto that particular donkey, the slap on the piebald rump at the gate—and then the beast heading purposefully away into the pitiless maelstrom, past the gate-cairn, head down, back bowed under the dead weight of the mercer, fading and vanishing within moments and never, never, never coming back. Yes, Shumal thought, that must have been how it happened. And this scenario suited Shumal very well.

———— «◇» ————

And now they were nearly to the gateway of the sixth shelter. Shumal knew Chief Kalef's habit. The trainmaster would stand just outside the gate, counting each beast as it passed, greeting the merchants, nodding to the drovers. The late mercer's animals were well down the string. The time had come.

Ignoring the flutter of nerves in the pit of his stomach, Shumal slipped his hand under the packsheet of the black-headed camel and pulled out the grey cloak he had bought from his old friend in the Oxmarket on that last morning in Iklankish. Then he moved a short distance away from the caravan, not so far as to lose sight of it—that could be fatal— but far enough so that the other men would not see him clearly. At a silent run, he moved up the caravan, pulling on the grey cloak as he went. He stopped when he was no more than a daring few armlengths from the sand-shadowed form of Chief Kalef, at his post by the gate; then he stood stock still and stared at Kalef from deep under the hood of the grey cloak.

Twenty-one, twenty-two, twenty-three. Chief Kalef was counting the animals. He raised his hand to the grain broker, waved the drover in, dropped his eyes to make a note on the tablet in his hand—and then froze. Slowly, his head lifted. He stared straight at Shumal. The tablet jerked. Shumal immediately shuffled back a few paces until he could no longer see Kalef through the sand, then turned and ran like the deadly wind itself, back up the line to the mercer's animals. Dimly, he heard a shout from the direction of the gate.

It was a close race. He just had time to push the cloak back under the camel's packsheet before Chief Kalef burst through the veils of sand behind him and thrust his head close to Shumal's.

"Shumal, did you see him? Did he pass you?"

Shumal pretended to adjust the packsheet. He hoped Chief Kalef would not notice his panting. "Who do you mean, Chief?"

"I—never mind who. Did anyone pass you?"

Shumal whacked the black-headed camel. "When, Chief?"

"Just now!"

"Just now, Chief?"

"Oh, never mind, you tupping idiot." And Kalef turned and ran on down the caravan.

Smiling, Shumal finished tucking the cloak securely under the packsheet. He felt that little drama had gone rather well. He hoped he had presented Chief Kalef with just the right sort of picture: the vague phantom of a grey-cloaked figure standing in mute accusation on the edge of the high desert where the mercer's body lay unshriven, unburied by human hands. If only, Shumal thought wistfully, there had been some way to present the Chief with the donkey's ghost as well.

———— «» ————

The Chief's hands shook as he measured the wine into Shumal's beaker, and he fumbled with the strings of the wineskin as he tied it shut. He glanced around the dim interior of the resthouse, then leaned his head close to Shumal's.

"How many souls do you make us today, Shumal?"

Shumal glanced around the room, counting. "Fourteen in here, including us, Chief. Kros and Miklish are still watering, and that makes sixteen, and Lukim is busy with the load of carpets that shifted, seventeen, and—oh yes, that fellow in the grey cloak was out by the gate, but I don't know his name, and he makes eighteen. Who is he, anyway, Chief?"

The trainmaster turned away without speaking and paced to the door, where he paused as if reluctant to go outside. Shumal grinned at his back. The wind rose in a chorus of devil howls and slammed the door against the frame—Chief Kalef jumped. Then he wrestled the door open, letting in a shrieking phantom-shape of blowing sand, and he pushed out into the courtyard and dragged the door shut behind him. Shumal, feeling almost grateful, clucked his tongue. How beautifully the trainmaster was playing his part!

"Raksh save him," he said to the company at large, "I think Chief Kalef has something terrible on his mind, far too terrible for me to tell you anything about it." And he dropped his voice so that the others would move closer, then proceeded to tell them the story he had worked out with such care.

———— «» ————

When Chief Kalef fought his way back into the resthouse about half an hour later, a number of serious conclaves broke up immediately and a silence descended. The feeling in the room was partly fear, but a significant proportion was simple embarrassment. What did one say to a haunted man? A man, moreover, who bloody well deserved to be haunted, if what the drover Shumal said was even halfway true. A dozen of these men had made the outward journey with Kalef's caravan and were feverishly searching their memories for details of the mercer's last appearance, in this very resthouse. Equally feverishly, they were avoiding the dark corners. There was even more reluctance than usual to go out into the sand-whipped enclosure to check on the animals.

Kalef did not seem to notice the silence. He strode across to the wineskin, untied it with exaggerated care, and poured himself a beakerful. Quite outside his rations, but who would dare remonstrate with him? Gradually the little groups reformed, a couple of games of chance started up, several men rolled themselves in their bedrolls for sleep... but not one man among them went near Chief Kalef except Shumal himself. The Chief grunted as Shumal thumped down beside him.

"Something wrong, Chief?" asked Shumal with a show of cheerfulness.

Kalef had pulled his face coverings apart only far enough to get the beaker near his mouth. Now he pulled the cloth away from his face entirely, and Shumal was surprised, and rather heartened, to see how drawn the Chief looked. The Chief glanced around the room and beckoned to Shumal to move a little closer.

"That fellow in the grey cloak, Shumal. Did you recognize him?"

Shumal shrugged and looked puzzled. "Chief?" he said.

The trainmaster drained the beaker and poured himself another; then, in an unusual gesture of generosity, he slopped at least a half-measure into Shumal's beaker as well.

"Let's put it this way, then," he said. "Did he remind you of anybody?"

Shumal put his head on one side and pretended to consider. "He was rather like my cousin Mitfalt's husband, short and plump, you know, moved to Safar a few years ago to open his own tailoring shop, or maybe like that tupping kahwa-seller who cheated me once on the Fishtail in Iklankish, and then there's—"

"Did he remind you," Kalef interrupted in a terrible whisper, "of anyone you've seen recently?"

Shumal frowned in thought. "Yes, now that you mention it, I believe he did. Now who is it I'm thinking of? Wait, I know—he was a little like your poor brother-in-law, Raksh rest him, the fourth one, I mean, the mercer that wandered off from the caravan, not the Omelian silk importer, or the fish broker, or the—"

"All right," said Kalef fiercely. He was silent for a moment, and then he leaned so close to Shumal that their foreheads touched. "I saw him out there just now, Shumal. And I saw him by the gate earlier, while the string was still coming into the shelter, and both times he was looking at me. And you've seen him too! The eighteenth man! Shumal, you know we are only seventeen on this crossing."

Shumal said nothing. He was pleasantly surprised to hear that Kalef was now seeing the phantom of Irshek without Shumal having to arrange the apparition, but he could understand how it might happen. How many phantoms had he seen with his own eyes, rearing out of the sand that shrilled and gyred across the Windy Swathe? Madness was always close here, as close as the next blast of devil-wind in your face, and he had learned long ago not to believe in the monsters that his eyes conjured up out of no more than sand and agitated air. It was a lesson that Kalef would also have learned—how interesting, then, and how gratifying, that a bit of judicious suggestion could have had such a powerful effect.

Kalef had emptied the second beaker of wine and was looking thoughtfully at the wineskin. When Shumal touched him on the shoulder, the beaker twitched out of his hands and half-buried itself in the soft sand of the floor.

"Chief? Shall I go out with you to have a look? Perhaps we have a hanger-on who hasn't paid his guidefee, and I could help you catch him."

Dully, Kalef considered this. "All right. There's nothing to lose. Just a moment." Carefully, counting just under his breath, he tallied up the fifteen other human souls in the resthouse, twice and then a third time. Then he pulled the headcloth back over his face and motioned to Shumal to follow.

It was mid-morning, but the sun's only effects were a harsh edge to the light filtering through the devil-dancing sand, and a heavy hotness in the air. The inferno blast of midday was still an hour or so away. Shumal and Chief Kalef picked their way towards the gate, between the rows of crouching animals. Under the cloak, Shumal's hand fumbled for the heavy drover staff he had thrust through his sash.

Suddenly Chief Kalef stopped short, with Shumal right behind him. "There!" he cried, "there he is, Shumal, do you see him?"

But Shumal was concentrating on the heft of the staff in his hand as he swung it above his head. He brought the heavy knob of it down with a crack on the back of Kalef's neck, smartly enough to crush the bones through several layers of headcloth, the kind of blow he'd learned to deliver in his brief career in a Kishti abattoir. The Chief collapsed like an ox in a butcher's killing stall.

Shumal waited a few moments, counting under his breath, keeping the staff ready for another blow, but no breath stirred the swatch of yellow headcloth that muffled the Chief's nose and mouth. At the count of fifty, Shumal flipped the body onto its back. He felt sick as the head lolled to a terrible angle, hating the loose flopping weight of it as his fingers worked the mercer's heavy golden chain from around the dead neck. Then he delved through Chief Kalef's complicated apparel to pull out the necessary seals and signet ring, the scroll of accounts, the purse of gold. The latter was rather heavy. There was no blood.

The donkey came next, and the rope. Any donkey would do; Shumal was just going to borrow it. There was no donkey he could trust to plod uncaring through the gate and into the screaming desert and never come back, no donkey to share Kalef's fate, as the other poor beast had shared Irshek's. Moving quickly, he selected one of the date grower's animals, one that knew him already because he used to be in charge of that string, and hoisted Kalef's body onto its back like a sack of badly bagged dates.

After that, he had to pause for breath, but he did not dare to wait too long. He took the big coil of rope from where he had left it in readiness, on top of the black-headed camel's load; tied one end securely to a hitching ring just inside the gate, and the other end around his own waist.

"Come along now, my pretty," he called into the donkey's ear. "Just a little stroll, my beauty, and then some extra corn for you, and some lovely water, and a nice soft place to lie down in the lee of the resthouse. Come along, my lovely. Come, my precious jewel."

This rarely works with donkeys, and didn't with this one. Shumal wasted more valuable moments tugging at the halter, and then a few more bashing at the beast's rump with his drover staff before he could persuade it to stump grudgingly through the gate and past the gate-cairn. The heat was rising steadily, and the light had that filthy quality that meant the sun was high in the sky over the Windy Swathe. Under his cloak, Shumal was already sweating.

He drove the donkey ahead of him with threats and blows, playing the rope out behind him. It was a good rope, a strong rope, and it needed to be, for Shumal's life depended on it. If it broke, he might never find the cairnway or the shelter again, and he would end up under his own yellow-grey hillock of sand, like Mercer Irshek, like Chief Kalef…

He jerked his eyes to the side. His imagination was toying with him—that had not been, could never have been, a man-shaped, man-sized figure in grey a few armlengths off to his right; it was a swirl of wind, a little vortex spawned by the greater vortex that whirled around him, a momentary uprushing twist of greyish sand. That was all. The impression of black emptiness under the mirage of a hood was just another trick of Shumal's eyes. He cursed himself. It was one matter to set Chief Kalef to seeing things, quite another to start seeing things himself. He fixed his gaze on the donkey and on its burden, not enjoying the lively way the dangling arms waved about, the boneless pendulum motion of the head, but preferring those definable infelicities to the chaos of grey images the sand was throwing up all around him. And then the rope jerked him to a halt, and he whooped with the shock, remembered himself, breathed a funerary prayer, and dumped Kalef's body without further ceremony off the donkey's back. He was glad to see, even as it hit the ground, how the sand began to build up against it as another dune was born.

———— «»————

The rope did not break or come loose. Tugging the donkey behind him, Shumal let out a sob of relief when the gate-cairn of the sixth shelter loomed up out of the veils of sand, and another sob a moment later when he saw that nobody was yet out in the enclosure. Shaking, he returned the donkey to the date grower's string and trudged toward the resthouse, rehearsing what he had to say next.

Once, halfway there, he whirled around to peer towards the gate. It seemed to him that a movement had flickered in the corner of his eye, but all he could see now was the ceaseless turbulence, the phantoms that rose and capered for a few moments before vanishing back into the shrieking veils of sand, sand, sand. That was all it was, he told himself: a wind ghost. Reassured, he paused for a moment outside the door to gather his words, then hurled it open. Fifteen pairs of eyes turned towards him.

———— «»————

Of course, he told them, he had tried to restrain Chief Kalef, but it is impossible to hold back the mad, especially the guilt-mad. No, no, he assured them, he himself had not seen the phantom of lost Irshek, though he thought he had heard, over the wild incessant howls of the wind, a voice even wilder, even more compelling, calling Chief Kalef by name…and at the sound of that voice, the Chief had fallen to his knees on the sand and prayed to Raksh and Rikasht, and Taskrisht the bitch-goddess of the Windy Swathe, and the Hounds of Fortune as well. In the end he had turned his face to Shumal and his eyes were already those of a dead man. Then he had put his ring and seals and documents into Shumal's hand, and the incriminating golden chain of Mercer Irshek around Shumal's neck, and made him swear, swear on his own inner thigh, that the chain would be given as an offering to Taskrisht, with prayers for the gentle treatment of the lost souls of Irshek and Kalef. In return (Shumal watched his audience through narrowed eyelids as he told them this) Shumal must marry Kalef's sister, the widow of Irshek, and carry on in Chief Kalef's stead.

There was quiet consternation at this last pronouncement. Shumal caught an incredulous look passing between the date grower and the kitchenware merchant—were they now to trust their valued lives and loads to Shumal the ne'er-do-well, Shumal the layabout, the born underling, the butt of so many of Chief Kalef's jokes? The kitchenware merchant opened his mouth to protest, but Shumal hastened to cut him off.

"And then," he said in a low, thrilling voice, fixing the kitchenware merchant with a piercing gaze, "Chief Kalef tore back his headcloth and opened his eyes and his mouth to the wind. I tried to hold him back, but he threw me off and stumbled out through the gate like a man already blinded—and just before he vanished, I thought I saw a grey form waiting for him, deep, deep in the mists of sand, and then they were both gone—Raksh rest them—and I knew there was nothing I could do but keep my solemn oath to a dying man. And that is all." He bowed his head humbly.

"I thought you said you didn't see the mercer's spirit," said one of the other drovers, Lukim, in a tone of deep suspicion.

"Not at the beginning," said Shumal with dignity, "though Chief Kalef claimed he did, and wailed and tore his cloak at the sight. And I could not tell you whether the grey form I saw with the trainmaster at the end was Mercer Irshek. It could have been Taskrisht herself, for all I know. Everything I saw and everything I know, I have told you."

He bowed his head again, waiting for their reaction. The signs were good. During his story, the merchants had gradually drawn closer together, keeping to the inner square that was well lit by the lamps hanging from the rafters. Even the drovers, a hard-bitten bunch of toughs, were keeping well clear of the shadows. Only the kitchenware merchant continued to frown skeptically. Outside the resthouse, the wind keened.

"Hark," Shumal snapped. "Did you hear it? Did you hear it? That voice in the wind..."

"It's true! I heard it too!" cried the date trader. All ears pricked up; a few even pulled their headcloths further open to hear better. The lamps flickered in a draft. Sand hissed through the crack under the door and danced just above the floor.

"A sign!" the date trader said in a hushed voice. "A sign, Chief Shumal!"

Chief Shumal. The new incumbent tucked his chin deeper into his headcloth to hide a grin. He liked the sound of that. In the frightened hush, he raised his head again to issue his first command.

"We must sleep now, we will need our strength for tonight's journey. But I shall call on all of you to bear witness of my oath to Kalef before his family and the priestesses of Taskrisht when we reach Kishti, and to join me in prayers at the temple. And each drover shall have a half-goldweight as a bonus in honour of the memory of our late Chief, and each merchant a rebate of one goldweight. Agreed? Now take your rest."

And to set a good example, as befits the trainmaster of a caravan, Shumal rolled himself in his own bedding and pretended to fall into a deep sleep—but he was watching through his lashes. He saw the others look to the kitchenware merchant with questions on their half-exposed faces. He saw the kitchenware merchant purse his lips in thought. Shumal held his breath: was one goldweight enough of an incentive? Should he have said two? But after a few moments, the kitchenware merchant shrugged, pulled his fine blanket up around his shoulders, and curled himself up on the pallet. Shumal let his eyes close for real in relief. Before long, the resthouse was filled with the sounds of slumber.

Shumal could not sleep, though. His heart was chattering to itself in excitement and elation—he had won! He had gained his own caravan! And the bribes just offered out of Chief Kalef's own purse would be an investment he could well afford; for when the caravan reached Kishti, he would be in a position to win Chief Kalef's lovely sister as well, with all her dowry, the late mercer's warehouse, the bags and bags of gold. Quite enough to justify the little lies he had told; more than enough to justify the murder of a guilty man.

—— 《》 ——

The caravan moved in an orderly manner out of the sixth shelter, beast by beast, with Shumal standing self-importantly by the gate and counting them off as they passed. The drovers bobbed their heads respectfully as they went by, the merchants nodded as to an equal. The world looked bright to Shumal at that moment, despite the gritty moon-soiled chaos just beyond the lamplight.

The last animal passed, a camel under a clanking load of metal tools, beakers, and trivets. With a flourish, Shumal made a note on the tablet and tucked it away in his pocket beside the heavy purse of gold. Then he turned to follow the caravan, briskly—the last camel was just disappearing into the shrieking curtain of sand, the lamp affixed to the top of its load making a diffuse globe of brighter yellow-grey in the bilious dark.

*Shumal…Shumaaaal…*

Frowning under his headcloth, Shumal turned to gaze back through the gateway. He could have sworn he heard his name being called, echoing off the walls of the resthouse, but no unusual shadows shifted in the enclosure.

*Shumaaaal…*

Only the wind, he told himself. Only the wind. He started after the caravan at a lively walk, all the livelier because too many seconds had passed, and he could no longer see the last camel nor the dirty glow of its lamp through the whirling sand. He broke into a run for a few paces but stopped short when nothing appeared in the roiling fog ahead of him.

"Hoy!" he shouted. "Hoy! Hoy!"

Nothing.

Then: *Shumal... Shumaaaal...*

He whirled to look behind him and saw nothing. Even the gate-cairn of the sixth shelter had already vanished behind the veils of sand.

"Hoy!" he shouted again; then he shut his mouth, not liking the way the wind seemed to be answering him. He squared his chin under the swaddlings of headcloth. The important thing was not to panic.

He took stock of his position. The gate-cairn, though he could not see it, must be just *there*. The first cairn, then, must be *there*, only about fifteen paces away, and the caravan could be no more than forty or fifty paces in *that* direction, though steadily drawing away from him. He bent and examined the ground for footprints, hoofprints, droppings, though he knew too well that the sand would have covered or scoured the traces within moments.

He hovered a heartbeat longer, but the thought of the caravan serenely plodding away from him, like a ship sailing on from a man who has fallen overboard, stabbed at him again. He chose his direction and began to jog, shouting "Hoy! Hoy!" and scanning the ground, raising his eyes to peer through the sand clouds for the lamp or the cairns, straining his ears for the sound of voices or the clatter of the last camel's load. He was rewarded by a dim spot of more definite yellow in the swirling yellow-grey void ahead of him, a little to his left. The lamp!

He veered towards it, still jogging. It appeared to be no more than twelve or fifteen paces ahead; in the corner of his eye, to the right, he glimpsed a dim standing shape that he took thankfully to be one of the cairns, confirming he was on the right course. He pounded on, speeding up to a full run, but did not allow himself to shout again. How humiliating it would be if the others learned how nearly the Windy Swathe had captured him, especially in his first outing as trainmaster. Who would want to ship out with him after that?

But what a pace the caravan was keeping! Trot along as he might, he could not bring the yellow smear of lamplight closer. How silently it moved, too, no irate donkey noises, no clattering of loads or flapping of loose packsheets over the shrieking of the wind. At last he slowed to a walk, puzzled and side-stitched, keeping his eyes fixed on the vital yellow blotch ahead of him. He could not afford to lose it, although, he realized gratefully, he would still have the trail of cairns to guide him and eventually he would catch up.

There was another of the cairns already, he saw, grey and misty in the sand-filtered moonlight. An unusually small cairn this one, though, obviously in need of building up again by the work crew from Iklankish; half as high as it should be, by Raksh, not much higher than a man...

Shumal stopped and squinted through the slit in his headcloth.

Not much higher than a short man...a short, plump man...

Shumal screamed. He screamed again, lustily, forgetting his dignity as trainmaster, forgetting the stitch in his side, and bounded in great leaps towards the guiding yellow blotch ahead of him. But the cairn that was not a cairn kept pace; indeed, it seemed a little closer with every panicky sideways glance, the lines of the grey cloak a little clearer, the dark void under the hood starting to show a glitter of pale eyes.

"But I avenged you!" he cried out once, over his shoulder. There was no reply.

*Shumaaal... Shumaaaal...*

The call was coming from directly ahead, where the yellow glimmer was slowly becoming better defined. Ignoring the grey horror at his elbow, Shumal gathered the last of his strength and burst into a despairing sprint, the heavy gold chain battering his breastbone, until under the yellow lamp-glimmer he saw the whitish form of the camel begin to take shape, closer and closer, nearly safe now, and he tucked his head down and pumped his legs and sobbed as he ran...

*Shumal.* A whisper ahead of him, like the rustle of sand grains rubbing together.

He raised his head and saw the yellow glimmer a few paces away; only it was not a lamp, but a sand-sifted remnant of moonlight on a yellow headcloth; and not the swaying white rump of a camel, but the outline of a dirty white cloak; and the sand whispered around him with many voices, saying *Shumal, Shumal*.

——— «◊» ———

The evil reputation of the sixth shelter from Iklankish dated from that season. The winds thereafter seemed to batter it with special viciousness, the sand devils to take more malevolent shapes, the shadows to cluster more thickly in the corners of the resthouse. Beasts and men rested uneasily within its enclosure.

And a tradition sprang up that it was bad luck to count a caravan's complement within those cursed walls: for often, the count would be three too many at the sixth shelter, and one too few at the next.

# The Hanging Room

**He might have** stood there indefinitely, staring at the cottage, if Corinne had not nudged him with the sharp point of her elbow.

"Look lively, Jason," she said. "It could rain in a minute. Though I agree, it's worth drooling over."

"I'm not drooling."

"Well, I am. Unashamedly." Corinne grinned at him, a chic double curve of crimson. "Just look at it! Even the Clarkes' precious oast house in Dorset can't touch this. Plus, we won't have to do much to fix it up. Dear old Aunt Thingy kept it in marvellous shape."

"Great-Aunt Maude," he corrected her somberly, "the late lamented. I must say, Corinne, you could show a little less glee."

"Well, I'd never met her, had I? I didn't know she existed until the executors got in touch. And you hadn't seen her since you were—what, thirteen?"

"Twelve," he said, looking back at the cottage.

"So she's hardly an object of grief, right? You can pretend if you want to, but why should I?"

"That's not it."

"What is it, then?"

Jason looked at her gloomily. There was no way he could tell her how the sight of Peking Cottage had dusted off a fear long ago stored away in the murkiest cellar of his memory. He knew what she would do if he told her the place was haunted; she would scream with delight and crow over the supernatural deficiencies of the Clarkes' oast house, and the enormous cachet of owning a family ghost. "I'm not sure she did us such a great favour, that's all," he said at last. "An old house is a major responsibility."

"Don't be silly, darling. Let's go in."

Unhappily, Jason suffered himself to be led through the rustic garden to the fanlighted front door. It was a cottage orné rather than a real cottage, a faux-Regency folly, built in Victorian times expressly to be picturesque. It was artfully asymmetrical, a bit too tall to be authentic, and the neo-Gothic points of the first-floor windows were perhaps a little overdone. But it had charm, enormous charm—even Jason had to admit that to himself. Buxom roses swarmed over the door; little leaded panes, some nearly impenetrable, gridded the bow window. There was even a band of pargeting, half-hidden by ivy, which drew a shriek of joy from Corinne before Jason turned the key in the lock.

Corinne whirled in the flagged hall, danced into and out of the parlour, peered into the back garden through the dining room windows, ecstatic. "It's too perfect, Jason. Molly Clarke will be *puce* with envy. That furniture, priceless some of it, I'm sure that's Chippendale, and the dining chairs are William Morris. And the paintings! They did say we get *all* the contents of the house, didn't they?"

"Yes." Jason was not intentionally short with her. He was preoccupied; his own twelve-year-old ghost was standing in his shoes and peering fearfully up the stairs. He shook himself. "What? Sorry?"

"I said, a little indirect lighting will do wonders for that parlour. Understated, of course, nothing too IKEA, we'll want to maintain the period ambience. Oh, Jason, just look at that china cabinet. Chinoiserie, isn't it?"

"I suppose so. I remember a chair and some other stuff in the same Chinese style upstairs, lots of carved dragons and things." Jason swallowed hard. He did not like to think about that chair, that room: the front spare bedroom in theory, but never used in practice. To the best of his memory, they had never stayed with his mother's Aunt Maude, just driven down for the day and left after teatime. Even then, his great-aunt had been both old and old-fashioned, sweater sets and pearls, grey hair corrugated in the style of her girlhood, as frozen in time as Peking Cottage itself. Whenever he had dutifully kissed her cheek, her skin had been like velvet rose petals, even to the scent. Perhaps that explained, he thought suddenly, why he had never felt comfortable with roses.

Corinne returned bright-eyed from a flying reconnaissance of the kitchen. "Spode," she said cryptically. "Scads of it. Let's look upstairs."

She was halfway up before Jason could make his feet move. Then he ran, leaping up the stairs two at a time. He could not tell if this was from dread of being left behind, or fear for Corinne. He reached her just as she flung open the door of Great-Aunt Maude's bedroom, then waited patiently for her raptures to subside.

"Jason, the view is superb. Fields! An orchard! The Clarkes' oast house looks out on a council estate, you know. Phew! The old girl certainly favoured rosewater, didn't she!"

Jason threw a quick glance around. He had never been in Great-Aunt Maude's bedroom, but everything was predictable, even to the well-remembered string of pearls on the dresser, and the Bible next to the bed. And there was nothing that felt *wrong* in the room, and that was predictable too, or else how could the old lady have slept in it unharmed for so many years? The atmosphere of roses made him choke.

"Just a few rooms left to see, darling, and a quick dip into the cellar, then we can go back to that precious little pub in the village to make plans." Corinne was past him before he could stop her. He heard the quick tapping of her heels down the hall and forced himself to follow. Her hand was on the knob of the front-facing spare room.

"No!" he cried.

She frowned at him, surprised. "There's no need to shout, darling." She opened the door and stepped through. Jason took a deep breath and moved between the jambs so he could see into the room without crossing the threshold.

The ceiling was high, higher than would be expected in an authentic cottager's cottage. Directly opposite the door, the chinoiserie chair he remembered was pushed against the wall, its dragon-clawed feet resting delicately on the Persian carpet. Beside it was the matching opium table, squat and polished under the dust, its short legs curling inward. Jason tried to focus on it, but his eyes dragged themselves against his will to the exposed wooden crossbeam running the length of the room, and followed it to where it disappeared into the far wall. Nothing had changed.

Corinne was silent for the first time since entering the cottage, standing still in the middle of the carpet. Abruptly she turned and moved back to the doorway, to link her arm through Jason's. Under the makeup, her face was pale.

"Curious," she said, "but I don't like this room much. It should be charming, that little window nook is absolutely sweet, but I feel...I feel..."

"Watched?" he suggested.

"Yes, rather. How did you know? When I first came in, I was sure for a minute there was somebody here. I'll tell you one thing, though, I don't think anyone's dusted in here for years."

Jason shivered and pulled her unresisting out of the room and closed the door behind them. Even through the solid wooden panels, he could feel that strong sense of presence. If he put his hand to the knob, some other hand would be on the other side, helping him turn it, willing him to enter again. And inside, the crossbeam would be waiting. He ushered Corinne along the corridor and stopped her at the door to a sunny and innocuous room that Great-Aunt Maude had used for sewing.

"Corinne? Did you hear anything in there?"

"Sorry? What?"

"Did you hear anything in that front room?"

"Jason!" She pulled her arm away from his. "What's wrong with you? The room did feel a bit off, but—hearing things? You're talking like the place is haunted."

She stopped dead with her hand on the sewing room door, her face lighting up with pleased supposition. "You *do* think the place is haunted, don't you? That's why you've been such a misery since we arrived. Oh Jason, how thrilling! Tell me all about it."

"Not now, Corinne. Not here."

"But you do think the house is haunted, right?"

"There's no such thing as ghosts."

"Then why are you so pale? You look like you've seen one—a ghost, that is. Don't be silly, tell me about our ghost."

Jason followed her unhappily into the sewing room. "There were some stories. I never knew the details. That front-facing room is where my great-uncle hanged himself, not long after he and Maudie were married, but I never got the impression he was the ghost."

She was already not listening, measuring the room with a practiced eye. "Brilliant, this is just big enough for a second guest room. That means we can manage house parties for six, including us. And I bet that old Singer is worth a bob or two. What was that about your uncle?"

"He hanged himself," Jason grated, "in the front-facing spare room."

"Well, we won't mention that to the guests." And then she was off again, for appreciative glances into the Art Nouveau tiled bathrooms and the cellar, and an inspection of the flowerbeds and mature shade trees in the back garden. She was smiling dreamily by the time they reached the car. "I can't wait to show it to Molly," she said as she opened the car door. "Do you think we should get the roof thatched?" she added.

"I think we should burn the place down," Jason said.

⸺ «» ⸺

In the course of the next two hours, in the precious little pub in the village and during the short drive into London, Jason stubbornly endangered the future of his marriage. Corinne did not actually mention divorce, but she mentioned many other things, numerous times and with much eloquence. The price and extreme desirability of country property, for example. The outrageous good fortune of having such a gem willed to them, with enough cash to cover the estate taxes, and a houseful of gorgeous antiques thrown in on top. The Clarke's oast house in Dorset received due attention, including calculation of the horrendous sums the Clarkes had spent on conversion, wiring, plumbing, suitably antique furniture, and a sewer connection. The dominant theme, however, was Jason's outrageous pigheadedness.

"I simply can't understand you, " she said for the twentieth time, as they swung onto King's Road. "You were nothing like this when we talked with the executors. Then one look at the cottage, and you're ready to tear it down. Why, Jason? You owe me an explanation."

"I've already told you."

"What, that cock-and-bull about the haunted room? It didn't bother you before."

"I hadn't thought about it in years, not until I saw the cottage again. Seeing the cottage reminded me."

"What, repressed memory? How convenient. Honestly, Jason."

Jason was silent while he slotted the car into a space in front of their building. Then he closed his eyes and slumped back against the seat. "It wasn't repressed, just forgotten. Listen, Corinne. I wasn't the only person ever to feel something wrong in that spare room. Everyone did, as far as I remember. Even you did, just today. I recall hearing bits and pieces of the story, the sort of fragments that kids pick up when the grownups think they aren't listening, and it always slightly scared me to go to Maudie's house, but it was an adventure, too. Until the final visit, my last visit, when something happened. Mother still went down after that, but she never took me again."

"What happened?" Corinne's tone was frosty but interested.

"On that last visit? I was sent out to play in the garden while my mother chatted with Maudie, but I wanted to see the haunted room for myself. It hadn't been used for decades, ever since Great-Uncle Jack's suicide, but there was no lock on the door. So I tiptoed up the stairs and along the hall, and went in and closed the door behind me."

"And?"

"Well, you went in there. You felt it too. A feeling that somebody—or something—was already in the room and pleased to see me, in a not terribly pleasant way."

"I think I can explain that," Corinne began in a businesslike voice, but Jason continued as if she had not spoken.

"Twelve year olds can be very brave. I was frightened, but I started to poke around anyway. Proving myself to myself, something childish like that. Then the voice started."

"Oh really, Jason!"

"It's true. It was just by my ear, or maybe even inside my head. It was more like a whisper than a voice, hoarse and not very loud, and I couldn't tell whether it was a man or a woman, or even human. It gives me shivers just to think about it, even now."

"What did it say?"

"It said I didn't need a rope. My school tie would do nicely."

Corinne exploded with laughter. In the darkness of the car, Jason looked at her with genuine dislike. "So that was your message from the spirit world!" she choked at last. "How absurd, darling!"

"Not really. It made sense to me then. By the time my mother and Maudie charged into the room, I had already pulled a chair under the crossbeam and was trying to get the end of my tie over the detached bit to make a noose. They heard me dragging the chair across the floor. Another few minutes, and I might have managed the knot and kicked the chair away."

"You were trying to hang yourself?"

"Exactly."

"For heaven's sake, why?"

"I didn't know then, and I don't know now. *Someone* was there, urging me to go ahead; the voice was being friendly and helpful, telling me what to do. It seemed like the most natural thing in the world. For a moment after my mother pulled me off the chair and out of the room, I was actually angry with her."

Corinne stared straight ahead. "What happened then?"

"Nothing. Mother took me home and never mentioned the affair again. I forgot all about it after a while. Now I remember another thing, though. While Great-Aunt Maude was seeing us off at the gate, twisting a tiny lace handkerchief in her hands, she said a funny thing, something about poor Jack and *the others*. So I guessed then that Great-Uncle Jack was not the first person to string himself up from the crossbeam in the spare room."

Corinne was silent for a moment. "So what?" she said at last.

"What?"

"So what? Power of suggestion, that's all. You've just proven it. Copycat suicides, like those copycat murders one reads about. There's nothing wrong with the room, Jason, nothing that a good dusting and a fresh coat of paint won't solve. Not to mention a bit of common sense."

"The answer is no."

"Really, darling? On account of a load of superstitious nonsense, you'd waste the most perfect cottage orné in the Home Counties?"

"Yes. "

"We'll see about that." Corinne pulled petulantly at the handle, bounced out of the car, and slammed the door behind her.

⸻ «» ⸻

In the end, there was little Corinne could do. Jason was adamant, and Peking Cottage had been left to him personally. He would neither use it for the smart weekend house parties that Corinne was wild to offer to a select acquaintanceship, nor allow it to be put on the market for some unsuspecting stranger to buy. He would not, he said, have some other poor sod's death on his conscience. It occurred to him that Maudie might have felt the same way—maybe that was why she spent sixty-odd years living there as a widow after Jack's suicide, keeping the world safe from some noxious presence in the spare room. At any rate, the house as it stood was a dire moral responsibility. Thank heavens it was not listed. As soon as the permits were through, he would have the legal right to have the damned place knocked down altogether if he thought that was the only solution. The site alone would bring in a pretty penny.

What a pity there was nobody in the family he could ask about the history of Peking Cottage! He knew only the bare bones of the story. His great-great-grandfather Charles Gerson had bought it in the 1880s with a fortune accrued in the Far East, and he had changed the name from Roseton Cottage to Peking Cottage in commemoration. The old man was the grandfather of Great-Aunt Maude and Jason's grandmother Lucille. On his death in 1910 the cottage passed on to his bachelor son Hubert, and then to Hubert's brother, Maude's father, in 1937, and then to Maude herself when she married her handsome Group Captain Jack Christopher after the war. If only Jason had thought to visit Maudie in the last few years, when he might still have drawn the minutiae of the story from her! But now she was gone, and her sister Lucille was a demented nonagenarian in a care home in Wiltshire, and Jason's mother was five years dead of cancer, and his father had moved to Australia after the divorce, so long ago that Jason barely remembered him. There were no surviving cousins closer than Canada, no aunts and uncles; the family tree was a straggly little shrub, and he was one of the few surviving twigs.

A local historian was helpful in a largely negative way— Peking Cottage had no history of trouble before Charles Gerson brought it into the family in the 1880s, nor for some time after. The patriarch himself had been well-regarded, a grand old son of the British Empire, a decorated hero of the Second Opium War that had brought the stubborn Chinese to heel and showed them who *really* ruled the world. A pamphlet in the historian's collection preserved some of Colonel Gerson's own colourful tales of the 1860 campaign, the vicious one-sided battles, the subhuman savagery of the Chinese, the sacking and burning of the fabulous Old Summer Palace near Peking. The old soldier titillated the reader with accounts of the treasures looted from the doomed palace compound, the architectural gems immolated; he described the charred cadavers of faithful eunuchs and maids who had barricaded themselves fatally in the burning summerhouses, the bulging eyes and lolling tongues of those who killed themselves before the English and French troops broke into the surviving structures. It was strong stuff, bound to appeal to the imperialistic fervour of the 19th century, but embarrassing and even shameful to the post-imperial twenty-first...

Anyway, none of this sounded relevant to Jason. Yes, there were clippings in the collection regarding tragic deaths in Peking Cottage, but not until long after Colonel Gerson died peacefully in his bed in 1910. The series began in his son Hubert's regime, with the suicide of a housemaid in 1919; the inquest disposed of the poor girl's case in under a page. The deaths of two separate house guests, a carpenter engaged in repairs, another housemaid, and a burglar who left a sack of family silver below his dangling feet were spread across the twenties and thirties, before the known series ended with Great-Uncle Jack in 1946. If there were others before or since, they were not recorded.

Corinne was bored by Jason's morbid research and mystified by the strength of his abhorrence for Peking Cottage, but there were compensations for her. She lunched out with her friends on the story of her husband's idiocy, and received some status from the possession of a cottage too haunted to live in. Most important, reluctantly and under a great deal of pressure, Jason made a major concession: Corinne could bring a selection of the antiques from Great-Aunt Maud's house, and use some of the proceeds from auctioning the rest, to refurbish the London flat.

Corinne was delighted, seeing it as the first breach in Jason's defenses. In the meantime, she hurled herself into the new project with enthusiasm and the help of a swanlike lady from Sloane Square who had been recommended by Molly Clarke. The three of them (Molly was desperate to see the haunted cottage) drove out one morning to check the executors' inventory and select a few choice pieces for the flat. When Jason returned from the office that evening, he found Corinne curled up with a dry sherry and a thoughtful look.

"Any progress?" Jason poured himself a sherry.

"Oh, Lady Angela was over the moon. She's suggesting a Chinese theme, building around those fabulous chinoiserie antiques from the cottage. The cabinet and vases from the dining room, the escritoire from the parlour, the chair, opium table and lacquered tea chest from the spare room, a few of the tapestries and all the jade bibelots." She paused for a moment, frowning. "Lady Angela didn't much like that spare room, either. She thinks it's something to do with the shape of the room, or the angle of the lighting—a kind of negative subliminal effect, yes? Anyway, Lady Angela was sure she could exorcise your ghost with a bit of conversion work and a new colour scheme."

"No! It's bad enough that you took them in there."

"I had to, we'll be taking some pieces from that room. Anyway, you didn't say not to," she added, pouting.

"Oh, never mind," said Jason. "With three of you, you were probably all right. " He noted that she looked poised between wanting a fight and wanting to be comforted. The thought of either made him tired.

"Tell me more about Lady Angela's plans," he said.

It was a good move. Within five minutes, most horizontal surfaces in the room were drifted over with fabric swatches, colour squares, and snippets of expensive wallpaper, and Corinne was smiling again.

———— «» ————

Lady Angela was terrifyingly efficient. Less than two weeks later, the two affected rooms in the London flat had been stripped of Swedish pine furniture, beanbag cushions, track lighting, and earth-toned dhurrie carpets. The walls had been lacquered a glossy crimson, accented with black; a dragon-headed iron chandelier had been obtained at considerable cost from one of the hushed antique shops on Pimlico Road. As Jason gloomily surveyed the bill for top-quality bamboo matting, he reflected that converting an oast house might have been cheaper in the long run.

"Well, we have to live up to the china cabinet," Corinne said, rather snippily, when he mentioned it to her. "Which reminds me. The man from Sotheby's phoned; he's finished his valuation of the things you want to put up for auction. By the way, he was not sure the chair and escritoire and other stuff are chinoiserie after all—he thought they might be authentic Chinese craftsmanship, 19th or even 18th century, rather high-end, and he'd like to bring a specialist over on the weekend to have a look."

"But we weren't planning to go down this weekend."

"No matter, the stuff will be here. Lady Angela's van is going down tomorrow to pick up the things we selected, which includes the Chinese collection. But darling, I've got my yoga in the morning. Any chance you could pop down with them?"

"No chance at all," Jason said firmly. "I'll be working from home tomorrow, and one of the accountants is coming over."

"Oh, never mind. Lady Ange will give them a list."

He looked at her darkly. "Mention to Lady Ange that they should work in pairs."

"There's only two of them," she retorted, "and they always work together. Lady Ange says they're thoroughly reliable."

"Bully for Lady Ange," he said, but so softly she could pretend not to have heard.

———— «》 ————

The van was in front of the building when Corinne returned from her yoga class and the purpose-defeating lunch with her friends that always followed. Jason was in the entrance hall checking items off a list as the movers hauled them up the stairs and into the empty sitting room.

"All accounted for," he said as she edged past them into the flat, "except the tea chest from the spare room. You couldn't find it?" he asked the movers.

They exchanged embarrassed glances. "Yes, that's it," said the elder, hesitantly. His feet shifted on the floor. He looked up at Jason with what might have been pleading.

"I quite understand," Jason said.

"Well, I don't," said Corinne sharply. "Lady Ange says the tea chest is crucial to the balance of the sitting room. It's the one piece that will focus the entire composition and bring it into harmony. It was right on the bookshelf in the spare room, I can't imagine how you missed it."

The movers looked uneasy. Jason could imagine all too well how they missed it. He could hardly blame them, either.

"Never mind, Corinne," he said. He saw the men to the door and slipped a generous tip into the elder's hand. When he turned back to face Corinne, she was livid.

"You should have sent them right back to fetch it," she snapped. "Lady Ange is coming tonight, and she's bringing her *feng shui* expert to help compose the sitting room, and they can't hope to get the resonance values and energy channels right without the tea chest. It's *critical*."

"Is that really how she talks?"

"What?"

"Composing the sitting room? Resonance values? Energy channels? All she's going to do is arrange the bloody furniture."

Corinne's lips compressed. Without a word, she pulled her coat back on, wound the long Gucci scarf around her neck, and scooped the cottage keys off the hall table, where the movers had left them. She stalked past Jason, head high.

"Don't be an idiot, Corinne. You can't go there alone."

"Try and stop me. Or come with me."

"I can't, as you know perfectly well. Dan will be back in half an hour with some urgent papers. I'll go down with you tomorrow."

"Lady Angela and Doctor Fong are coming tonight. Anyway, I don't want you to come with me. I've had it up to *here* with your insane delusions about the spare room."

He was stung, but he ignored it. "Then promise me. Straight in, grab the damned chest, then straight out. No hanging around, all right?"

"Under the circumstances," Corinne flared, "that's a fine choice of words." She slammed the door behind her.

———— «》 ————

She fumed onto the motorway, and then off it. Just past the exit, the route led her onto a narrow meandering road verged with lush grass on one side and dense hawthorn hedges on the other. It wound along the edge of a broad valley, then dipped into dark woods that crowded the roadside, meeting overhead so that Corinne seemed to be driving through a green-tinted tunnel. There were few other cars. Corinne began to feel very alone.

She worked hard on maintaining her angry bravado. "Bloody nonsense," she muttered. Something fluttered out of the trees; she swerved the car wildly to avoid it and jerked to a stop. In the road behind her, a pheasant preened itself. Shaking, Corinne drove on.

"Jason and his stupid ghost," she told herself, "have destroyed my nerves."

A sharp turn onto a narrow lane and she was in the open again, out of the glooming woods, through the tiny picture-postcard village with its quaint pub, and up the gentle slope that led to Great-Aunt Maude's house. She parked by the gate and stood beside the car, gazing at Peking Cottage.

Under the gunmetal sky, it seemed less innocent, more aware. Why hadn't she noticed before that the upper windows were like eye sockets, the fanlight a gaping nasal cavity, the cottage a rose-covered death's-head? Tightening her lips, Corinne walked purposefully through the garden and let herself in the front door.

The scent of stale roses greeted her. It was cold in the cottage, several degrees colder than outside, and she gave the scarf an extra turn around her throat as she stood at the foot of the stairs. It seemed a long way up, and very dark at the top. Halfway up she realized she was walking on tiptoe, and forced herself to clatter the rest of the way. "So there," she said defiantly. Her heels clacked along the hallway.

Outside the door of the spare room, she paused. In the company of Molly Clarke and Lady Angela, it had been easy. Corinne had joked about the haunted room, had flung the door open with a flourish and a trill of laughter, had carelessly preceded her guests through the doorway. They had followed, smiling with correct appreciation—and then had stopped. Even Molly, with all the imagination of a wedge of cheddar cheese, had looked troubled. Lady Angela had propounded her theory of negative subliminal cues at some length, but only (Corinne now realized) from outside the door. They were almost as silly as Jason, Corinne told herself, and the thought of what Jason would say if she went home empty-handed acted as a goad. Straightening her shoulders, she pushed the door open and stepped into the room.

She was holding her breath. She let it out slowly, drew another. Nothing. She looked around the room with growing boldness. It was empty. Furnished, yes, but *empty*. Nobody was there. Nothing moved invisibly at her shoulder or watched her from the shadowy corners. Outside the tiny panes, roses nodded innocently on their vines.

Corinne laughed; then stopped, shocked by the irreverent sound of her own voice, and then laughed again, louder.

She was not completely comfortable, but the discomfort was different—no more, now, than the awareness that she was alone in an old house, a house with nerve-wracking but explicable creaks and groans, not a haunted house at all. Wonderingly, she moved to the bookshelf and picked up the lacquered chest, which was, of course, in plain sight. At the door she paused and turned around to survey the room again. It was charming, really. The little window nook was enchanting; the exposed crossbeam lent a pleasantly Tudoresque touch.

It was not until she was through the little village that the implications hit her. The ghost had mysteriously been exorcised. She could not imagine how, but it was so. The important thing, the dazzling and glorious thing, was that Jason could no longer object to using the cottage. Corinne wasted no time on the mechanics of the exorcism, though she did spend a very few moments regretting the loss of a prestigious family ghost. After that, her musings were pure pleasure: Lady Angela would design the decor, naturally, although Corinne had a few ideas of her own. They would need to buy some antiques to replace the ones taken to London, but there was still a handsome sum left from darling Maudie's legacy. As Corinne drew up outside the flat, she was composing the first weekend guest list.

In the flat, she deposited the lacquered chest triumphantly on the hall table. "Jason! You'll never guess!" she called. "Your family ghost has done a midnight flit. Jason?"

The flat was silent. Corinne pouted. It was too bad of Jason to be out when she had such glorious news. She poured herself a glass of sherry from the bottle in the kitchen, then walked through into the sitting room.

"Oh, there you are," she said automatically, so strong was her sense that someone was already in the room. She looked up and screamed. She was being watched, but not by Jason, though he was in a sense present. He was dangling by his tie from one arm of the dragon chandelier, and the chinoiserie chair was overturned below him. A draft swung him around, and she screamed again at the sight of his face, the bulging eyes, the lolling tongue.

Panicky, she scrambled to set the chair upright. It warmed to her touch, welcoming her, soothing her. There was a whisper in her ear.

"You don't need a rope," it said, "your scarf will do nicely."

Corinne finished righting the chair. Calm now, she studied the chandelier, trying to decide whether Jason had left enough room.

# Cold Case

**"Well, at least** she got finished off proper," said the sheriff.

"True enough," said Catherine. "The stake's in the eye, though. You don't often see that."

"Long as it goes deep enough, it'll do." The sheriff bent over and pulled the girl's yellow daisy-print dress down over her splayed privates. In the old days, Catherine reflected, that small gift of modesty would not have been possible, not until the photographer had snapped enough pictures to fill a wedding album, and the pathologist had poked and prodded, and the scene-of-crime crew had examined every molecule in the immediate area. Now there was just Catherine and that good old boy, Sheriff Wiley, plus Jed and Jimmy, the two undertakers, waiting with their buckboard and their shroud, and not one of them had so much as a pair of latex gloves or an evidence bag, or even a camera. Catherine knelt by the dead girl's side.

Just another body, flat on its back in the fresh spring grass. Catherine had seen thousands of them—tens of thousands on the hoof, maybe, counting the ravening herds seen from a distance. This one was just fresher than most. No green cast to the face, no festering rips in the skin, no fingers or limbs or patches of scalp sloughed off in the aimless postmortem wander. No bloating either, no signs of blowfly larvae, no rigor mortis, which could point in a different direction. This girl hardly looked dead at all, just sleeping. She was not the first such, though. She was at least the third, as far as Catherine knew.

"Something's wrong here, Sheriff."

"The whole world's wrong, case you hadn't noticed. Let's just get her shrouded up."

"I think we should take this further. Why is she—"

"She is what she is, and that's dead and out of her misery. I don't see no signs of rape. Far as I can see, she was a wanderer, and that's the end of it. All we need to investigate is where she got through the barrier, so's we can let the Border Force know to plug it up. Do a ride-about, Cathy, report back. We're done here." The sheriff motioned to the undertakers, who moved forward holding the shroud between them.

"Is that all we're going to do? What about those others? Two could be coincidence, but three's a pattern. And that dress isn't dirty enough for a wanderer. Her sandals look new."

The sheriff picked up the girl's hand, let it drop. "No rigor mortis. Wanderers don't stiffen up."

"I know, Sheriff, but we can't assume it never set in at all. She might have been lying here for a day or more, and that's long enough for rigor mortis to come and go. What if she didn't come through the barrier, what if—"

"What if you go off and do the ride-about, like I told you." The sheriff was already turning towards the horses, Jed and Jimmy were bending down to tuck the shroud around the girl's body, the buckboard was waiting. There would be a short trip to the cemetery about a mile away, a respectful depositing of the body into the open line-grave, a few spadefuls of dirt. No mourners for this one, no funeral beyond the kind offices of the undertakers. The shroud would be dipped in bleach and returned to the cemetery shed, ready for the next time.

"But what if she was alive when she came into Holcomb? What if she got killed here? We can't just ignore that."

"If the corpse ain't moving," the sheriff said over his shoulder, "we actually can ignore it. What's one more dead body, these days? Git, Cathy. You got near a couple hours daylight. Ride the line."

Catherine rode the line, backtracking to start at the building site where brick and cement were slowly pushing eastward to replace the chain-link and barbed wire fencing that still enclosed much of the townsite's current outer perimeter. The metal fencing was not bad, but it could be breached. Occasionally a tree might fall across the line, or a critical mass of wanderers might pile up against it; when such things happened between inspections, a few of the wanderers got through and drifted into the townsite, and that was bad. But still. If that girl in the yellow-print dress had taken a single step on dead feet before the stake went into her eye, Catherine would eat the sheriff's hat. Likewise for the camo-clad little redhead five weeks ago, and the pretty black girl with the tattoo sleeves a couple of months before that. Catherine had felt edgy about those ones, too. They were fresh, all three of them. After six years, you got a feel for how long since wanderers had stopped breathing.

She found one weakness in the barrier, way out in the fields, where the rains since the last inspection had washed out a post. A short section of chain-link was sagging to the point where it could be easily crossed, but the two wanderers in the hayfield on the other side did not appear to notice until Cathy stopped near the sag with her horse. She took care of them with the crossbow, used the radio in her pack to call the Border Force for a repair crew, and rode on.

Nothing else to see. The east gate, where the fence crossed the line of the highway out of Holcomb, was manned by the Border Force and had no troubles to report. They gave her a cup of coffee and a bagel. By just after sunset she reached the end of the circuit, the new watchtower outside the northeast edge of the townsite, where the brick fortifications resumed. Catherine rode through the quiet streets, past the darkened Methodist church and the one noisy bar, and cut through the alley behind Carter Street to the stable attached to the station house. Something was niggling at her again, something from the world-before.

Elvira was typing up reports at the reception desk, Harmon was eating a sandwich next to the coffee machine. Catherine had expected to see Charlie, but she remembered now that the evening and graveyard shifts had just swapped over. Anyway, Harmon was okay. He had been a beat cop for twenty years in the old days, somewhere in the western states. Catherine considered him easier to talk to than the sheriff, if only because he was younger, whereas the sheriff was next thing to a fossil. Harmon had arrived a couple of years ago with his wife, Gretchen, who worked part-time in the Foodstocks Office and evidently took pride in packing good lunchboxes for her man. Catherine had only met her a couple of times, and had not been drawn to her, but there was nothing wrong with her lunches. The couple had even qualified for a house of their own, a tiny bungalow with enough yard for a chicken coop and a vegetable garden, which accounted for the near-nightly menu of egg salad sandwiches. Now Catherine looked at Harmon questioningly, and he nodded, and she helped herself to a sandwich. Gretchen made her own mayonnaise and pickles and bread, and always packed too much.

"We found another dead girl," Catherine said.

"Yep, Sheriff mentioned that. A wanderer, he said. You find where she got through?"

"There was a sag in the fencing near the waterhole, but she was found a long way from there. A good three fields from the barrier altogether. It was a birdwatcher who reported her. She was wearing a yellow-print dress with flowers on it, he sighted the yellow in his field-glasses."

"A birdwatcher."

"Exactly. Gives me hope that there are still people in this world who want to watch birds."

Harmon shrugged and offered Catherine one of Gretchen's gherkins. "Was she like the other two?"

"Pretty much. Fresh. No panties, but no signs she had been interfered with, either. Stake through the eye."

"That's different," said Harmon.

"Somewhat, maybe. The black girl was through the ear. The redhead was up through the nose into the brain. Thing is, it was a stake every time, and the stake was left in."

"That's not much to go on, not these days."

Catherine reached for another sandwich. "I'm thinking there's a chance they were none of them wanderers. It's worth checking out whether this girl was a new arrival, and when. Though it's harder to tell now, since the Welcoming Committee ran out of Polaroid. I want to go back through the files, say, three months. No, let's make it four months. See if the previous two show up as well."

Elvira, up at the reception desk, cleared her throat. "Did you say a yellow dress with a flower print?" she called over her shoulder.

"Yeah."

"Little white daisy-type flowers on a yellow background?"

"How did you know?"

"My Sandra has one like that. Just got it new. The bolt only came in last month, and the dresses went into Stemple's about two weeks ago. If you ever went shopping, girl, you might've seen them."

"Hmm," said Catherine. Harmon took another sandwich.

《》

Two hundred and twenty-seven live humans had been absorbed by the Holcomb enclave in the past four months, two large groups, seven smaller ones, and quite a few pairs and singletons. It appeared the enclave's reputation was spreading, even as its fortifications pushed farther into the surrounding prairie. Those who had arrived in the large groups could be skipped on this first run, since any disappearances would more likely have been noticed and reported by others in the group. Even so, it was a daunting pile, and the carbon copies sent over daily by the Welcoming Committee were not always easy to read. By the fortieth record, Catherine found herself nodding off, and Elvira sent her home to bed. She and Harmon, Elvira said, would check out the rest and pull any that seemed promising. "Your shift was over hours ago," said Elvira.

"Yours is just about up."

"I had a good sleep in the day, you didn't. I can keep Harmon company till we're done or Charlie clocks in. You git on home and git your head down." Catherine saw the sense in it.

But tossing on the cot in her studio apartment was not the same thing as getting some sleep. The girl's delicate face from different angles, one blue eye open, the other full of wood and rayed with dry blood, played in a loop against the inside of Catherine's eyelids. She got up after a while, poured out a precious finger of her hoarded rum, lay down again. No change. Why was that bell ringing so persistently in the back of her brain?

No signs of rape. No blood or glisten of bodily fluids on the naked thighs, just like the other two. The five doctors in the Holcomb enclave had just under nine thousand breathing people to look after now, and no time to play pathologist, so it was no use trying to call them in without good reason. But the daisy-print dress…it would be worth dropping in at Stemple's in the morning, to see if it looked like the fabric had come from the same bolt. If it matched, there was a good chance the girl had been alive until very recently, and was inside the enclave as a breathing human until somebody changed that for her. The prospect of a solid chore in the morning soothed Catherine. She slid towards sleep…

And then she jerked as if falling in a dream, and sat up sharply. Synapses had snapped and fired with electrons in that hypnagogic moment; connections had been forged. The stakes. No signs of interference. *That guy.* The notorious one, the one that got away—the last known killing was when Catherine was still doing traffic stops, four years before the end of the world, but every cop and true crime junkie in the country had known the details. At least thirteen linked deaths, spreading out from southern Washington State to Northern California over a period of seven years. When the series stopped, everyone assumed the monster had either kicked the bucket, got himself jailed, or aged out of the urge, like a lot of serial killers did. And he had always pounded the stakes into the heart, hence the nickname bestowed upon him by the press. But what self-respecting murderer would put a stake through the heart these days? Hearts were useless. He would want his victims to stay dead.

So now she had two things to do in the morning.

———— «◇» ————

Somehow Catherine slept, though not for long. Due to start her shift by ten, she found herself striding through the black morning along Carter Street just after five o'clock, heading for the one pool of light ahead, the station house. She paused in front of Stemple's Department Store and peered through the window into the darkness, past the shelves of mason jars and tools and general salvage, but the dress racks were too far from the window. Stemple's opened at seven; she could wait.

She was happy to see Charlie manning the desk, even happier to see the coffee machine was half full and still hot. Elvira and Harmon had long since gone off shift. No one else was around at this hour. Charlie watched her quizzically as she poured herself a coffee and wrapped her cold hands around it.

"I figured you'd be in before your shift, from what Harmon said." Charlie was ex-military, an MP, tall and black and funny and remote. He did not talk about his family or his life in the world-before, which was fine. Catherine didn't talk about hers, either. He had joined Holcomb about nine months before.

"Couldn't sleep much," she said, "Listen, Charlie. I got a question. Do you remember the Fearless Vampire Killer?"

He looked at her hard, hesitating. "I'm guessing you don't mean the Roman Polanski movie."

"Nope."

His eyes narrowed. "Then that's a righteous blast from the past. Also a mighty strange question to start the day with."

"But do you remember?

"Course I do, now you bring it up. That psycho was memorable in the worst possible way."

"Did Harmon tell you about the dead girl yesterday?"

"He filled me in. He and Elvira left you a little heap of files to check out. So what's the connection with the Fearless Vampire Killer? The stakes? That's pretty thin. Sometimes a stake is just a pointy piece of wood."

"The stakes are one thing," said Catherine, "though that could be coincidental. But I think it's worth checking out the dead girl again before the maggots get hold of her."

Charlie grimaced and passed one hand over his dark, shaven head. "You're thinking about the words on the belly, the inscriptions. And soap traces on the thighs."

"Yeah."

"You want to wait till the sheriff comes in?"

"Nope," said Catherine. "I'm going out there now."

"That's natural. But I can't go with you, Catherine, I'm on duty. Someone has to be here."

"Of course," said Catherine. "I just want you to know where I'm going, and why. I'll be back quick as I can."

"It's a stretch, you know. That sicko wasn't heard from for years, even before things in the world went sideways. What are the chances he'd survive in the first place, with all that shit that went down, and then become active again in the new world, and end up in little old Holcomb? It's been, what, eight, nine years and a whole pile of trouble since the last murder?"

"The last *known* murder," she said, "and the answer is ten years. I'm borrowing the scissors from Elvira's drawer. See you later."

———— «» ————

She chose the big roan from the stable this time, placid and dependable. By the time she left the town streets and struck out towards the cemetery, the eastern sky was just beginning to lighten where it met the prairie, but the fields were still dark. The shed was by the cemetery gate, rarely used for anything more than keeping Jed and Jimmy's shovels and shrouds out of the weather. Why keep watch? Nobody but the undertakers and the odd mourner went near the line-graves unless they were certifiably dead in all current senses of the word. A few birds called from the trees, and then went quiet. Six years ago, she might have been spooked by the silence of the birds, the shadows dancing under the trees in the light wind. Nothing could spook her now. One had to make a choice at some point: to be spooked by everything, or never be spooked at all.

Even before Catherine passed the shed, the grave stink was subtle but present. She paused on the lip of the line-grave. Six feet deep, six feet wide, fifty feet long. Jed and Jimmy were digging a new line-grave even as they filled in the current one, the earth from the new one finding a new home on top of the corpses in the other. Poking through the layer of dirt at the end of the current row of bodies, about halfway along the trench, a fold of light-coloured fabric shone pale in the pre-dawn twilight. Catherine tethered the roan to a tree and fetched the undertakers' ladder from the shed.

Kerchief over her nose, Catherine climbed down into the pit and gingerly, gently, brushed the dirt away from the face-end of the last mound of dirt. It was the girl in the print dress, no doubt about it. Catherine brushed away more dirt. The dead girl was neatly laid out on her back, arms by her sides, shoulder to shoulder with the next cadaver. The stake had been removed, and the ruined socket seemed to stare past Catherine's face, up towards the thin crescent moon. Catherine cut a small square from the bottom edge of the dress with Elvira's scissors, and tucked it into her pack. Then she hesitated: the moment of truth. Why did she feel like she was violating the dead girl all over again? She pulled the skirt up and carefully lifted the bodice to expose the belly. And there was her answer.

———— «» ————

Stemple's was still not open by the time Catherine got back to Carter Street, so she went straight to the station house. Charlie looked up from the reception desk, eyebrows raised.

"It's him," she said, "or else a damn good copycat with a long memory."

Charlie's expression did not change, but he put his pen down and sat back in his chair.

"Same as before?"

"Felt-tip, probably a permanent marker. The lines hadn't smudged. But it was red capitals outlined in black, couple of inches high. NOT MY FAULT. If only we had access to a handwriting expert to confirm it, but still..."

"Soap traces?"

"Couldn't tell either way. Not till we get her back here."

He shook his head. "It's hard to believe. What are the odds he'd survive the troubles, and then set up shop here, a thousand miles and a whole mountain range away?"

"What are the odds this girl would have a stake in her flesh and a felt-tip disclaimer on her belly, just like the Vampire Killer's victims? Come on, Charlie."

"Okay, it's hinky as hell. What did you do with her?"

"Covered her up with a shroud for the moment. I'll need help getting her out of the trench, and a buckboard for transport. I want to get her inside into the cool before the day gets too hot. I'll go just after eight, once the newbs are here to help." Catherine hesitated. "It seems to me the sheriff will have to listen to me now."

"The sheriff," said Charlie, "usually listens to what he wants to hear. But he's not an idiot, far from it. And if the body's already in the station house, he might have trouble shutting his ears. He may not be happy, though."

"Too bad for him," said Catherine.

《》

Sharp at seven o'clock in the morning, Catherine walked along Carter Street to the Central Communal Goods Depot. Nobody called it that except in official documents. The Old Holcombers, the folks who were resident here in the world-before, had always called it Stemple's, and now the newcomers did too—a venerable brick edifice established in 1910, and managed by a great-grandson of the original Stemple at the time the world ended. Now the last of the Stemples was in the first of the line-graves, and the store was a curious mix of socialist and capitalist enterprise. Newcomers accepted into the enclave were given vouchers for food and new clothes for a month—after that, purchases worked on barter and Holcomb's own scrip, produced on the enclave's only operational photocopier, up in the old insurance office. This week's special was a load of cookware brought in by a team foraging forty miles south in Aspen Ford. Two weeks ago, Catherine now knew, the special was clothing run up by the Holcomb seamstresses from a pallet of cloth bolts brought in from Millerville, sixty miles west.

Miss Lilly, whose clerkship at Stemple's had survived the collapse of western civilization, appeared magically beside a rack of salvaged rubber boots. The dresses from the Millerville bolts? Right there at the back, and mighty tasty they looked, there was a maroon paisley that would just suit the deputy's colouring, the seamstresses would be happy to do alterations if need be. Catherine thanked Miss Lilly and moved to the rack, pushed a few hangers along, sought out the remaining yellow daisy-print dresses. There were three of them. The fabric sample from the dead girl's dress was a match. Catherine folded the sample away again in her pack and beckoned to Miss Lilly.

Those cute little daisy-print dresses? Real popular those were, the seamstresses made up ten from that particular bolt, seven went like hotcakes, but the maroon paisley would be far more flattering, or maybe that black-and-white houndstooth pantsuit, if the deputy preferred that to a dress? Who bought the other seven dresses? Well, that would surely be in the ledger, here we go, five were scrip, one was barter, one was a welcome voucher, but no names except for the barter-buyer. Louisa was in charge for those mornings, maybe she'd remember the buyers, but the poor woman had a touch of tummy bug, didn't come in yesterday and wasn't expected today. Catherine thanked Miss Lilly once more and escaped before the subject of maroon paisley could be raised again.

———— «» ————

"The fabric matches," Catherine told Sheriff Wiley three hours later, "and one of the dresses was paid for with a welcome voucher. What if our victim was the girl with the voucher? I've never known a wanderer to go dress shopping."

The sheriff's jowls still had that dull red glow they got when he was annoyed, but he was listening. The blonde girl was safely in the cool of the cellar, naked under a gaudy checked tablecloth. On her own authority, Catherine had taken the newbs and the station buckboard to collect the body, dropped a note off at the clinic to request assistance from one of the doctors, and gone over the body and the daisy-print dress with a magnifying glass and tweezers, all before the sheriff arrived at the station house. And she had put her nose to the skin of the girl's thighs and taken a good long sniff, and then a scraping from the surface into a test tube. Soapy, with a hint of lilac.

Across the glass, in the outer office, the newbs had been watching the process from the beginning. Ethan, an ex-security guard from Wisconsin, was a newb only to the police, having transferred after working a few months in the Border Force; Abby, a brawny thirtyish woman who had worked as a law clerk in the world-before, had joined the enclave only three weeks past, and was clearly still in her honeymoon phase with Holcomb. Catherine remembered feeling like that. Now Holcomb was just real life.

"So let's just imagine this is your show, Cathy. What would you figure on doing next?" Sheriff Wiley's voice was as flat as the prairie enfolding the enclave.

Catherine's list was firm in her head. "First, I've already dropped a note for the doctors, see if one of them can come around and look at her and tell us anything we don't already know."

"Should of checked with me before pestering the docs. Never mind, go on."

"Second, I've started going through some files of recent newcomers, potential victims, that Harmon and Elvira pulled overnight. I'll give the list of possibles to Abby, get her to check out the employment and housing allocations listed in the files, see if all those women are where they're supposed to be. We already eliminated two, since they're in the same hostel as Abby, and she can confirm they're alive."

"Sounds sensible," said the sheriff.

"But most of all, I want to bring the Welcoming Committee over to take a look at the victim. If she entered Holcomb recently, one of them should remember her face. And we should bring in Louisa from Stemple's as well, make sure that's the girl who used the voucher to buy the daisy-print dress."

"Fine. Go for it. But better keep the smelling salts handy for Miss Louisa, she always was a touch nervy." The sheriff sat back in his swivel chair. His jowls were only normally ruddy again. "I'll say this once, Cathy. You were right about that gal, she was no wanderer. But don't let it go to your head."

——— «» ———

Three years before, when Catherine first stumbled into Holcomb along with a random cluster of survivors, there were just over four thousand breathing people in a town built for twice that number. The population had more than doubled since then, to more than before the apocalypse, while not falling into the pitfalls Catherine had observed and escaped elsewhere—the ghastly experiments in social engineering thrown up in those first terrible years, the messiahs and warlords, the visionaries and gang bosses, the feudal hells and doomed idealistic utopias. Holcomb, for all its faults, had somehow felt its way into a brand of reasonable governance. Who would have predicted that civilization's secret weapon was bureaucracy?

Bureaucracy, that is, plus a habit of dogged decency in the face of the unthinkable. When the unthinkable happened, Holcomb was kept together by the sheriff, the town librarian, the manager of the feed store, and the redoubtable grandmother who had run the post office for more than forty years. The first barrier, enclosing a good chunk of the town, was in place within the first six weeks, its innards cleansed of wanderers, the supplies catalogued and rationed, livestock and survivors and rolls of barbed wire brought in from the outlying ranches. By the end of the first year, the barriers had expanded to include the rest of the town and some surrounding fields. The wind farm substation a mile out of town had been fortified and staffed with surviving technicians brought in from all the wind farms within an eighty-mile radius. The chicken hatchery was back in operation, seeds from Elbert & Sons Farm Supplies were burgeoning in the fields, school was in session, and more refugees had arrived, including a doctor and two nurses. And, notably, the new bureaucratic infrastructure had been hammered out over that year, ratified, and put into operation: the Foodstocks Office, the Central Communal Goods Registry, the Manpower Bureau, Infrastructure and Maintenance, and the Security Service.

The Welcoming Committee, a subsection of the Manpower Bureau, dealt with anything related to incoming survivors. Catherine, like all other incomers, had passed through their hands. After the horrors of lone survival and dire social experiments, she had found it curiously soothing to be faced with a lengthy questionnaire regarding her qualifications, employment history, skills, and—yes—her hobbies. She had been seen by a doctor and given a hot shower, a delousing, and a change of clothes, followed by a decent meal, a vitamin injection, and a night in a clean bed. If the Welcoming Committee had assessed her as a potential troublemaker, she would have been escorted politely but firmly out of the gate the next morning and advised never to return. Instead she had been given a choice between the Border Force and the sheriff's station house; she chose the latter, and thereafter advanced rapidly from newb to deputy, roughly equivalent to the rank she had held in the world-before. Catherine had every reason to bless the Welcoming Committee and the Holcomb bureaucracy.

———— «» ————

Two-thirds of the Welcoming Committee arrived at the station a little before four o'clock, when Catherine had just finished combing through the files set aside by Harmon and Elvira. Nineteen files from the last four months. Two had already been eliminated by Abby, leaving seventeen. Of those, five black women in the right age range had entered the enclave between sixteen and thirteen weeks ago, when the first assumed victim had been found. Only two redheads had been recorded between sixteen and five weeks ago. Ten blondes or light-browns within the search parameters had been recorded over the entire period. Catherine laid the last file down and looked up as Ethan ushered Miss Ella and Miss Michelle into her office. She rose and greeted them warmly. "Only two of you?" she asked.

"Julie's holding down the fort at the office. She'll come in later. No newcomers in the last couple days, but you never know when some poor lost soul might stumble in." A plump, apple-cheeked relic of the old Holcomb, ex-postmistress and the only remaining founding member of the Welcoming Committee, Miss Ella was the one who had processed Catherine on her arrival. Miss Michelle, who had taken over from Miss Linda just under a year ago, was a hefty woman on the far side of fifty, a social worker in the world-before. She was the one who had installed pots of mixed flowers in the reception office and painted the walls a cheery yellow, to set the tone for new arrivals. How threatening could the enclave be, when shocked and brutalized newcomers were processed in a sunny yellow room filled with flowers? Miss Julie, an ex-human resources executive who had joined the Committee owing to the recent onset of Miss Ava's dementia, was known to Catherine only by sight.

"Perhaps we should get it over with," said Miss Michelle.

Down in the station basement, a chilly space filled with filing cabinets and stationery supplies and guns, the dead girl lay on a table under her improvised shroud. It was the coldest part of the station, but Catherine could already see bloating in the abdominal area. She drew back the top edge of the tablecloth. Miss Ella and Miss Michelle, who had both seen much worse, bent down for a good close look. After a moment Miss Ella covered the girl's ruined eye with one hand, frowned at the undamaged portion of the face, dropped her hand, shook her head. "Nope," she said, "I never seen this poor girl."

"I don't remember seeing her either," said Miss Michelle.

That was not what Catherine wanted to hear. "Okay, but do you get to see everyone that gets processed, even if you're not dealing with them yourselves?"

"Girl, far as I know, I seen every face that come into Holcomb in the last six years, even the poor lost souls that we had to send right back out again the next day. And I never seen this one." Miss Ella crossed her arms on her stout bosom in a posture of certitude.

"I don't recognize the face at all," said Miss Michelle in her quiet, dry voice, "but of course we do see a lot of people."

"Well," said Miss Ella, "we never did see this one, 'specially not if it was in the last few days, like young Ethan said."

"How about the other two? A black girl with sleeves... with tattoos all the way up her arms, and a redhead in a camo outfit?"

Miss Ella shrugged. Miss Michelle said, "Without pictures, we really can't say. So sorry."

"It's fine," said Catherine. Then she pulled the tablecloth back over the livid cheeks, the black-rimmed cavity where an eye used to be. "Thanks for coming, ladies," she added.

——— «» ———

That was the first dead end. The second was reached not long after Catherine saw off two-thirds of the Welcoming Committee with a reminder to send Miss Julie along as soon as she was free. That was when one of the doctors paid a hurried visit, examined the girl in the basement, confirmed there was no sign she had been penetrated and had probably died from a stake through one eye into the brain, and rushed back to the clinic. None of that was exactly news to Catherine. The third dead end was when Abby returned to the station with her list of seventeen names all neatly ticked off.

"You're sure?" said Catherine. "You checked them all?"

"Every single one. Helped by the fact that eight of them still live in the big women's hostel on Belcher, where they were first assigned. Two of those ones were home, and confirmed the other six were all alive and well as of last night. Then I visited workplaces for the remaining nine and spoke to them all. I'll go back to the hostel this evening to confirm the ones I didn't see with my own eyes, but it's looking like everyone on your list can be accounted for. None of these files match any one of our victims."

"Good work," said Catherine without enthusiasm. She saw a long night ahead, combing through the files again to see whether Elvira and Harmon had missed someone. Charlie would help when he came on shift after two in the morning, if she lasted that long, but she already knew in her heart that it would be wasted effort. One victim, Harmon and Elvira might have missed. Missing all three was highly unlikely. Even more unlikely, though, was the coincidence of a fatally administered wooden stake and a familiar phrase neatly inscribed on the victim's belly. NOT MY FAULT. She waved Abby back to the outer office and indulged herself briefly by putting her face in her hands. Sleep would be wonderful, especially dreamless sleep.

A light touch on her shoulder. A fresh cup of coffee at her elbow.

"Hey, Charlie," she said, "you're hours early. Harmon's not even in yet."

"Couldn't sleep. Couldn't keep away. Remember how the last case we handled was some moron shoplifting at the bakery? A murder case is more like old times."

"You mean, when death still meant something?"

"Death will always mean something. Just means different things now. Can you fill me in on how things are going?"

"They're going nowhere." Catherine summarized the nothingness arising from the Welcoming Committee, the doctor, the checklist of seventeen women who seemed to be, happily but inconveniently, still breathing and exactly where they should be. "All we have left for now," she finished, "is to talk with Miss Julie from the Welcoming Committee, and Miss Louisa from Stemple's. Maybe the guys on the gate as well. We've got loads of DNA but we can't use it, found some possible soap residue on her thighs but can't analyze it, we've got nowhere to send the hair samples I took off the dress, nothing to compare her fingerprints with."

"I know it's frustrating." Charlie pulled up a chair. "All those space-age diagnostic tools we used to have, all gone. Nowadays, doing forensics is like trying to watch a movie on a radio. But I did bring you something."

"Yeah? What?"

"Miss Louisa from Stemple's. She was coming out of the pharmacy when I passed by, and I asked her to come along asap. She just walked in."

Miss Louisa, chatting with Ethan in the outer office, was a birdlike Old Holcomber whom Catherine recognized from the store, and from the senior ladies' barbershop quartet at the last two Christmas concerts. She was still wan from her tummy bug, and Catherine wondered about the wisdom of showing her the dead girl's body with no smelling salts to hand, as per the sheriff's warning. But Miss Louisa trod lightly down the stairs to the basement ahead of Ethan and Charlie and pulled the tablecloth aside before Catherine could stop her.

"Why, yes," said Miss Louisa, peering down, "I do remember her, poor girl. Size six, the smallest we had in stock in the adult section. She didn't love the pattern, said she didn't much care for florals, but it was the only one on the rack that fit her."

Catherine controlled her breathing. "What was the pattern? Do you remember?"

"Of course I remember. That pretty daisy print. She warmed to it in the end, said she had one like it when she was a kid, before the world went bad. Nice girl, such a pity."

"Did she tell you anything else? Her name, where she came from, when she arrived, who she came in with, anything like that?"

"Not a thing, not even her name. I figured she was a newcomer, though, and you know what they're like. Takes them a few days to get used to being safe."

Catherine nodded. She knew very well. "So there's nothing else you can tell us?"

"No. Well, yes. That would be Wednesday morning, early, not long after I opened up. I know it was Wednesday because I told her about the church social that evening, invited her to come along, but she said someone was waiting for her and she'd have to check with them. And my tummy bug kicked in that afternoon, so I never did get to the church social anyways."

Wednesday morning. Three days ago, the dead girl was alive in Holcomb. That was two days before the body was found. "Did she say who was waiting? Did you see anyone out on the sidewalk, or which way she turned when she left the store?"

"Deputy Cathy, I got better things to do with my time than watch customers leave the store. We had a new shipment in to sort out, those nice pots and pans from Aspen Ford."

Catherine drew the tablecloth back over the dead girl's face. "Did she change back into her old clothes before leaving?"

"Nope, she walked out in her new dress, with her old clothes in a parcel. Believe you me, the duds she had on just needed burning. How about her shoes?"

"What?"

"The poor gal bought a new pair of shoes, too, as I recall. Some pretty sandals."

Catherine crossed the room, opened a drawer, pulled out the new white sandals lying beside the daisy-print dress. "These the ones?"

"I'd say so. Most of the sandals in the store right now are from that same Millerville shipment, and those look about right."

"Thank you, Miss Louisa," said Catherine. "You've been very helpful."

———— «»————

"So she was alive Wednesday morning," Charlie said to Catherine. "And she was dead no more than a day and a half before she was found, judging by the state of the body. It's Saturday now, and she was spotted yesterday afternoon. So it looks like the stake went into her eye some time on Wednesday night, or early Thursday morning at the latest."

"I don't want to think about that yet," said Catherine.

Charlie hesitated. "It's relevant."

"Sure, but we shouldn't get ahead of ourselves. Focus on Wednesday morning. Louisa confirmed the girl got to Stemple's early. That means she must have been processed by the Welcoming Committee as early as Tuesday night, and that means she should have been recorded in the carbons sent over on Wednesday night, or Thursday at the outside— but two of the ladies from the Welcoming Committee didn't recognize her, and we didn't find her in the carbons."

Charlie's face was blank as he nodded. "We need to talk to Miss Julie." He picked up the receiver and held it out to her. "It's your case. You make the call."

Reluctantly, she pulled the phone closer and took the receiver from him. There were no cell phones in the new world. The phone engineer who joined the enclave about the same time as Catherine had scavenged enough old-fashioned hardware to connect the main town offices, the police station, the gates, the Manpower Bureau, the Foodstocks Coordinator, and a few public phones in the library and outside the bar. Private lines were a thing of the past, a dream of the future. The police station was sufficiently high priority to merit a punch pad rather than a rotary dial. Catherine punched in the fast-dial for the Welcoming Committee. The voice that answered spoke in Miss Ella's flat Holcomb-native accent.

"Julie? She's gone for the evening. She had night duty the last few days, wanted to get on home and catch up on chores. Said she'd stop in at the station in the morning."

Catherine thanked her and put down the phone. She stared into the air above the shabby desk.

"You want to bring Miss Julie in to view the girl? Harmon will be in at six, I can cover the station till he gets here. And Ethan hasn't left yet, you could send him."

"Not yet," Catherine said.

"You got a thought?"

She gulped her coffee, turned to him. "We're assuming she had only just arrived in the enclave. So we have to look at the process. When I first came to the enclave, I arrived in the early afternoon with five others, nobody I knew well, just some other people I had met on the road here. The guards opened the outer gate, disarmed us, let us into the holding pen, looked us over, escorted us to the office of the Welcoming Committee. Miss Ella was the one who gave out the questionnaires, ordered in some food, and gave us room assignments for the night, upstairs from the welcoming office, but all of them saw us the next morning. Miss Ella, Miss Linda, Miss Ava. What happened with you?"

Charlie frowned through a long moment of silence. "Different. I came in alone. I got up to the gate after midnight with a pack of wanderers not far behind, they'd been following me for hours. I was about done when I saw that red flashing beacon at the gate and stumbled right to it. The Border Force opened up when they heard me shouting, and yanked me inside, and I never bothered to ask what happened with the wanderers after that. Alvin, big curly-headed guy in the Border Force, checked me over then took me across the street to the office and woke up Miss Ava, who was on duty that night. The ladies have that little bedroom behind the office for whoever's on night duty, and I guess mostly they just get a good night's sleep if nobody shows up at the gate. Miss Ava saw the state I was in, gave me some soup, put me to bed in one of the rooms upstairs, and processed me early in the morning. Good thing I didn't have lice or bad intentions."

"Did you see the others?"

"Yeah, Miss Ella came in about nine while I was filling out the forms, Miss Michelle a little later."

"What happened then?"

"I had a shower and some breakfast then fell asleep again in the chair. At about noon they woke me up for the doctor, and then told me I was okay to stay in Holcomb, gave me vouchers and a map. Then there was the station house, the store, the bachelors' hostel. You know the rest."

Catherine did. She had been on duty when he showed up at the station, straight from the welcoming office. "None of them offered to guide you?"

"The map was fine."

"Do you remember anything else?"

Charlie hesitated. "Miss Ella was a bit sharp with Miss Ava when she came in. Said she should have called for the doctor's exam and made me have a shower and the delousing shampoo before giving me a bed, now they'd have to boil that bedding just in case. She shouldn't have sent Alvin away, either. Against safety regulations. Seems there's protocols for after-hours arrivals, and Miss Ava broke them. But then, she was already showing signs of going gaga. Miss Julie took over from her a couple months later."

"So only Alvin and his guys and Miss Ava would have known you were there until Miss Ella came in at nine."

He nodded slowly. "Guess we should talk with Miss Julie asap. And then check with the guys on the gate."

«›»

Miss Julie's boarding house was a few blocks away, conveniently close to the welcoming office and across the street from the charging station where three of the enclave's four foraging trucks were plugged up in a row, like suckling puppies. Catherine and Ethan crossed the road to the pleasant brick mansion, previously the home of the Stemple dynasty. What had once been a sweep of emerald lawn behind wrought-iron fences was now an array of vegetable patches where tomatoes, beets, and peppers were already a foot high. Several women were weeding the beds, hatless in the approaching dusk, and Catherine recognized one of them as Miss Julie—tall, slender, with an elegance of carriage that must have served her well as an HR executive, and survived despite the grubby jeans and plaid shirt. She turned and smiled as Catherine and Ethan came up the drive.

"Ethan, isn't it?" she called out. "How have you settled in?"

Catherine glanced at Ethan with raised eyebrows.

"You didn't tell me we were coming for her," he murmured.

"She's the one who checked you in?"

But Miss Julie was advancing to meet them, stripping off her gardening gloves, and he had no time to answer Catherine. "I settled in fine, Miss Julie. This place is heaven, after…you know, out there."

"I'm happy we could help." The smile was warm and professional, and held firmly on her face as she turned to Catherine. "And you must be Deputy Cathy. I've heard all about you."

A practiced schmoozer, thought Catherine. She realized how much she disliked Miss Julie. "We need you to come to the station with us," she said, "and have a look at a body we found yesterday. Your colleagues came by already. We had hoped you'd come as soon as you left the office."

"Oh, sorry, my bad. I didn't realize it was urgent."

"She's starting to bloat," Catherine said bluntly. "Sooner we can get her back in the line-grave, the better. Don't bother changing. Ethan, you go rustle up Alvin and find out who was on the gate on Tuesday night."

———— «» ————

"Poor girl," said Miss Julie, gazing down with what looked like authentic pity. "No, I don't recognize her. She didn't come in on my watch, anyway."

Catherine stared at the dead face, now showing a greenish tinge and some foamy discharge at the nostrils, the side of the mouth. "Who was on duty Tuesday night?"

"I was. It was supposed to be Mickey, but she had a date."

"Mickey?"

"Michelle. It's not a big deal who stays overnight in the office, you know, since we mostly get to sleep anyway. It's not like any of us have families to get home to. I enjoy the night duty, get a lot of reading done. And I got a lot done that night, because nobody came in."

"Nobody?"

"Not a soul."

"Thanks, Miss Julie. You can get back to your gardening now." Catherine drew the tablecloth back over the dead girl's face, for what she thought might be the last time. Who else had to view the body? It was possible now that, whoever the girl was, she had not gone through the normal entry procedure—unless Miss Julie was lying. It was unlikely one of the doctors had seen her, so unlikely that it was hardly worth dragging the other four doctors in to have a look at her. Catherine listened to Miss Julie's feet retreating up the stairs. After a decent interval, she followed.

———— «» ————

"She arrived late Tuesday night or early Wednesday morning. That's clear. Early enough to get to Stemple's about the time it opened."

Charlie poured out the rest of the coffee into Catherine's mug. "But she wasn't recorded. There were no carbons for Tuesday night or Wednesday morning, no newcomers until late Wednesday afternoon, when a group of three was processed. So either Miss Julie is lying about not seeing her, or she never reached the welcoming office in the first place."

"What about the gate log?"

"Nothing there." Charlie had the carbons out already. "Ethan checked with Alvin and the other guys on the gate that night. Nobody came through. And it turns out Ethan frequently hangs out at the gate with his old buddies on the Border Force and was playing poker with them until long after midnight."

"The east gate?"

"Nothing reported."

"Then somebody could be lying. But who? If it was someone on the Border Force who took her, how did she get the voucher? Those bits of paper are tightly controlled. But if the Border Force did hand her over to the Welcoming Committee at some ungodly hour, how come there's no record of her coming through the gate? I can't believe all of them are lying, especially including Ethan."

Charlie had no answer. They sat in silence, listening to the voices in the outer office. It was after seven; Elvira was typing reports at reception, while Harmon had arrived at six for his shift. Raised voices at the desk—a citizen of Holcomb with a complaint about a neighbour. Some things in the world never changed. Abby came in the front door, stopped for a quick word with Elvira, and hurried through the outer office. Catherine waved her in.

"Well? How were things at the women's hostel?"

"Everybody's there," said Abby, "so all the women on your list are accounted for."

Catherine sighed. Was it wrong to be disappointed? She forced herself to nod approvingly. "Good work, Abby. Guess you're done for the day now, have a good night." She looked down at the pile of carbons on her desk, but Abby did not move. "Something more?"

"Yes, Deputy. Funny thing—one of the new girls at the hostel, she came in about two weeks ago, was wearing that same kind of dress, that yellow daisy print. And similar sandals. Thought you'd like to know." And when Catherine nodded but said nothing, Abby left. There was a long silence after the door closed behind her.

"I'm an idiot," Catherine said at last.

"We're both idiots," said Charlie.

"We didn't think to confirm. We just assumed."

"It seemed reasonable at the time." Charlie pulled out the master list of current addresses in the enclave and ran his finger down the columns. "She's at 17 Brook Street, a couple doors down from your place."

"I know where it is." Catherine was already at the door.

———— «·» ————

"Sugar? Milk? A shot of something?" Miss Louisa's kitchen was a museum diorama of the mid-20th century, except for a much older wood-burning stove in the corner. The room sparkled with decades of loving care. Miss Louisa poured the tea into three teacups of a pattern Catherine recognized from her great-grandmother's house, far back in the dead past of the world before.

"We don't want to take up your time," said Catherine. She did not want tea—she wanted an answer; but Miss Louisa, like many of the little old women of Holcomb, was a force of nature. Catherine accepted sugar and milk and averted her eyes from the sight of Charlie stirring his tea with a dainty vintage teaspoon. "Miss Louisa, please. That girl who bought the dress, the one whose body we showed you—do you remember if she used a welcome voucher?"

Miss Louisa was busy producing an ancient cookie tin from the cupboard. "That one? No, I was surprised because she seemed so much like a new arrival, I expected her to pull out a voucher. No, she paid with scrip. The young lady with the voucher came in a few days earlier."

"Scrip," repeated Catherine. "You're sure the dead girl used scrip?"

"Sure as I'm standing here."

"Why didn't you tell us this before?"

Miss Louisa opened the cookie tin and placed it in the centre of the table. "I don't recall being asked about it, Deputy Cathy. Have a cookie."

———— «》 ————

Five busy hours later.

Sheriff Wiley managed to retain his good-old-boy vibe in a plaid bathrobe, scuffed carpet slippers, and a worn leather recliner chair, comfortable in his own home and his own skin. "Susan got up, she'll bring in some coffee directly. So what you got that's worth pulling me out of a warm bed at one o'clock in the morning? This is about that poor little dead gal, right?"

"It is, Sheriff," Catherine said from one end of an aggressively floral chesterfield.

"And you two got your panties in a twist because she paid with scrip at Stemple's?"

Catherine drew a deep breath. "Basically, yes. Scrip that she must have been given by someone she met in Holcomb. Sheriff, you were right about her coming through the fence in the night, instead of through the gate. But she was breathing when she came through the fence."

"That sag you found by the waterhole? How do you figure that?"

"Because it was the only weakness I saw in the fence a couple of days later, and we're certain she didn't come through either of the gates. The Border Force didn't see her, neither did Miss Julie at the welcoming office. That's what they say, and I believe them. She came through the fence late Tuesday or early Wednesday, in the dark hours."

"Okay. What else you got?"

Charlie cleared his throat. "I cross-checked the duty rosters against the approximate times when the redhead and the black girl most likely came through, based on what dates their bodies were found. The dates were consistent. Here's my notes."

"What else?"

"I checked the repair records from the Border Force." Catherine laid a page on the coffee table in front of the sheriff, three lines highlighted. "In all three cases, a weakness in the fence was repaired within one to three days after the body was found. And one more thing."

"Okay."

"We brought that young doctor back in to cut open her stomach," Catherine said flatly. "Looks like pickled gherkins and boiled egg last a while in the gut." She laid her last paper on top of the others.

The sheriff gave her a hard look, transferred it to Charlie, grunted, picked up the papers. He took his time reading through the notes, then laid them down. "So paint me the picture," he said. "What do you figure happened?"

"We figure she'd heard about Holcomb, was heading for the gate, maybe some wanderers were chasing her—"

"Hold up, Catherine. Which one you talking about?"

"All three of them, and maybe more, for all we know, but we'll focus on the blonde girl. She saw that sag in the fence, climbed inside, headed toward the faint glow over the town, for what she hoped was safety and shelter."

"Why didn't she head for the beacon at the gate?"

Charlie said, "You can't see the beacon from there. We checked it tonight. Going by the repair records, the redhead would have come from the north, the black girl from about the same angle as the blonde. None of them would have headed for a beacon they couldn't see."

"Fair enough," said the sheriff, "and maybe something we should correct. Then what?"

"Sheriff, put yourself in her place," said Catherine. "She heads for town in the dead of night, comes out onto Carter Street, and the only bright light she sees is the station house. After the bar shuts down, it's the brightest light in town. And where does a citizen go to feel safe? A police station."

"It happened once while I was on graveyard," said Charlie. "I just phoned the Border Force to pick the guy up and drop him off at the welcoming office. He was processed normally."

"You checked the roster for Tuesday night?" the sheriff interrupted.

"Consistent. Catherine and the newbs signed out at six, when I took over," said Charlie. "Elvira came in for her evening shift at seven, clocked out at midnight, Harmon relieved me at two. He was alone in the station house until Ethan and Abby signed in again at eight."

Susan Wiley came in with a tray holding three steaming mugs, deposited them on the coffee table, and withdrew.

"So blondie crosses the fence early in the morning and finds the station house, and Harmon's alone there, and he... what, gives her a coffee?"

"And a sandwich, based on her stomach contents. Gretchen always packs more than he can eat." Egg salad sandwiches. Catherine felt her gorge rise and stuffed it back down. "But Harmon knows the newbs are coming in shortly, so he gives the girl some scrip and sends her to Stemple's when it opens, tells her to buy a new dress and wait for him on the street."

"And then?"

Catherine hesitated over her mug of coffee. "Can't say exactly. But we checked with Abby, and she says Harmon went out on a call not long after she got there. Nothing about a call in the station log, though."

"What do you reckon?"

Catherine hesitated again, and this time Charlie answered. "We think Harmon faked a call-out and took the girl home. His home. Gretchen might have been out of the house by then, she starts work at nine."

"They've got the Bristow's old house." Susan Wiley's voice, from the door. "It's got a cold room in the cellar. Ellie

Bristow put a lock on it after that tramp broke in and stole some preserves in about '02. Far as I know, it's still there."

"So he had a place to lock her in until Gretchen left for work." Catherine felt a moment of triumph, pieces coming together, the jigsaw making sense. "When I relieved him at ten, he went home and…"

"And did what? No signs of rape or torture."

Catherine and Charlie traded glances. "No signs of penetration, anyway. But whatever was done to her, he cleaned her up afterward with soap and water. That's consistent with the Fearless Vampire Killer, as well. And then he…"

"…Drove a stake into her eye. And dumped her body before relieving Charlie at two on Thursday morning."

"That's about the size of it, Sheriff."

"Wednesday?" Susan's voice from the door. "Wednesday's a problem, folks. Far as I know, Gretchen didn't go into work on Wednesday. Bella was supposed to do the church flyers with me at lunchtime, but she had to cover the office since Gretchen didn't show up. She said Harmon dropped over in the morning to let her know."

"Woman, go back to bed. This ain't your problem."

Susan advanced into the room. "If there's a killer in Holcomb, Joe Bob, it's everyone's problem. And the answer's lit up like a Christmas tree. She's a strange woman, that one, crazy as a coot according to some. And she got her husband on a leash like a whipped puppy. But sure, I'll leave you to it." She went out and padded up the stairs, leaving an uncomfortable, even shocked, silence in the living room.

"I'll get dressed," said the sheriff.

———— «·» ————

Five minutes to two o'clock in the morning. About the time Charlie would have arrived anyway, to relieve Harmon. About the time that Harmon had relieved Charlie in the early hours of Wednesday morning, before the shift swap took place. The lights of the station house splashed across the darkness of Carter Street as they straggled past Stemple's. Inside at the reception desk, Harmon stretched his arms above his head and smiled at Charlie as he led the way through the door. The smile faded as Catherine and Sheriff Wiley followed.

"What is this?"

"I reckon you know," said the sheriff.

"Stay where you are," said Catherine, "and keep your hands high, just where they are." She followed Charlie around the reception desk.

Harmon stared straight ahead, across the desk, into Sheriff Wiley's eyes. "It wasn't my fault," he said.

Charlie had the handcuffs out.

"I just did what she needed me to do. It wasn't my fault. Wasn't hers either."

"Guess we need to pay a visit to the house next," said the sheriff. Harmon screamed then, but Charlie and Catherine grabbed a wrist each and clicked the handcuffs behind his back, and the handcuffs were carbon-steel relics from the world-before.

———— «» ————

Afternoon. It was six years since Catherine had driven a vehicle, but old skills were strong and traffic was nonexistent. The truck had a range of a little over 160 miles in this weather and with this minimal load, and they would need much less than half that according to the report from the technicians manning the newly recommissioned Breisling wind farm. Thirty miles there, thirty miles back, tops.

"You can't do this," said Harmon from the back seat of the cab. Gretchen had said nothing from the time they went to arrest her in the small hours of that morning, but she had smiled without ceasing except when she wept for the chickens she was leaving behind.

"You can't do this," Harmon repeated, "it's not right, it's not legal."

"It's legal under the Holcomb municipal by-laws," said the sheriff, "as updated five years ago with the consent of the citizens of Holcomb. Any persons deemed by the Welcoming Committee to be a danger to the community will be invited to leave, without further process. Unquote. This morning, the ladies deemed. So we're inviting you to leave."

"What happened to a fair trial? You're violating her constitutional rights."

"There ain't no constitution, son, not no more. Turn right on the gravel road up ahead, Cathy."

Catherine made the turn. A cloud roiled close to the ground not far to the east, a dirty brown cloud billowing below the shining pinwheels of the Breisling wind farm. She thought of the paintings she had seen from two centuries ago, when the hooves of the bison churned the prairies to dust. But these beasts were on two legs apiece, not four.

"She's not responsible. It's not her fault." Harmon was fighting the ropes again.

"Don't matter if it was your fault or hers. Don't care who of you did the raping and who did the killing. Don't care why you did it. We just can't have you around no more. See that up ahead, Cathy?"

For the first time since she had taken refuge in Holcomb, Catherine saw it: the vanguard of a herd, scattered and drifting ahead of the main mass, distant dots of ruined faces turning towards the sound of tires on gravel. The technicians were safe overhead in their fortified eyrie, but Catherine knew she would need to drive hard afterward to get beyond the herd's eyes and ears before turning back towards Holcomb. She checked the charge on the engine, saw that it was good. "It doesn't matter now, Harmon," she said, "but I'm curious. Why the stake in the heart, back in the day?"

"It was quick," Harmon said sullenly, "and didn't hurt them much. She never wanted to hurt them."

Gretchen perked up. "They were pretty," she said. "He always brought pretty ones."

Catherine absorbed that, watching the vanguard through the dusty windshield. The nearest cluster was maybe a hundred and fifty yards away. She pulled up in a patch of open ground between two rows of towering turbines. "One more thing. Why did the Fearless Vampire Killer go quiet all that time?"

In the mirror, Harmon's face was a mask of tragedy. "Her meds were changed, she was okay for years, but after things went bad the supply dried up. It wasn't her fault."

"Enough talk," said the sheriff. "Out."

"You can't, Sheriff! This is a death sentence."

"Son, there's no room for capital punishment in the Holcomb by-laws. If you get out right now, you might even have a chance of getting clear. Thanks for your service, you were a good cop as far as that went. Just don't come back to Holcomb." When Harmon didn't stir, the sheriff hopped out, yanked the rear door open, and hauled Gretchen out. Harmon followed hastily. The first of the vanguard was no more than a hundred yards away now, and moving faster.

"At least cut our hands free."

"Heck, Harmon, seems I forgot my knife." The sheriff climbed into the truck and slammed the door.

———— «◊» ————

There were two mourners at the graveside.

"Pity about the tablecloth," said Charlie, staring down into the trench. "Elvira said it was the last of the ones they always put out for Fourth of July. Not that they'd ever want to use it again, not after this."

"Those stains would be stubborn, all right," Catherine agreed. Jimmy and Jed had surveyed the sad little form on the table when they arrived at the station house in the cemetery buckboard, then simply wrapped a regulation shroud around her, tablecloth and all. At this moment they were positioning her carefully in the line-grave, one body-width over from the space she had occupied two days before.

Charlie said, "You're sure they're dead? The sheriff just grunted when I asked him."

"They're dead. Trust me." Catherine had watched the end play out in the rearview mirror: Gretchen smiling up at the sky; Harmon trying to protect her to the last moment.

The undertakers climbed out of the line-grave and began raining spadefuls of earth onto the bright tablecloth.

# End Notes

**Miracle, in Sand:** Envision a future where the aging process has been conquered, but humans run up against a hardwired death-wish at about 115 years of age. Death has evolved into an all-inclusive holiday with no return ticket, but with a dizzying array of choices – at a price. This story was a reaction to the Hallmarking trend of this century and the last, where the most venerable of our rituals and celebrations have been blown up into commercial bonanzas.

**The New Forty:** This story was commissioned by Nancy Kirkpatrick for Evolve: Vampire Stories of the New Undead (EDGE, 2010), a collection examining how vampires may progress into the 21st century. It was amusing to write, drawing largely on my inner curmudgeon (post-menopausal variety.)

**Kids These Days:** First published in Tesseracts 13 (EDGE, 2009), this story is, I have been told, the saddest variant on the zombie-apocalypse trope possible. I'll take that. Indeed, I will admit to weeping over my keyboard while writing certain scenes. Enjoy.

**The Fremont Collection:** Legendary creatures are fun to research, and the story was huge fun to write. For about ten years, I wrote a blog called the Lateral Truth on the Skeptic Ink network and always enjoyed deep skeptical dives into the literature of Bigfoot, Nessie, Ogopogo, Mothman, bunyips in Australia, anachronistic dinosaurs in Africa, and the like. Throw in some gourmet food fantasies and a version of Lara Croft with the equivalent of a big butterfly net, and there you have this story.

**Condominium:** We open with some gold-painted stones in a rockery—these actually existed, a few doors down from the late, great Marie Jakober's apartment building in Sunnyside. The rest is a fantasia on how writing sometimes feels, especially when there are dishes that really need to be washed.

**Red Carpet:** Soft sci-fi story "Red Carpet" came out of nowhere, as a kind of irreverent shaggy-dog twist on the First Contact theme. I do enjoy mixing solemnity with farce. And sometimes writers just wanna have fun.

**An Inspector Calls:** Commissioned by Nancy Kirkpatrick for Expiration Date (EDGE, 2015), "An Inspector Calls" takes its title from J.B.Priestley's classic play, and its content from years lecturing about Ancient Egyptian funerary and business practices. Hey, Egyptian funeral directors had to make a living, too.

**The Scrolls of Bishop Eubulus:** This is the story I waited all my life to write—well, the last sixty years anyway, ever since I first read "The Dunwich Horror" at age twelve and spent the next two nights on a mattress outside my parents' bedroom door because I was too scared to sleep upstairs. Yes, this is my first foray into the Cthulhu Mythos. Another main strand goes back to evening bull sessions on the excavations at Qasr Ibrim in Lower Nubia in the 1980s, where the team fantasized hilariously about writing a murder mystery called "The Scrolls of Bishop Timotheos, or The Body in the Backdirt." All that background stuff I had to read for my thesis came in handy too, for the first time in thirty-odd years. As for the 17K word-length, I had aimed at about 10K, but the story had other ideas.

**Small World:** Riding upstairs in a London bus, looking down at the people swarming in Trafalgar Square, I had two tiny epiphanies. First, I could be connected in many ways, both direct and indirect, with any one of them, but I would never know. Second, that I had most likely experienced my one and only brief contact with each of those people and would never knowingly see them again. Then I got off the bus, but the weird feeling remained with me and eventually turned into a story.

**Operation Hand of God:** Okay, this was written during Donald Trump's first term and has suddenly become current again. The immediate triggers were separate discussions of drones and nanotechnology on CBC radio one morning as we drove between Calgary and Edmonton, interrupted by a news report of some eyebrow-raising rhetoric south of the border. By the time we reached Edmonton, the story was already written in my head.

**The Shrieking Sand:** Iklankish, where this ghost story is set, is the evil empire in the first volume of my Gil Trilogy, published in the 1990s. The story involves elements that I realize must be close to my heart, because they show up in so much of my writing: desert, nasty winds, nasty heat, and camels. (See also "The Scrolls of Bishop Eubulus.") I suppose this goes back to vivid and often uncomfortable memories of trudging across, bumping over in shockless Landrovers, swaying along sore-butted on camels, or digging into the sands of the Nile Valley. Don't get me wrong, I loved every minute, especially in retrospect.

**The Hanging Room:** The first version of "The Hanging Room" was written in Hong Kong in the early 1990s for a self-published volume of short stories, Hong Kong Macabre, which did about as well as could be expected. But I always thought this particular ghost story had some unrealized potential that would be entertaining to develop—giving it more of a back-story, principally, and giving myself an excuse for some nifty historical background reading.

**Cold Case:** I suffered through many seasons of The Walking Dead but gave up on it forever on the day Negan introduced Glenn to his little friend Lucille. It was all so dreary, as if the Hobbesian critique would inescapably team up with Murphy's Law after the catastrophic collapse of civilization. Why couldn't at least one of those post-apocalyptic societies survive and thrive by retaining some degree of commonsense decency, not to mention a functioning police department? Also, I've always wanted to write a police procedural, and this seemed like a golden opportunity.

# About the Author

**Rebecca Bradley, born** in Vancouver, is an archaeologist and author specializing in Nile Valley studies. Her global journey spanned Northern Ireland, Kuwait, and Hong Kong before returning to Western Canada. She's known for The Gil Trilogy, Temutma, Cadon, Hunter, and two short story collections. A former blogger, she explored skepticism, pseudoarchaeology, and the history of religion

# Need something new to read?

If you liked The Scrolls of Bishop Eubulus, and Other Stories, you should also consider these other EDGE titles…

# Pishtaco:
Lord of the Lost Inca Gold

## by Mark Patton

### *An All-Powerful Evil Shaman Wakes to Protect Lost Inca Gold*

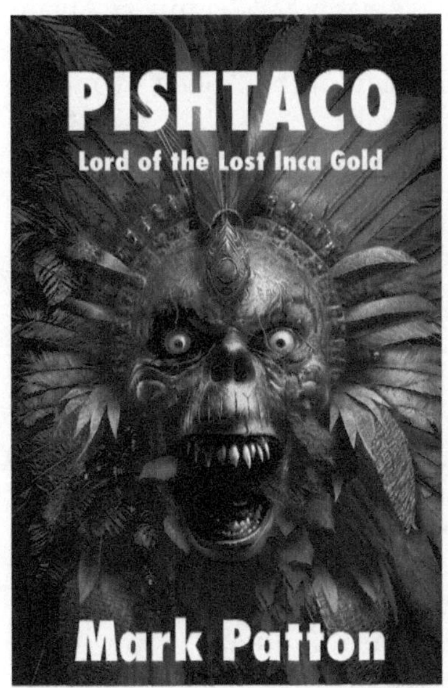

Penelope Augusta Gertrude Farquhar, a woman struggling with schizophrenia, finds herself lost in the Amazon rainforest after a fateful airplane crash. But she's not alone: her voices, now personified as historical figures such as René Descartes, Ada Lovelace, and Ernest Shackleton, accompany her on a quest to find the fabled city of Paititi and destroy the evil shaman Pishtaco, who has amassed the lost Inca gold of Atahualpa.

"Pishtaco: Lord of the Lost Inca Gold" is a thrilling historical fantasy that takes you on a journey through the mystical and mysterious world of the Inca people. Along the way, you'll encounter the pantheon of Inca gods and goddesses, as well as the tribal people of the Amazon rainforest, and learn about their cultures and beliefs. This offbeat adventure is filled with humor, twists and turns, and a unique blend of history and mythology.

Mark Patton's well-researched and engaging writing transports you to another world, while delving into themes of mental health and the nature of reality. "Pishtaco: Lord of the Lost Inca Gold" is a must-read for fans of adventure, history, and mythology.

# The Haunting of Westminster Abbey

## by Mark Patton

### *Romance Amidst Chaos...*

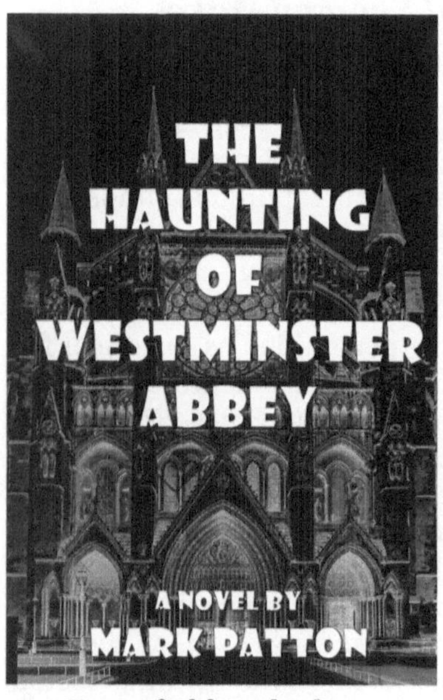

British architect Wallace Butterfield's invitation to design a new tower for Westminster Abbey has come as a summons from the chairman of the Abbey's Foundation itself.

Though Butterfield feels he may not be the right choice, especially given that his most recent work was the design of 'le Mareschal's Supermarket,' a large and unimpressive glass and chrome rectangle, he's decided to give it a try.

After all, work is work. And work shouldn't interfere with his desire to live his life and possibly find a romantic relationship in a local coffee shop.

Butterfield is clueless. He might be talented, but he's unaware of the world around him. Especially when, in looking for love, he ends up involved with a coven of absinthe-drinking Witches who take an interest in what they perceive to be his special qualities.

But he doesn't feel special, and he can't understand why they are conspiring against him, plotting to do everything in their power (kidnapping, torture, or burning at the stake) to get what they want from him.

Given the incredible circumstances in which he finds himself, how will Butterfield survive the pursuit of the coven, an onslaught of ghosts from the Abbey's tombs, and, more importantly, the disappointment of the Abbey's chairman himself?

Worse, how can Butterfield even contemplate finding romance amidst the chaos?

The answers to these questions can only be found in the book. Buy your copy today.

# Gaslight Gothic:
### Strange Tales of Sherlock Holmes

## edited by J. R. Campbell
## and Charles Prepolec

### *Cloaked in gothic shadows, soaked in blood, darkness descends on the world of Sherlock Holmes.*

"I have heard, Mr. Holmes, that you can see deeply into the manifold wickedness of the human heart."

Vengeance from beyond, forbidden passions and sadistic cruelty draw the great detective and his faithful companions into storms of madness and otherworldly violence which threaten to cloud the clarity of logic. Facing the eldritch reach of ancient talismans and arcane science, from the streets of London and Paris to the loneliest of manor houses, the great detective battles the weird and uncanny. Can steadfast reason hold against unspeakable terror when Sherlock Holmes can no longer eliminate the impossible? Follow the great detective through ten new tales of terror as he doggedly pursues investigations leading him to the edge of reason and beyond!

With contributions by:

David Stuart Davies, Lyndsay Faye, Nancy Holder, Mark A. Latham, James Lovegrove, Mark Morris, Charles Prepolec, Josh Reynolds, Angela Slatter, Kevin P. Thornton, and Stephen Volk

# For more EDGE titles and information about upcoming speculative fiction please visit us at:

www.edgewebsite.com

Don't forget to sign-up for our Special Offers

www.ingramcontent.com/pod-product-compliance
Lightning Source LLC
Chambersburg PA
CBHW060544190726
48283CB00003B/862